⌘ ⌘ ⌘

"**An excellent read!** Wiens provides a thoroughly enjoyable read as she takes her readers through one family's journey from public school to home education."

—PAUL D. FARIS
    Executive Director and Senior Legal Counsel, HSLDA Canada

Bringing Them Home

Elizabeth Wiens

OAKTARA

WATERFORD, VIRGINIA

Bringing Them Home

Published in the U.S. by:
OakTara Publishers
P.O. Box 8
Waterford, VA 20197

Visit OakTara at
www.oaktara.com

Cover design by Red River Design Office
Cover images © iStockphoto.com/Vetta stock photo
Author photo © 2010 by Jessica Wiens

ISBN: 978-1-60290-220-0

Bringing Them Home is a work of fiction. References to real people, events, establishments, organizations, or locales are intended only to provide a sense of authenticity and are used fictitiously. All other characters, incidents, and dialogue are drawn from the author's imagination.

⌘ ⌘ ⌘

To the Pioneers
of the Modern Homeschool Movement

Many of whom had to fight government legislation
and stand strong in the face of opposition.
Some families even endured threats of being charged
with child abuse and having their children taken away—
all because of their effort to win the right
to follow their convictions to homeschool.

Because of their hard-fought battle,
we can enjoy this wonderful freedom today!

Acknowledgments

First and foremost, I would like to thank Gary, my husband, who first caught the vision for homeschooling and who faithfully pursued the matter even when his hesitant wife wasn't sure she could handle teaching her children at home. He has been by my side through it all.

Secondly, I would like to thank our four girls: Jessica, Jylisa, Justina, and Tamara, who have made this adventure so rewarding and so much fun. I will always cherish our days of reading together and our Bible story plays! Thanks, all of you, for allowing me the time to write this book.

Finally, thanks to all the families in the Mountain View Homeschool Association, who have provided encouragement, support, and friendship. Without our local homeschool support groups, homeschooling would be a much tougher road to travel.

Foreword

In writing this book, my goal has been to paint a picture of a homeschool family, as well as their journey in deciding to bring their children home. Homeschooling is not merely a reaction to the school system, but a philosophy and way of life. I believe that God has placed children into family units and has given parents the ultimate responsibility to train and raise them for the Lord. How that is accomplished may look different for each family—and the challenges you face will differ, depending on whether you choose public school, private school, or homeschooling.

Although I believe parents whose children are in the public school face a very difficult task of monitoring what their children are learning and combatting the unbiblical content taught there, I do see Christian parents who get actively involved in their local schools and in the relationships their children develop. Many of these parents strive to provide their children with a biblical foundation at home, and their children learn discernment in hard situations. However, this process can be complicated and confusing—especially for younger children.

If your children attend a public school, I would encourage you to read the article at the end of this book concerning the global curriculum and New Age agenda being pushed in our schools, as many parents are not aware of what is truly happening in our public schools. Keep in mind that your children will spend more than 15,000 hours in that system by the time they graduate—even more reason for parents to evaluate this choice for their children prayerfully. The more information they have prior to making that decision, the better.

Christian schools have become a valid alternative for parents where such schools are accessible. Government regulations and curriculum guidelines, however, can sometimes make it difficult for Christian schools to choose their resources freely. Some Christian schools choose to use the same textbooks as the public school. This can make it more difficult to effectively weave biblical truth and a Christian perspective into that curriculum from the foundation up, in an effort to present a truly biblical worldview. However, I know that many Christian teachers work hard to accomplish this and seek to provide a godly atmosphere within their school. Unfortunately, the tuition and busing costs for private schools can make this option financially prohibitive for many families—especially those with multiple children. Parents who choose this route often have to budget carefully and sacrifice in other areas to do so.

One drawback for either of these educational choices is that children spend many hours in school and with their peers, making it a challenge for parents to establish their authority and to cultivate strong relationships with their children. Today's families are being pulled in so many directions, it's hard to maintain both quality and quantity time together. Though the school can be a resource to help parents train their children, ultimately God has entrusted a child's education, character development, and spiritual discipleship to Mom and Dad. Parents must decide how much of that responsibility they will delegate to others and be intentionally involved in the process.

Finally, I wish to address the choice of homeschooling. Teaching your children at home is a huge commitment and usually means limiting your involvement in other areas. It's a challenge to seek good resources, to discover each child's style of learning, and requires much patience and flexibility. But I've found the blessings to far outweigh the challenges.

Homeschoolers choose to teach their children at home for many reasons. However most, if not all, experience some degree of opposition because of this decision—whether from school administrators, neighbors, or family members. Often they feel misunderstood in what they are trying to accomplish because their approach may be very different from that found in a typical classroom.

For my family, the decision to homeschool was like a journey into uncharted waters. We did not fully understand the concept and process ourselves until we started living it, and slowly our philosophy of family and education changed as we experienced this new lifestyle. At the same time, it's hard to share that experience with others who have not yet experienced it for themselves.

Most of you are familiar with what the school classroom looks like—you've been there. Many of you may be considering homeschooling, or know someone who homeschools, but you don't really understand what it's all about. There are many approaches and styles of homeschooling—the story I share in this book is only one of them. But I'm convinced that education is more than the prepackaged box developed by the government, and homeschooling allows us to discover the world of resources and methods outside that box. Will you dare to join me in stepping outside that box for a little while to see what it looks like and why we do what we do?

Bringing Them Home is my desire to reflect my family's heartfelt journey to honor God and to raise godly children. In doing so, I hope to strengthen your desire to spiritually mentor your children—no matter how you choose for them to be schooled. If I succeed in challenging Christian parents with the awesome responsibility God has placed on them to bring up their children "in the training and instruction of the Lord" (Ephesians 6:4), I have accomplished my goal. This task is getting increasingly harder in our post-Christian society, and no matter where your children are being educated, you need to work diligently at home to instill into their lives a strong faith in Christ. May God bless you as you endeavor to do that!

—*Elizabeth Wiens*

Family Tree

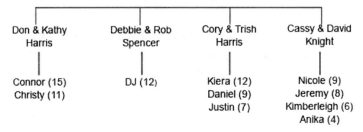

Cassy's Family
Mike & Joyce Harris
(Pastor in B.C.)

Don & Kathy Harris	Debbie & Rob Spencer	Cory & Trish Harris	Cassy & David Knight
Connor (15)	DJ (12)	Kiera (12)	Nicole (9)
Christy (11)		Daniel (9)	Jeremy (8)
		Justin (7)	Kimberleigh (6)
			Anika (4)

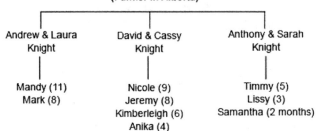

David's Family
Paul & Jean Knight
(Farmer in Alberta)

Andrew & Laura Knight	David & Cassy Knight	Anthony & Sarah Knight
Mandy (11)	Nicole (9)	Timmy (5)
Mark (8)	Jeremy (8)	Lissy (3)
	Kimberleigh (6)	Samantha (2 months)
	Anika (4)	

1

The Dilemma

Quiet! With a tired sigh Cassy Knight drew up her legs and tucked them snuggly beneath her on the couch. A steaming cup of coffee rested on the worn end table within easy reach. It was one of those rare, peaceful moments cherished by any mom with young children, and she intended to take full advantage of it. Anika was playing quietly in her room, and it would be several hours before her three older children would be home from school, narrowing the chances of her finding a few stolen moments of solitude. May sunshine filtered through the south-facing bay window and onto the couch where she sat, bringing a welcome warmth after the long winter.

Cassy sipped her coffee and opened the cover of the magazine in her lap. Scanning the table of contents, she noticed an article titled "Twenty Tips for Working Mothers." Though Cassy had been out of the workforce for almost ten years, she planned to head back to work once Anika entered kindergarten in a year. She flipped a few pages and began to read. An unwelcome ring broke the silence before Cassy had even finished the first paragraph. With a frown she set her mug back on the table, flipped her magazine upside-down on the cushion and trudged to the kitchen to answer the phone.

"Hello, Mrs. Knight?"

"Speaking." Cassy shifted the phone as she attempted to identify the voice on the other end.

"This is Shawna from Thompson Elementary School. I'm afraid I have to ask you to pick up your son, Jeremy."

"Is he sick?" Cassy's brows wrinkled with worry.

"No, he was in a fight at recess. Since this is his first offense, we will not suspend him, but you need to take him home for the rest of the day."

"I don't get it." Cassy sank into a nearby chair. "Why would Jeremy get in a fight?"

"You'll have to ask him that question when you get here, since he started it," the woman answered crisply before hanging up.

Cassy's shoulders slumped as she stared at the phone in her hand for a moment before setting it down on the kitchen table. Jeremy was obviously not hurt too badly or the secretary would have said so, but what could have caused her eight-year-old son to pick a fight?

"So much for my peaceful afternoon." Cassy shook her head as she rose to collect her purse and keys. "Anika," she called down the hall.

"What, Mommy?"

"Come here, honey. We have to go get your brother from school."

Immediately the four-year-old came bounding from her room where she had been playing, her blond ponytail bobbing as she ran. "Are Nico'e and Kimmy coming home, too?"

"Not right now. They'll come home on the bus. We're picking up your brother because he's in trouble."

"Oooh." Anika's face turned serious.

It was a twenty-minute drive from their acreage to the elementary school on the south end of Red Deer. Cassy was quiet as she drove, her mind focused on deciding what punishment would be appropriate to administer for her son's behavior. Her fingers tapped the wheel as if keeping rhythm with her turbulent thoughts.

After they arrived, Cassy unbuckled Anika from her booster seat and led her into the school office. She recognized Shawna sitting behind the massive reception desk, working at a computer. The school secretary paused long enough to point toward the corner of the room where Jeremy fidgeted in his seat, head down. Taking in her son's disheveled appearance, Cassy strode in his direction. At her movement Jeremy glanced up, and Cassy immediately noticed the purplish color already appearing along the curve of his cheek just under his left eye. She threw her son a disapproving look, causing him to turn away, his lips clamped tight and his arms crossed against his chest.

Not wanting to discuss the matter in the presence of the secretary,

Cassy gripped her son's shoulder. "Come on." Without a word, Jeremy followed his mother out to the van and climbed in.

"What happened to your eye?" Anika asked her brother once she had been buckled into her seat.

"Nothing."

"Are you in trouble?" Anika persisted.

"Be quiet," Jeremy snapped.

"You want to tell me what this is all about?" Cassy stared at her son in the rearview mirror, her keys resting idly in the ignition.

"It's nothing!"

"You picking a fight with someone isn't nothing. I want to know what happened."

Jeremy met his mother's steely blue gaze in the mirror. "Randy started it," he declared.

"The secretary said you started it."

"Randy was calling me names. He's always picking on me, and I'm tired of it!" As Jeremy's lower lip started to quiver, the defiance left his face.

Cassy noticed the tears beginning to pool in his eyes, and her heart softened. She turned to face her son, who was seated directly behind her. "What did he call you?"

"He said I was the dumbest kid in third grade and should go back to kindergarten." Jeremy turned to stare out the window, but Cassy could see a tear spill over and make a trail down his cheek.

"That's not very nice," Anika said solemnly.

Jeremy glanced over at his little sister before shifting his gaze toward the window once again.

"I'm sorry he hurt you, Jeremy. Randy was being nasty, but fighting never solves anything. You know your dad and I don't approve of such behavior." At Jeremy's silent nod, Cassy turned around. "We'll talk about this more when your dad gets home," she added before starting the van.

It was a quiet ride home.

When Kimberleigh and Nicole came in the back door a couple of hours later, Anika ran to meet them. "Jeremy got in a fight at schoo', and his eye is aw funny co'wers," she announced, obviously proud to be the bearer of such news.

"I bet he's in big trouble!" six-year-old Kimberleigh declared as she threw down her backpack and hurried off to investigate the situation.

"Is he okay?" Nicole asked quietly. "I was wondering what happened when my teacher told me he wouldn't be on the bus."

"Oh, he's awright. He's just mad because a mean boy caw'ed him names."

Nicole's forehead creased in a frown. Hanging up her jacket, she went in search of her brother. She found Jeremy sprawled on his bed, his face buried in his arms. Kimberleigh was standing beside him, jabbing his shoulder and pleading with him to show her his black eye, but Jeremy was ignoring her.

"Don't bug him, Kimmy," Nicole admonished her sister.

"Fine—he can't hide forever!" Kimberleigh flounced from the room.

"You okay?" Nicole asked tentatively.

Jeremy peeked over the edge of his arm and scanned the room. "Yeah," he said quietly.

"Don't listen to those boys, whatever they said."

"It's just Randy. I wish he'd leave me alone. I can't help it I'm so stupid."

"You're not stupid; you just don't like school, is all. I bet you can do all kinds of things Randy can't do."

Cassy, in the midst of folding laundry in her bedroom, heard the exchange between her children. She had been glad when Nicole headed into Jeremy's room. He had moped all afternoon, and she knew if anyone could cheer him up, it would be her tenderhearted daughter. Placing the last pair of socks in the appropriate pile, Cassy headed to the kitchen and busied herself with supper preparations. She had called David on his cell phone earlier, and her husband was planning to come home a little early to deal with Jeremy's episode at school. David ran a construction business with his brother, Anthony, so his time was somewhat flexible when need be, though Cassy tried not to abuse it.

As soon as David came in the back door, he made his way to the kitchen. "How's Jeremy?" He leaned against the counter at his wife's elbow.

"Okay, I guess. He was mad at first, but I think he's more hurt than anything. I don't know how long this bullying has been going on."

"I'll go talk to him." David squeezed his wife's shoulder before he left.

Whether from Nicole's comforting words or David's talk with his son, Jeremy seemed more himself when he came to the table a half hour later. No one mentioned the fight over supper, and Cassy was glad that tomorrow was Saturday. Jeremy's eye would have the weekend to heal a bit before heading back to school, though she was sure the evidence would last well into the following week. Cassy decided to chalk her son's behavior up to an isolated incident and hoped it wouldn't happen again.

⌘⌘⌘

The following afternoon Cassy had just started to mix up a batch of cookies when Jeremy came running in from outdoors. The next moment he was at his mother's side.

"Look what I found!"

Cassy turned to find herself eye-to-eye with a garter snake. She jerked back and let out a shriek. "Jeremy David, you get that thing out of the house this instant!" Cassy dropped the egg she was holding, and it was now dripping down the front of the cupboard where it had landed. She glared at her son, who at least had the common sense to take a step back.

"But Mom, he's so cool! Can't I keep him, please?" Jeremy held up the twelve-inch snake once more in hopes his mother would see its colorful stripe and boyish appeal. The snake's tongue darted in and out and the reptile gracefully coiled its tail more tightly around its captor's hand. "See, Ziggy likes you."

Pressing her back more firmly against the cupboard behind her, Cassy cocked her face away from the snake's beady eyes and flicking tongue. She frantically shooed Jeremy to take it away. "I said no. Now get him out of my face!" She spat the words through gritted teeth in exasperation.

Jeremy gave a dejected sigh as he turned and headed for the back door. "Don't worry, Ziggy, she didn't mean it. She just needs a chance to get to know you better."

Cassy rolled her eyes and involuntarily shivered. In relief she heard the door close behind her son. *How am I ever going to survive Jeremy's infatuation with disgusting critters?* Cassy wondered as she grabbed a paper towel and began cleaning up the messy egg.

Cassy was sure God had given her a son like Jeremy to test her patience, and most days she felt she was failing that test miserably. As the young mother washed her hands, she glanced out the window and spotted her son. He was still talking to the snake he held clutched in one hand, while he yanked out some grass with the other and flung it into a large, empty flower pot on the back deck. Jeremy stopped to stroke his pet before gently placing it into the planter. His chin rested between his hands on the curved rim of the snake's new home. Then Jeremy began talking animatedly to Shasta, their brown cocker spaniel, who was parked at his side, tail wagging.

Cassy sighed and shook her head. So much for the petunias clustered among the flats of bedding plants on the deck soaking up the sunshine. She had hoped to get them transplanted into that pot next week if the warm weather held. She could only hope Ziggy would have tired of his new home by then.

Turning from the window, Cassy decided to go in search of the girls. Anika would be disappointed if she discovered her mother had baked some cookies without her. Making her way down the hall, Cassy paused and glanced in Nicole's open door on the right. Her eldest was sprawled on her belly across the bed, her ankles crossed behind her. She was propped up on both elbows, a large book in her hands. The nine-year-old's brows were knit in concentration.

"What are you reading?" Cassy braced herself on the doorframe.

"Oh, just this book on dinosaurs I got from the school library." Nicole looked up with a frown.

"Looks pretty serious. So why the sudden interest in dinosaurs?"

"You remember our fieldtrip to the Royal Tyrrell Museum last Wednesday?" At her mother's nod, Nicole continued, "Well, it just doesn't make sense."

"What do you mean?" Cassy slipped into her daughter's room and sat on the edge of the bed.

"You know, all that stuff about everything evolving from a single cell and all. That's not what the Bible says happened, is it?"

"Well, we didn't come from apes, if that's what you mean. Though sometimes I wonder when I watch your brother climb a tree." Instead of the smile Cassy expected, a small tear trickled down her daughter's face. Cassy reached to put a hand on Nicole's shoulder. "I'm sorry, Nicole. What's really bugging you?"

"When I told Mrs. Owen the Bible says God created everything, she laughed at me and said the Bible is just a storybook and that evolution is science. Then she told me not to talk about the Bible anymore." More tears came now, and Cassy pulled her troubled daughter onto her lap. "That was wrong of her to say that to you," Cassy struggled to keep the anger from her voice. "The Bible is not just stories, it's God's Word. He gave us all those stories so we would know what really happened and so we'd know more about Him. Mrs. Owen has just chosen not to believe the Bible."

"But Mom, what about the dinosaurs and all that? The lady at the museum said the dinosaurs lived millions of years before man. If man was created only a few days after God created the earth, how could they have lived before the earth was created?" Nicole wiped at her tears, frustration still keen in her voice.

"Hmm, so that explains the dinosaur book." Cassy had never been able to clearly understand this herself. "Well you see, some people believe the six days of creation were not real days like we know them today; they might actually have been longer periods of time."

Nicole raised her eyebrows incredulously, not looking very convinced.

"Or, some people think God created a world before ours with dinosaurs and prehistoric things, but then, for some reason, He destroyed it about the time He kicked Satan out of Heaven and started over."

"Oh, why would He have done that? I didn't know that was in the Bible." Nicole looked into her mother's eyes.

"It's not really in the Bible, but sometimes God doesn't give us the whole picture, and we may not fully understand it all until we get to Heaven. Does that make sense?"

"I guess so. I just wish God had told us the whole story so we could know."

Cassy could tell the answer she'd given hadn't really pleased her daughter, but she was unsure what else to say. When she thought about it, Cassy realized she'd never settled this dilemma in her own mind but long ago had filed it away as unanswerable. However, she was not pleased with Nicole's teacher and her response concerning the Bible. She would definitely talk to David about that later.

"I wish I had all the answers for you, Nicole. Maybe I'll ask Pastor Nelson about it if I get a chance. Whatever you do, don't let anyone make you doubt the Bible is God's Word and that it's true. Okay?" She situated her daughter back on the bed.

Nicole nodded silently as she flipped the page in her library book.

Cassy gave her daughter's shoulder a reassuring pat and headed down the hall. Reaching Anika and Kimberleigh's room, she found the door slightly ajar. Gently Cassy eased it open and peeked inside. Her youngest daughters sat on the floor surrounded by doll clothes and paraphernalia, and each held a small doll.

"Miss Stacy, I would be so delighted if you could join me tonight at the ball. I will send my carriage to pick you up promptly at 7:00," Kimberleigh drawled with a flourish.

"What's a ba'w, Kimmy?"

"I'm not Kimmy! I'm Lady Violet, and a ball is a fancy party with lots of princes and everything."

"What should Miss Stacy wear?" Anika rummaged through a pile of clothes on the floor.

"Quit asking questions." Kimberleigh sounded exasperated. "You're supposed to say, 'I would be honored to come to your ball. It sounds lovely, Lady Violet!'"

"I can't remember all that stuff, and if I don't ask what to wear, you a'ways make me change cwothes, and it's too hard for me to get those dresses on right." At Anika's obvious frustration, Cassy stepped in before Kimberleigh had a chance to respond.

"How would Miss Stacy like to come help me make cookies, since I can't find Anika?"

"Yeah, cookies, cookies!" Anika dropped Miss Stacy and jumped up and down. "I'm right here, Mom, I'm Anika! You're being siwy."

Cassy laughed at her daughter's exuberance. "Well, hurry and put Miss Stacy away because the cookie dough is already started, and I need a taste-tester."

"I'm a taste-tester. I can do it!" Anika was quickly stuffing Miss Stacy and her clothes away in a box, as though afraid the position might be filled if she didn't hurry.

"Mom, what about Lady Violet's ball? I need Anika to bring Miss Stacy!"

"You can help make cookies too if you want."

"But I'm the taste-tester, right, Mom?" Anika crinkled her brow.

"I think I could use two taste-testers today. What do you think?"

"Well, okay. But Kimmy can't bring Wady Viowet to help make cookies, 'cause she's too bossy!"

Struggling to hide her smile, Cassy told the girls to join her in the kitchen as soon as their dolls were picked up. She would have to hurry to get the cookies baked in time to get supper on.

Even though the nicer weather meant busier days for David, he was conscientious about guarding his supper time and evenings with his family. For that Cassy was grateful, and she liked to have a nice hot meal ready when he got home. She knew he was usually tired and very hungry after a day of heavy work.

Barely did she make it back to her cookie dough before Anika was at her side, clamoring to be lifted to sit on the counter. Kimberleigh was not far behind, dragging a chair from the table to stand on. They took turns adding the remaining ingredients and stirring the dough until it got too stiff, then Cassy once again took over.

Eager hands waited for the small mound of chocolate chips they knew they'd each get. Kimberleigh quickly grasped Anika's hand before she could eat any and counted the chips to compare against her own handful. Cassy waited with the chip bag to even it off if necessary.

"You got it right, Mom!" Kimberleigh announced.

"I've had lots of practice ever since you learned to count!" Cassy tweaked her daughter's nose, and Kimberleigh giggled.

It didn't take long once the first pan was out of the oven for Nicole and Jeremy to find their way to the kitchen for a warm cookie. Cassy put out her hand to stop Jeremy just out of reach of the cookie rack.

"Did you wash your hands when you came in?" Cassy knew the answer before her son moaned and headed for the sink.

"They're not dirty." Jeremy studied his hands before he turned on the tap, ran his hands quickly under the water, and turned it off again.

"Use soap!" Cassy didn't even need to turn around—she knew her son well enough.

With another moan, Jeremy turned on the water again for a little longer this time. After a swipe of his hands across the towel, Jeremy snatched a warm cookie from the rack. The whole thing almost disappeared in one bite. Cassy shook her head as she glanced from him to Nicole, who sat daintily nibbling her cookie at the table. How could her children be so different? *Lord, help me to mold each one to your will*, she silently prayed.

When Cassy heard her husband come in the back door awhile later, she hurried to finish supper preparations. David headed to the bathroom to get cleaned up before coming to give his wife a kiss.

"You could teach your son a thing or two about washing up when he comes in from outside," she teased.

"I'm afraid he comes by that honestly; it took my mom a long time to drill that habit into her sons."

"Thanks a lot!"

As Cassy put the last dish on the table, Jeremy came bounding into the kitchen. "Daddy!"

"Hey Bud, what's up?"

"Daddy, can I keep Ziggy?" the small boy implored.

"And who's Ziggy?"

Jeremy glanced at his mom, who was giving him a warning look, before continuing. "He's my snake I found and he's only little. He might die if I leave him outside, and I'll take real good care of him." His words tumbled over one another.

David smirked as he looked from his son to his wife, and at the threatening expression on Cassy's face, he laughed outright. "I think God made snakes to like living outside, so let's see if we can find a good spot to keep him out there. Besides," David stooped to whisper loudly in his son's ear, "I rather like having your mother live in the house. Don't you?"

Jeremy sighed in defeat. "Yeah, I guess so."

"You guess so!" Cassy gave her son a light swat and he smirked as he scooted to the table.

"And Jeremy," David spoke to his son more sternly this time, "I get the distinct feeling you've already had this discussion with your mother. Am I right?"

"Yes, sir." Jeremy dropped his gaze.

"Then should you come and ask me if Mom already gave you an answer?"

"No, sir." Jeremy glanced again toward his mom and Cassy saw the genuine remorse in her son's eyes. She tousled his hair and threw David a thankful smile before calling the girls to the table.

⌘ ⌘ ⌘

Later that night, as Cassy lay beside her husband in bed, she remembered her discussion with Nicole. "David?"

"What?" he answered sleepily as he shifted to face his wife.

"Do you think we're wrong to have the kids in the public school with teachers who don't believe the Bible?"

"Well, I don't think the public school hurt us too much—they're just teaching basic facts. I think as long as we're aware of what's going on, the kids are okay. Why?"

Cassy propped herself up on one elbow. "Nicole had a run-in with her teacher the other day, and it made me mad. You know, they went to the Royal Tyrrell Museum and it's very evolutionary. When Nicole told her teacher that the Bible says God created everything, her teacher made fun of the Bible and said it was just a storybook and that evolution was science."

David sat up now. "I'm not sure how to reconcile all of science with the Bible—they do seem to contradict each other—but she had no right to say that! How did Nicole take it?"

"She seemed confused and wanted answers to when the dinosaurs lived and all that. I'm not sure I helped her very much—I didn't know what to tell her. I mean, in some respects, I don't think it really matters when they lived or how they died, and God doesn't tell us everything. But Nicole brought home a book on dinosaurs from the library to look through. Now that I think about it, she's been awfully quiet the last couple of days. I thought she was just tired, but I'm sure what her teacher said is really bothering her. What if she hadn't told me what Mrs. Owen had said, and she started believing it?" Fear edged Cassy's voice.

Sighing, David nodded. "I think we need to talk to Mrs. Owen and see what she says. I'll talk to Nicole tomorrow and try to encourage her, but I don't think one comment is going to make her stop believing the Bible."

Cassy flopped back on her pillow. "I know," she huffed, "it just made me so mad, that's all."

David lay down, placed his arm around his wife, and soon was quiet again. But try as she might, Cassy couldn't block the vision of Nicole's tears of hurt and doubt. Without warning, questions from her own childhood long ago came back to haunt her. Questions about the billions of years credited to the earth, the cave men and where they fit, and the many evidences for evolution she'd been exposed to throughout the years.

Cassy remembered bits and pieces of the different theories she'd heard that tried to fit evolution with the Bible. Some explanations she'd heard from her own father who'd picked up different theories from his years in seminary, but the details seemed hazy to her now. *Could anyone know the answers for certain?* she wondered. She didn't think so, but for some reason she felt compelled to try. What difference it would make in her life she didn't know, but she would try. As Cassy prayed about it, peace stole over her and sleep finally came.

2

The Confrontation

Frazzled, Cassy hurried to buckle Anika into her booster seat before collapsing into her own seat for the ride to church. Kimberleigh had been in one of her moods again that morning where none of her dresses "looked right" or "fit right," except the one that was sitting in the basket of dirty clothes in the laundry room. Cassy had finally picked a dress and ordered her to put it on. Kimberleigh knew better than to openly defy her mother, but she had been sulky and dawdled all through breakfast.

Then Jeremy, in his rush to beat Nicole to the Cheerios, had brought the cereal box back right into his glass of milk, tipping it over so that it ran into Anika's lap. Cassy carried her crying daughter from the room to change her clothes, while David oversaw the cleanup in the kitchen by a subdued little boy. Only Nicole looked happy as she reached triumphantly for the abandoned cereal box.

The twenty-minute drive to church was a quiet one. As Cassy hurried the children to their respective Sunday school classes, she tried to lay the tension of the morning aside and focus on why she was there. *It must get better when the kids get older,* she told herself, as she rushed to her own Sunday school class.

As Cassy's frustration subsided, she was able to enjoy the morning. However, by the time Pastor Nelson stood to preach, Cassy found her mind wandering once again to her thoughts of the night before. She found it difficult to concentrate on the message, and after they were dismissed, Cassy waited for the cloud of greeters to clear from around the pastor. When there was a break, she made her approach with Anika in tow.

"Good morning, Cassy, how are you?" Pastor Nelson greeted warmly.

"Good morning, I'm fine, but I have a question for you." She highly respected the elder gentleman.

"Sure, what is it?"

"I was wondering if you could suggest any books I might read that would give answers to some of the claims of evolution in light of the Bible. You see," Cassy continued, "Nicole had a problem with her teacher the other day because the Bible doesn't line up with evolution, and I was wondering how to answer that. How do we support the Bible and creation, and at the same time give our children answers to what they are learning in science?"

"Ah, I've done a fair bit of reading on that myself and it's actually not as complicated to fit it all together as you might think. I have a good book in my library I'll lend you called *Understanding God and Time*. It's a study in progressive creationism, and I found it quite informative. It makes sense, though I don't think we'll ever have it all figured out until we get to Heaven. It's not like the method of creation is a core doctrine that affects our faith, so I wouldn't worry about it too much."

"Yeah, I guess so." Cassy shrugged.

"It makes for an interesting read if you're into that sort of thing. Just wait a minute, and I'll get it from my office." Pastor Nelson excused himself, and Cassy turned to find Lauren Andrews waiting quietly behind her.

"I'm sorry, were you waiting to talk to the pastor?"

"Uh, no," Lauren stammered awkwardly. "Actually, I was walking by when I heard your question, and it caught my attention. You see, Richard and I have some DVDs we bought at a homeschool convention reinforcing the truth of the Bible while exposing the dangers and lies of evolution. They are very good. The DVDs are put together by a group of creation scientists from an organization called Foundations in Truth. I think you would find them quite helpful."

Cassy glanced to see if the pastor was returning yet, but there was no sign of him. She trusted his recommendation and wasn't sure how many resources she wanted to sort through at once. Cassy didn't know the young ginger-haired woman in front of her very well, other than the fact she had five children whom she homeschooled. Brianne was Nicole's age and James was in Anika's class, but Cassy had always thought homeschoolers were a little strange or fanatical.

Lauren seemed to sense Cassy's doubt and became a little bolder. "Please consider watching a couple of them; I can drop them by one day this week. The DVDs will give you a different perspective from the book Pastor Nelson mentioned, but they have given us answers to many difficult questions, and they have helped us learn how to teach our kids to have a solid foundation in Scripture."

Cassy could not help but see the conviction and sincerity in Lauren's eyes. "Sure, I'll watch them. Thanks."

"Will you be home Tuesday afternoon? I can drop them by on my way back from taking the kids to swim lessons, about 2:30."

"Sure. Do you know where I live?" Cassy quickly gave Lauren directions to their acreage. She vaguely remembered hearing that the Andrews lived in their vicinity and hoped she wasn't going too far out of her way.

Just then Pastor Nelson arrived with the book he had promised. "Sorry to keep you waiting, Cassy, I couldn't find it at first."

"Thank you," Cassy replied, as Lauren gave her a little wave before leaving. "I'll get it back to you as soon as I can."

"No hurry."

Cassy picked up Anika, who had been pulling impatiently on her skirt, and went in search of the rest of her family. She found David talking with his younger brother, Anthony, and his sister-in-law, Sarah. Their kids were all playing in a corner of the foyer, except for two-month-old Samantha who was sleeping contentedly on Sarah's shoulder. Anika squirmed from Cassy's arms and ran to join her cousins.

"Sarah invited us to come for dinner." David raised his eyebrows at Cassy.

"You're sure you guys aren't sick of each other and need a break?" Cassy teased Anthony. The two brothers worked together and saw each other almost every day, but Cassy didn't know if there were two men who had ever gotten along better. Anthony was three years younger, but they were both pushing six feet, had ebony hair, and looked a lot alike, though Anthony had a slightly slimmer build. Cassy was often amazed at his agility when she saw him climb limberly atop the open beams of a set of trusses. Anthony was even more of a tease than David, and her kids adored their uncle.

"Considering the fact that we were going home to leftovers today, that sounds great! Do we have time to run home and change so the kids can play outside?" Though they lived outside the city, Anthony and Sarah lived right on the edge, so it wasn't too far.

"Sure."

⌘ ⌘ ⌘

Cassy enjoyed visiting together over dinner, and when five-year-old Timothy and three-year-old Lissy invited their cousins to come try out their new swing set, the kids jumped eagerly from the table and raced for the door. Only Nicole lagged behind, offering to play with her baby cousin, whom she begged to hold every chance she could get. This gave the ladies a chance to clean off the table and do the dishes while the men reclined at the table with their coffee. Just as they were finishing, Anika came running into the house.

"Mommy!"

"What, honey?" Cassy hung up her dish towel and turned toward her daughter.

"Do I have to be the piggy this time?"

"The piggy?"

"Yeah. We're pwaying farm and Kimmy a'ways gets to be the horse, and she said Wissy gets to be the sheep, and I have to be the piggy. I a'ways have to be the piggy, and I don't wike piggies. I can't even make a good piggy noise. See..." Anika proceeded to crinkle her nose until her top lip curled up. Putting a hand to each cheek, she pushed her cheeks forward to make them look pudgy and snorted air in through her nose.

Anthony and David burst out laughing, and Cassy put a hand over her mouth to hide her smile.

"Daddy!" Anika turned and stomped her foot in indignation, her hands in little fists at her side.

"Sorry, honey," David said but he couldn't control his grin. "So, what do you want to be?"

"I want to be a buffa'wo wike on the farm by us."

"A buffalo?" Anthony smirked at his brother. "I thought she was going to pick a kitten or something," he whispered. Clearing his throat, he looked back at his niece and declared, "Yeah, I guess you would make a good buffalo. With those horns of yours, you look just perfect."

"Uncle Anthony, I don't have any horns!" Anika giggled.

"Oh yeah?" Anthony crossed the room and grabbed Anika's piggy tails and held them straight up. "What are these, hmm?"

Anika removed her hair from his grasp and giggled again. "Those are piggy tails siwy!"

"Ah hah," David exclaimed. "I knew you looked more like a piggy."

Anika raced to her dad, who grabbed her and started tickling until Anika couldn't stop laughing—a game they both enjoyed.

"I thought you were playing on the new swing set?" Cassy finally cut in, as Anika climbed up on her father's knee.

"We are," Anika informed her. "Jeremy's making it into our barn."

"How's he doing that?" Cassy wrinkled her brow.

"He cwimbed up on top and is hanging a big tarp over it," Anika answered matter-of-factly.

Cassy dashed for the back door, and David followed a little more slowly.

"Jeremy David, what are you doing up there?" she demanded, heading for the swing set. A large blue tarp had been draped over the tall wooden frame Anthony had built, and Jeremy was nonchalantly walking along the top cross-beam inspecting his work.

"I'm making a barn," he said with a grin. "It's easy. You just climb up from the top of the slide." He swiveled around on his toes to point.

"Yeah, well, you can just get down before you break your neck. What are you teaching Timmy?"

"Come on, buddy," David crossed the yard to help Jeremy down.

"I tell you, he'll climb anything. He's going to be the death of me yet." Cassy turned to go back in the house once her son's feet were safely on the ground.

"How do you think we got so good at climbing across rafters?" Anthony grinned from his place in the doorway.

"Yeah, but you didn't start when you were eight!"

Anthony and David just looked at each other and laughed. "You'd be surprised." Anthony gave his sister-in-law a goofy grin. "Didn't your brothers ever do things like that growing up?"

"Well, Don is seven years older than I am, and Cory is three years older, so I don't remember too much when they were this young, but now that you mention it, they did do some pretty stupid things."

"I don't know about *stupid*…well, okay, some things boys do might be stupid, but they need to be adventurous." Anthony defended his nephew.

"I know. I'm sure God took out more than Adam's rib when he made Eve!" Cassy huffed as she brushed past her brother-in-law and into the house. She was followed by the men's laughter.

As they were leaving late that afternoon, David made arrangements with Anthony to start early the next morning so that he could get off in time to join Cassy at the school. They were hoping to catch Mrs. Owen after class.

"I can't believe a teacher would come right out and say that to a student," Sarah remarked when she'd heard the story.

"I'm sure most teachers wouldn't," Cassy answered in all fairness, "but we thought we'd better follow up on this and see what she has to say about it."

"Of course. Let me know how it goes." Sarah waved to them from the doorway.

⌘ ⌘ ⌘

David and Cassy talked with Nicole before bed to make sure they had a clear understanding of what had transpired between their daughter and her teacher. As David tucked her into bed, he reassured Nicole that they would go see Mrs. Owen after school the next day.

That evening Cassy read the first couple of chapters in the book the pastor had given her, and though it was hard to follow some of the reasoning, she thought she understood the gist of the author's arguments. Basically he was saying that the days of creation were not literal days, but long periods of time. Each day represented a long age in which creation progressed slowly and followed natural processes. These processes followed some of the time-frame and evolutionary development of life as "proven" by science, but it was all God directed.

Cassy closed the book and got out her Bible to read the first chapter of Genesis. She frowned and read it through again more slowly, but she found it hard to see the long elements of time within the creation week that the book referred to. There were certainly no clear indications of it that she could see, but she was not a Bible scholar and had no way of comparing it to the original Hebrew. Maybe the author would explain the basis for his interpretation more thoroughly throughout his book. Cassy closed her Bible with a yawn. David had already headed to bed awhile ago. Pushing her troubled thoughts aside, Cassy went to join him.

⌘ ⌘ ⌘

By three o'clock the next afternoon, Cassy was seated in a chair where she could watch out the front window for her husband. She was hoping he didn't have any trouble getting away from the construction site on time. Cassy had managed to read a few more chapters of the book *Understanding God and Time,* while Anika napped. Though the author had made a strong case to support the old age of the earth and some evolutionary aspects of creation, Cassy felt little peace over it. Science certainly seemed to support what he said, but somehow Cassy couldn't reconcile this view of creation with what she felt the Bible described.

Just a few minutes past three, David's truck pulled in the drive. He hurried into the house to wash up and change, and he was soon ready to go. Cassy hoped Jeremy, Nicole, and Kimberleigh had remembered not to get on the bus.

Once at the elementary school, Cassy and David had little trouble finding both girls clustered beside Jeremy's locker. He was still trying to stuff his lunch kit and papers into his backpack.

"Nicole, you take Anika and the others to the bench by the front door and wait for us, okay?" Cassy instructed her eldest. "We shouldn't be too long. Did you give Mrs. Owen our note saying that we wanted to see her?"

"Yes, she's in her room." Nicole pointed down the noisy hall.

Making their way down the corridor, the Knights paused outside room 23. David gave his wife's hand a squeeze and offered a reassuring smile. Cassy hated confrontations.

Mrs. Owen was tidying her desk when the couple entered. She looked up and motioned them over. "What can I help you with, Mr. and Mrs. Knight?"

"We just wanted to clear up a little misunderstanding Nicole seems to have had with you last Wednesday," David said.

"Oh? And what might that be?" Mrs. Owen rose from her desk with a look of surprise.

"Well." David cleared his throat before continuing. "It seems that Nicole made a comment on your fieldtrip questioning the theory of evolution against our belief in creation. From Nicole's account, we felt that her belief in the Bible was undermined and we just wanted to hear your account of what happened."

Mrs. Owen visibly stiffened as she replied crisply, "If I offended you, I am sorry. But Mr. Knight, this is a public school and we are not here to teach or promote the Bible, and neither are the students."

"I hardly feel that Nicole was promoting the Bible; she was just standing up for her faith," David interjected. Though he appeared calm, Cassy sensed the tension in his voice.

"Precisely, Mr. Knight, and if you choose to fill her head with such stories at home I cannot stop you, but it must stay out of the classroom."

"It was a fieldtrip," Cassy objected, "not a classroom discussion."

"A class fieldtrip, and she made her comment in front of other students. Mrs. Knight—" the teacher's voice took on a condescending tone as if talking to a troublesome child—"we were being instructed with the simple facts of science, and if I allowed every child to question what is taught with their own opinions, I would accomplish nothing in the classroom."

"I realize you have to have order, but since when did evolution become a fact?" David questioned pointedly.

Mrs. Owen was clearly tiring of this line of questioning. "It is well known that most scientists support evolution. And though a few, like yourselves, choose to believe otherwise, it is the accepted science curriculum of the Board of Education. Though it is not necessarily in the core curriculum for fourth grade, it was a part of our fieldtrip and fully acceptable. We teach science in school, and you are free to teach the Bible in church. Even if I should choose to teach the Bible in my classroom, which I wouldn't, I would not be allowed to. If you have a problem with that, you can take it up with the principal. Now, if you have no other concerns, I must be going."

"Thank you for your time," David replied calmly. When Cassy looked with frustration at her husband, he placed his hand on her back and directed her from the room.

"I can't believe that," Cassy fumed angrily the moment they were out of earshot.

"She definitely holds Christianity in low regard, but she shouldn't let it cross into the classroom. We weren't going to get anywhere debating it with her, though. Let's just stop and check if the principal is in and see what he says."

After a five-minute wait, the Knights were escorted by the secretary into Mr. Johnson's office. Following a brief recounting of the issue at hand, Mr. Johnson addressed the concerned parents in front of him.

"Mr. Knight, we employ teachers with many varying belief and value systems. We try our best to keep these beliefs from being expressed in the classroom, but occasionally they do come through. It's inevitable, I guess. I'm sorry if Mrs. Owen's comment about the Bible troubled your daughter, but in a way she is right. We cannot teach the Bible, or any specific set of religious beliefs, within a public school system. I'm sure you can understand and appreciate why. If we should let one group in the door to teach their faith, we would have to let them all in, and then where would we be? That is why we must keep matters of religion out of the classroom and restrict our teachers to the curriculum set out by the government. We have to meet the objectives and standards they have established."

David sighed, his frustration evident. "Thank you very much for seeing us on such short notice. I know you're busy." He rose to go. "You've given me something to think about."

"Glad I could help," Mr. Johnson reached across his desk to shake David's hand.

"That went well," Cassy said sarcastically as they headed for the front door.

"I guess we shouldn't be surprised. After all, it's not a Christian school system. I know we have no right to force our faith on the teachers, but in a way, by leaving Christ out of the picture, aren't they imposing their faith on the students? It must be really frustrating for the Christian teachers out there trying to make a difference but forbidden to share anything about God."

"I guess I never thought of it much before. I'll have to say an extra prayer for Don, teaching in a public high school. It must be hard teaching history without God," Cassy mused.

She had grown up as a preacher's kid and knew her Bible well, but as she thought back, she didn't remember ever once hearing God mentioned as an integral part of history. God's interaction with man seemed to end with the Bible, though she knew in her heart this was not so. Cassy was hit with the distinct realization that she had missed something, perhaps something vital. Something that, until this moment, she had never realized was missing at all, and that saddened her. She was quiet all the way home, only absently mindful of the kids' chatter.

3

A New Friend

Tuesday morning Cassy's heart was heavy as she dragged Jeremy from bed and hurried to pack lunches while the kids sleepily ate their breakfast.

"You've got a spelling test today." Cassy patted Jeremy's shoulder. "Do you remember your words?"

Jeremy moaned before answering, "I forgot to write them out and practice them last night." He rested his head in his hands.

Cassy knew how much he hated reading and taking tests. "Maybe you can read them over on the bus," she encouraged gently.

"I guess so," he said, but he didn't sound enthused.

"Time to grab your backpacks; the bus should be here any minute." Cassy hurried her kids along. She shoved Jeremy's arms into his jacket to speed him up.

"I can't find my shoes," Kimberleigh wailed in panic. Cassy did a mad search through the shoes in the entrance way, but to no avail. Dashing down the hall she flipped on the light in Kimberleigh and Anika's room, waking Anika in the process. She found her daughter's shoes and hurried back to the entryway.

"They were under your bed," Cassy declared as she tied one shoe and reached for the other.

"Oh yeah, I forgot." Kimberleigh shrugged.

With a quick kiss Cassy shooed her children out the door just as she saw the bus rounding the corner. With them safely on their way, Cassy returned to the kitchen and her cold cup of coffee. Warming her cup in the microwave, she joined a sleepy Anika at the table.

Cassy was busy all day with housework and entertaining her

lonely preschooler, and she had forgotten about Lauren's promise to stop by until the doorbell rang. She jumped at the sound.

"Here are the DVDs I told you about on Sunday." Lauren smiled warmly at her.

"Oh thanks. Would you like to come in for a cup of coffee?"

"Sounds great, but I've got all the kids with me." She turned and motioned toward her minivan.

For a moment Cassy had forgotten Lauren's kids weren't in school, but she smiled and opened the door wider. "Great. Anika has been dying for company all day."

"You sure?" Lauren only hesitated a moment before motioning for her children to come in. Melissa helped her two little brothers from their car seats as nine-year-old Brianne and seven-year-old Christian bounded from the van.

Soon Anika was happily leading her unexpected playmates down the hall to her room.

"You want to keep an eye on James and Kegan?" Lauren asked her eleven-year-old daughter. Melissa nodded and followed her siblings down the hall.

"She's such a big help, I don't know what I'd do without her." Lauren turned to her hostess. She took the seat offered while Cassy went to the cupboard for two coffee mugs.

"I can't imagine keeping up with three little boys," Cassy shook her head in wonder. "I can hardly keep up with my one."

Lauren laughed. "They have lots of energy all right. There's never a dull moment around our house, but I can't imagine life without them."

"Yeah, I know," Cassy conceded, "though I could get along very well without some of Jeremy's pets!"

A horrible grimace crossed Lauren's face. "Thankfully James and Kegan aren't into that too much yet, but I once found a wad of dead worms in Christian's pocket when I was doing laundry. He was 'saving them to go fishing.' Now that was gross!"

A shiver ran down Cassy's spine and she shuddered. She set the mugs of coffee on the table. "Remind me to quit checking pockets! Although having them go through the washer and dryer would be horrible too," she added as an afterthought. "I'll have to threaten

Jeremy right now that if I ever find anything disgusting in one of his pockets, he's going to be doing the laundry for the rest of his life!" The women laughed as they chatted over their coffee.

"So, where'd you say you got these DVDs from again?" Cassy picked up one case to study it more closely.

"There's a booth at our homeschool conference each year run by a local creation science group, and they carry a lot of resources put out by the organization called Foundations in Truth."

"And what exactly is that?"

"It's an organization made up of top Christian scientists who specialize in a variety of fields, like geology, astronomy, biology and who knows what all. They produce a lot of books, DVDs and audio CD's explaining the evidence that supports a young earth, creation, a worldwide flood and all kinds of things. One of their goals is to expose the lies or false presuppositions behind evolution, so that Christians can defend their faith."

"But I thought evolution was supported by most scientists."

"Maybe most non-Christian scientists who approach science rejecting the Bible and the creation account, so they are looking for a way to explain life without God, though some of them will even acknowledge problems within evolution. The sad thing is, some Christians have bought into their ideas and have tried to fit them into the Bible. This has only caused Christians to doubt the authority of the Scripture, or to reinterpret what it says to fit man's ideas. Remember, evolution is not true science like they claim. It's only a belief system— one that rejects God. There's lots more information about all that on the DVDs. I've also got some good books if you're interested."

"Wow, sounds like you've studied this a lot." Cassy was impressed.

"Richard and I came across these DVDs a few years ago and they answered so many questions for us. For the first time I didn't have a bunch of doubts about Genesis and I realized how important it is as a foundation to all aspects of my faith."

"Really?" Cassy remembered Pastor Nelson's comment about the issue not being an important one, and she wondered.

"We've since picked up a lot more of their resources to use in teaching the kids. I want them to really be able to defend their faith and know they can trust the Bible."

"I don't know how you do it! The homeschooling, I mean. I could never do that, but I'm suddenly doubting the wisdom of having our kids in the public school system. I'd like to check out the Christian school more. That's where my brother Cory's kids go."

Lauren just smiled. "Homeschooling has been great for our family for many reasons. It's not always easy, but there's a ton of excellent curriculum and books out there to help. We've been homeschooling for six years now, and it definitely gets easier, or at least not so overwhelming."

"I don't know, I don't think I could handle it. At least with the Christian school, I could know the kids were in a better environment with Christian teachers and books and all. I think they could do a better job than I ever could."

"Yeah, it's good we have some options, but don't sell yourself short. I didn't think I could do it when I first started either. The first couple of years were the toughest and I had lots of doubts, but I also had some good support and felt it was what God wanted us to do. Now I wouldn't trade it for anything."

Just then there was a commotion from the bedroom, and moments later Melissa came down the hall carrying a fussy, three-year-old Kegan.

"What's the trouble?" Lauren rose to take her crying son.

"Kegan wanted to play with the same car James had."

"Jeremy has tons of cars in his room. Anika can get more," Cassy said, rising as well.

"That's okay. These two are too close in age and always have to compete for the same toy, no matter how many there are." Kegan was already settling down in his mother's arms. "We should get going anyway; your kids will be home soon."

Glancing at her watch, Cassy was surprised. She had been enjoying her visit more than she'd expected. "You don't have to rush on my account."

"Well, I think this guy's pretty tired, but let me know what you think of the DVDs. We can talk some more another time."

"Sure." Cassy thought she'd like that.

"And if you want to know more about homeschooling, just give me a call," Lauren added with a smile.

Cassy only nodded as Lauren headed for the hall to call the rest of her kids.

"Mommy, can't they stay wonger?" Anika whined as she followed them out of her bedroom.

"Not this time, but we'll have to see if they can come again sometime. How about that?"

"Why can't they stay for supper?"

Cassy turned to give her daughter a reproving look for suggesting that in front of company and putting her on the spot. She had pork chops out for supper, but not enough for an additional family of seven.

Lauren chuckled. "Just what every mother needs—someone to invite unexpected guests to supper at the last minute."

Sheepishly Cassy turned to her guest. "A bad habit of hers she's been warned about many times."

"I know what that's like. You'll have to come to my house for supper sometime," Lauren bargained with the little girl.

"Tonight?" Anika responded eagerly, drawing another laugh from Lauren and a groan from her mother.

"Not tonight, but soon." Lauren patted Anika's blond head.

"Okay," Anika let out an exaggerated sigh.

"You sure you don't need one more to take home with you," Cassy teased, tilting her head toward her impish daughter.

"Sorry, got my hands full." Lauren waved her family out the door. "Thanks for the coffee."

"Thanks for the DVDs. I'm looking forward to watching them," Cassy replied sincerely.

A short time later Cassy's older children came bustling in the door. Jeremy threw down his jacket and backpack and immediately headed to the kitchen for a cookie. Nicole and Kimberleigh stopped to tell Cassy about their day before joining their brother.

"How was your spelling test?" Cassy crossed the kitchen to stand beside her son.

Jeremy quickly stuffed the rest of his chocolate-chip cookie into his mouth to avoid answering. Not that he was usually so conscious of talking with his mouth full when they had company at the table.

"Not so good, eh?" Cassy gave her son a sympathetic look.

"Aw Mom," Jeremy said when he'd swallowed his mouthful. "It's just so stupid! Why does there have to be so many ways to spell the same sound? And whoever made up 'silent' letters. I mean, what's the point of sticking a 'GH' in the middle of a word if it's not going to say anything? It's like they're just out to trick ya on purpose. And then they have to make all these words that sound the same like *there, their,* and *they're,* and I'm supposed to know which one is which!" Jeremy rolled his eyes.

"So when do you use the word *their,* spelled t-h-e-i-r?" Cassy quizzed her son gently.

"See!" Jeremy threw up his hands and let them fall loudly against his legs. "You don't even know, and they expect me to know it!"

Cassy smothered her laugh. "I was seeing if you knew." She lifted her son's chin with one hand and peered intently into his eyes. "Let's see your test so that I can help you."

Jeremy shrugged and shuffled off to find his backpack, his head hanging. He returned a minute later, smoothing out a crumpled paper against his chest. Cassy took one look and saw all the teacher's red *X*s beside misspelled words and felt sorry for her son.

"I want you to learn to spell so that writing isn't so frustrating for you, and you can feel good about what you write, not so that you can get an *A* on your spelling test. Do you understand?"

"Yeah, but it's not like I'm ever going to write a book or anything."

"You never know," Cassy punched her son's shoulder playfully. "Besides, everyone has to do some writing, no matter what his job is. Even though your dad is in construction, he still has to write quotes for different jobs and things."

"Yeah, but he uses the computer. You don't have to know how to spell to use a computer."

"Not entirely true. And besides, you are to use the brain God has given you to the best of your ability."

Cassy proceeded to direct her obstinate son to the kitchen table, where she sat down and reviewed some of his spelling errors with him. She did her best to explain the sounds and encouraged Jeremy to write each of the words out correctly a couple of times for reinforcement, while she set about preparing supper.

⌘ ⌘ ⌘

That evening, once the children were all settled in bed, Cassy told David about her visit with Lauren. Showing him the DVDs she had dropped off, they decided to watch one. All three were presented by Dr. John Stout, the president of Foundations in Truth. One was a debate between him and a prominent evolutionist, one was on the importance of Genesis and the authority of Scripture, and the last was on the age of the earth, dinosaurs and the evidence for a world flood. David and Cassy decided on the latter, as it dealt most specifically with some of the questions they were facing with Nicole.

Throughout the hour long presentation, Cassy was astounded by the scientific evidence for a young earth and the explanations for the earth's layers, which seemed to suit the biblical flood so perfectly. She didn't remember hearing these facts or explanations in any of her school textbooks, or even in church, for that matter. She discovered that many of the secular dating methods are based on circular reasoning or premade assumptions that geological changes happened at a constant rate throughout history, and that the earth has to be old to allow for the evolutionary process and to explain the layers found in rock formations. Many scientists do not take into account the catastrophic changes that would have taken place in a worldwide flood or other natural disasters, and they don't have any way of knowing what God created to start with. What really agitated her, however, was the feeble and often fraudulent evidence purported by men in the name of science, which was used to promote evolution. For the first time Cassy realized that most of what was being presented as scientific fact was no more than an interpretation of the facts based on atheistic assumptions.

Cassy was impressed with the scope of Dr. Stout's knowledge and the assurance with which he supported the Bible as written—no hidden ages or contradictions. He claimed that the earth was about six thousand years old, that dinosaurs were created on day six, along with man, and that young dinosaurs would have even been on the ark. Cassy couldn't remember ever having considered such a possibility, but she found the thought intriguing. She realized that the main reason she hadn't considered this was because she had been duped into believing the dinosaurs were millions of years old.

"Nicole has to see this!" Cassy proclaimed the minute the presentation was over. "In fact, all the kids should see it."

"I remember seeing those same geological timecharts in my science textbooks in school, but I never really questioned them or understood how they dated all those layers. To think that there aren't even any such layers all stacked in that order anywhere in the world—it's deceiving!"

"But David, the book Pastor Nelson gave me is based on all of that! The author agrees that the earth is billions of years old and that creation didn't happen in six literal days, but in six long ages. If some pastors aren't even learning the truth in seminary, how are our kids supposed to learn the truth in school—especially in public school?"

"I guess I never realized. This is just one area of science, and it doesn't mean that the other aspects of science aren't presented accurately, but it does make you wonder."

Cassy and her husband were still discussing the matter as they drifted off to sleep.

4

Seeking the Truth

Over the following days, the Knights watched one of the DVDs with their children each night and discussed it with them afterwards to make sure they understood what was being presented. Cassy was more impressed with each session as she came to understand the importance of the issue. Dr. Stout pointed out that the foundations for salvation and all the Bible's major doctrines are found in the first eleven chapters of Genesis. Unfortunately, many "Bible scholars" undermine these chapters by claiming people can't take them literally or by reinterpreting what they say. Some even go so far as to call Genesis a collection of ancient fables with lessons of faith mixed in. By doing so, they undermine the authority of Scripture and open the whole Bible up to man's reinterpretations. If there was not a literal Adam and Eve, a literal act of disobedience resulting in death, why would anyone need a literal Savior? And if Christians can't declare the first book of the Bible to be wholly true, which explains who God is and man's relationship to Him, why should they expect anyone to believe the rest of the Bible?

Furthermore, if Christians capitulate to evolutionistic theories by accepting long ages and the Big Bang as more accurate than God's own account of His six days of creation, they might as well announce to the world that the Bible is unreliable as truth. In reality, these people are claiming that man, who wasn't there in the beginning, knows better than the God who was there and created them.

As the Knights discussed these ideas with their children, Nicole's face brightened. She was pleased to know that she had been right to defend the Bible against evolution and that she did not have to fit the two together. When they discussed the matter of dinosaurs being created on day six and that they were only about six thousand years old, the kids all started talking at once.

"Cool! Adam would have seen all the dinosaurs!" Jeremy jumped up and startled Shasta, who had been curled up at his feet. "I wish I could have been there!"

"Not only Adam," David corrected, "but many people down through history."

"But Dad," Nicole crinkled her face with concern, "that means all those books I got from the library are wrong. Why do they all say dinosaurs lived millions of years ago and before man?"

"I guess because the idea of evolution has taken such a strong hold on our world, that people have started accepting it as fact. Unfortunately, it seems the evidence against it is rarely published." David pulled his daughter onto his lap.

"But why wouldn't the scientists want people to know the truth?"

David thought for a moment. "Because it discredits all their theories, and they don't have the answers for that without accepting God as the Creator. I guess they're not ready to do that."

"They're wying!" Anika declared, eyes wide.

Cassy laughed. "I guess in a way they are lying, Anika—at least some of them. But many really believe they are right and are trying hard to prove it. That's why what Dr. Stout is doing is so important. Mrs. Andrews said there are many scientists who don't believe in evolution who are trying to tell people why it's wrong."

"Why don't we have some of their books in school?" Nicole questioned her mom.

"Well, that's a tough one, Nicole. The school system has accepted evolution and teaches it. They probably feel that evolution is based on true science while creationism is purely religious faith without any evidence. If the schools brought in books that contradicted their textbooks, the teachers wouldn't be able to teach evolution as fact anymore, and they aren't allowed to teach the Bible...."

"Don't they want to teach the truth?" Kimberleigh was aghast.

Cassy looked to her husband for help. This was all so new to them both, so how could they explain it to their children?

"I'm sure most teachers feel that they are teaching the truth," David addressed his daughter. "Maybe they haven't heard the real truth before."

"Well, when I get to schoo' I'm gonna te'w them." Anika stomped her foot with determination.

Jeremy laughed. "I'm sure they'll listen to you, Pipsqueak!"

"Yeah, Mrs. Owen sure didn't listen to me," Nicole shook her head. "I wish she could see these movies; then maybe she wouldn't make fun of the Bible!"

"She might not believe Dr. Stout anymore than she did you, kiddo." David gave his daughter a hug.

Cassy glanced at her watch. "It's way past bedtime, so away you go. And don't forget to brush your teeth," she added.

"It's Friday night and there's no school tomorrow," Jeremy pleaded with his mom.

"Don't argue with your mother," David reprimanded his son. At his father's stern look, Jeremy hung his head and shuffled from the room.

When they were alone, Cassy shifted her position on the couch and snuggled against her husband's arm, her head on his shoulder. "I almost feel tricked into questioning the Bible all these years. I mean, I didn't believe in full-blown evolution, but I did allow evolutionistic teaching to influence my thinking. I don't know why I couldn't just accept what the Bible was saying regardless of what I was taught."

David lifted his arm to encircle his wife and pull her against his chest. "I guess it is hard to question what you see printed or pictured in a textbook. The sad thing is, I don't remember ever hearing a Sunday school teacher or pastor take a stand against it. I don't feel that it affected my salvation, but I think it did affect my view of the Scriptures and made me more accepting of men manipulating the Scriptures to fit their ideas. It scares me to think where this could lead and that I've maybe accepted other errors."

"I'd like to see more of what Lauren has from this organization; we should have them over for dinner. I know that would make Anika happy." Cassy smiled to herself.

"What about Sunday?"

"That should work; I'll check with Lauren."

One by one four pajama-clad children came to give their parents good-night kisses before climbing into bed. Anika bounded in first and sprang onto her father's lap.

"I want a bear hug, Daddy." She slipped her arms around her father's neck in anticipation.

"A bear hug?" David lifted Anika up to peer into her eyes as he made a loud roar, bringing a delighted giggle from his daughter. "I'll give you a bear hug and then I'll eat you up, ah-hah!" he growled in a husky voice, engulfing his squirming daughter in a tight hug against his chest. When David dug his face under Anika's chin to attack her neck, she shrieked and laughed the harder, grabbing her father's cheeks to defend herself. Shasta barked at the commotion.

"Me too! Me too!" Kimberleigh danced at her father's knee.

David grabbed his second daughter, and with one girl under each arm he squeezed and tickled them both in turn until they were out of breath. Cassy couldn't help but laugh, even though she'd watched this spectacle many times before.

"Okay, off to bed both of you, before this hungry bear chases you there," David said. Immediately both girls slid from his lap and dashed for their room. Anika almost ran into the wall when she glanced back to see if her father was coming after her before disappearing around the corner. David just chuckled as he watched them go.

Nicole was a little more sedate as she came to give both parents a hug and kiss good night, but David gave his eldest a little squeeze as well. As usual, Jeremy was the last to make his appearance.

"Did you brush your teeth?" Cassy questioned her son.

"Yeah," Jeremy replied with a tinge of exasperation. "I need to go check on Ziggy and make sure he's all right."

"I'm sure he's fine; you checked on him after supper. Right now it's time for bed." Cassy had been relieved when David brought home a small aquarium for Ziggy a couple nights ago, and the reptile was now tucked safely away on a shelf in the garage.

"But he might be catching a cold out there, and I need to make sure he's warm enough."

As the image of a snake with a runny nose and cough flashed

across Cassy's mind, she had to laugh. Her son was a master at prolonging bedtime, but she had to give him credit for creativity. He rarely came up with the same excuse twice.

"Nice try, bud, but snakes live outside. He's plenty warm in the garage." David gave him a pointed look.

"Maybe he's too warm," Jeremy started before being cut off by both parents in unison.

"To bed!"

Reluctantly the boy admitted defeat and turned with a sigh. He trudged from the room with his head hanging. Cassy just shook her head, and David chuckled.

"He rivals Kimberleigh for dramatics when it comes to bedtime," Cassy mused. "Too bad he doesn't get marks in school for making up creative excuses; he'd get straight *A*s. I wish he didn't struggle with school so much." Cassy sighed. "Lauren was telling me about home-schooling the other day. She says I could teach the kids at home, but I don't think so."

"You could start with a lesson on the difference between being cold-blooded and warm-blooded," David teased.

"Yeah, could you see me teaching a class on reptiles and amphibians?"

"Not hardly."

Though the idea of teaching Jeremy about reptiles seemed ridiculous to Cassy, she admired what Lauren had shared the other day about the importance of teaching her children a foundation for their faith. Tackling the full education of her children, however, was a different story, and the idea overwhelmed her. No, even though Cassy enjoyed spending time with her children, homeschooling was out of the question! She dismissed the idea and turned the conversation toward a safer topic. By the time the couple headed to bed, Cassy felt she had put the idea of homeschooling behind her, so why did she still sense this nagging feeling to find out more? It was some time before she could finally still her thoughts and go to sleep.

⌘ ⌘ ⌘

The next morning Cassy phoned Lauren to inquire about dinner on Sunday. Cassy was pleased when she said they could come. Lauren insisted on bringing a salad and dessert, and the ladies chatted awhile longer before hanging up. The day passed quickly as Cassy transplanted bedding plants, straightened the house, and made preparations for the next day.

When David got home, the two discussed some of the questions they still had concerning the presentations by Dr. Stout. Cassy had finished the book from Pastor Nelson during the week as well, but after seeing the DVDs, she couldn't reconcile the process the author of the book used to manipulate the meaning of Scripture. Though he had gone into great detail to try and validate his arguments, Cassy felt he was compromising with the secular theories of science at the expense of the integrity of Scripture. It seemed a dangerous game to play.

After the service on Sunday, Cassy went to return the book to Pastor Nelson. When he asked how she liked it, Cassy felt uncomfortable.

"Well, I guess I don't agree with all his interpretations," she admitted, "but we're also looking at some information from an organization called Foundations in Truth, and we feel we've gotten some of our questions answered."

"Oh?" Pastor Nelson seemed a little taken aback. "I don't know much about them, but it doesn't hurt to compare different views, I guess."

"Yeah, well I appreciate your help," Cassy hoped she hadn't offended the pastor.

⌘ ⌘ ⌘

Once at home, Lauren joined Cassy in the kitchen as they hurried to finish off dinner and get it on the table. An extra table had been set up in the living room for the three older girls, Jeremy, and Christian, as the kitchen table would not fit thirteen people around it. In no time they were able to call everyone to sit down and David led them in prayer.

It didn't take long to discover Richard Andrews' love for discussing theological issues, and by the time the ladies were done fixing plates of food for their youngest children, the men were engrossed in friendly dialogue. The kids in the living room were laughing and seemed to be getting along well, and Cassy soon found herself absorbed in the discussion at her table. Topics flowed rapidly from the creation debate to the authority of Scripture, which led to other church issues. She was impressed with the knowledge and confidence with which Richard spoke. Glancing from time to time at her husband, she could see that David was totally enjoying himself.

Kimberleigh and Anika were busy chatting with James and Kegan, but when Richard started to comment on the growing divorce rate in the church, it caught Anika's attention.

Turning to pull on her mother's sleeve, Anika leaned toward Cassy and whispered loudly. "Mommy, is Mr. Andrews going to weave wike Amy's daddy did?" Mortified, Cassy shushed her daughter, but the Andrews only laughed.

"Definitely not!" Richard proclaimed to the little girl who was staring at him with wide eyes. "God gave me a very important job taking care of my family, and I love them very much! I would never leave them. Besides, God would be very sad if I did."

"Ooh," Anika said seriously. "Someone should tell Amy's daddy that, 'cause Amy reawy misses her daddy. It makes Amy sad, too!"

"Amy is our neighbor's daughter and Anika's little friend," Cassy explained, with tears in her eyes. "Her dad filed for divorce and left six months ago, and the family hasn't heard much from him since. It's been pretty hard on all of them. We've been trying to help them out a bit."

"They're not a Christian family," David explained, "but you're right. All too often Christian families do break apart, and the church is silent. Why?"

"I think that our focus so often is on showing love and being non-judgmental," Richard reasoned, "that we don't feel we can take a stand against it. Don't get me wrong, we definitely need to show love, but not at the expense of truth. I feel for all the single moms out there and the hurting families, but by not taking a stand, divorce has become more acceptable and we just have more casualties. We are not only watering down the Gospel, we have less to offer our hurting society as a result. I don't think God is pleased with that."

"I've heard people refer to many of the controversial issues as side issues and not core doctrines," David said. "Or I've heard different interpretations concerning some of Paul's teachings, declaring them to be cultural and not relevant for today. I guess I can see your point, though, that it all comes down to the authority of Scripture."

"You're right," responded Richard. "And when you start to question that authority in areas such as Genesis, it follows that you'll start to question it elsewhere. It's a dangerous place to be in to set yourself up as judge over the Bible to determine which verses are important to obey and which ones you can dismiss or reinterpret. I've heard many people delegate different commands of God to the status of 'secondary doctrines' as well, thereby diminishing their importance. But since when is obedience secondary to God? Just read the story of Achan again if you think God doesn't take obedience seriously. Not only did the Israelite nation suffer defeat because of his sin, but Achan and his whole family were killed because he chose to disobey God's command. God demands obedience, and it's not our prerogative to pick and choose what commands we want to obey. If we can't take a stand on all of Scripture, is it worth taking a stand on any of it?"

The Knights sat in thoughtful silence for a moment. When the children started to get restless, they were excused from the table. The whole gang hurried noisily outside to play. With the break in the conversation, Cassy turned to Lauren, directly across from her.

"So what made you decide to homeschool your kids?" The question had been plaguing her since the other night, and, though she had tried, Cassy hadn't been able to put it out of her mind.

"I've been waiting for you to ask." Lauren turned to her new friend with a smile. "Actually, when Melissa was four, Richard and I started discussing school options for our family. Of course we had both grown up in the public school system ourselves, but we weren't sure we wanted that for our kids. Not that some kids don't do all right in the public system, but we had recently heard a message on the radio about a parent's responsibility to train up their children in the Lord, and felt that we would have to answer to God someday on how well we had done that. The more we discussed it and searched the Scriptures, the more we felt that, for us, it would be much harder to do a good job if our kids were in a secular system devoid of God and surrounded everyday by non-Christian peers."

"But aren't we supposed to be the salt and light?" David questioned. "I know some Christian kids who have been a good witness to their friends at school."

"Some have; I don't deny it." Richard joined in. "But I have also seen many Christian kids stumble and fall in the process, or come out of high school with a very secular mindset and not knowing what they believe. Some merely survive with their faith still intact, but they don't really have a biblical worldview. As mature Christians, we are to be salt and light in our society, but can we really expect that from our five-year-olds, who haven't established a mature faith and convictions yet? I feel we need to train them and give them a good foundation before we send them out. Remember, contaminated salt isn't good for anything."

"I guess that makes sense."

"The Jewish nation constantly fought with the negative influences of the pagan cultures around them and repeatedly fell away from God," Lauren continued. "That's why God so often admonished them to train their children and teach them the things He had done, so they would not fall away. God would never have wanted the Israelites to send their small children to their pagan neighbors to be trained, expecting the children to be salt rather than being influenced by the pagan beliefs and practices."

"Wow, I never thought of it like that before." Cassy let out her breath in a rush, shaking her head.

"I'm sorry, I got carried away," Lauren stammered. "I didn't mean to be inconsiderate, or to hurt your feelings. It's just that I'm beginning to understand that no form of education is completely neutral, and as I've been teaching the kids from a Christian perspective and comparing it to my own education, I see the contrast," Lauren admitted.

Cassy could see her discomfort. "No, that's okay." Cassy got up to get the coffee pot and refill their cups. "I really want to know why you believe so strongly in homeschooling. I don't know much about it, but you still haven't answered why you chose homeschooling over the Christian school."

Lauren smiled with a look of relief. "Actually, we were planning on the Christian school. We had even registered Melissa in kindergarten when I came across a book at Lighthouse Books titled, *The Call to Homeschool.* For some reason it caught my interest and I bought it. It was all about the philosophy and advantages of homeschooling and I couldn't put it down. We had briefly considered the possibility, and I knew that a couple of families in our church homeschooled, but we hadn't really checked into what it was all about. After reading that book, I talked to Teresa Henderson, and she loaned me a couple more books. The more I read, the more I was hooked on the idea—scared to death, but hooked. Richard and I prayed about it and felt it was what God wanted us to do."

"So what was it that 'hooked' you?" Cassy persisted. She still didn't get it.

"Well, we liked the idea of keeping the family together for one thing, and we liked being more involved in what they were learning. It was nice to see that we could tailor their education to suit each child's needs and interests and let them work at their own pace."

"What do you mean 'tailor'?" David interjected. "Don't you have set curriculum that everyone has to follow?"

Lauren glanced at her husband and laughed. "That's what most people think because that's how they were raised. And if your kids were in a classroom, then they would have to follow the same material as their peers and keep pace because that's the only way to handle twenty-five to thirty kids and mark their work. Unfortunately, not all kids learn the same, or at the same rate, so often some of them are bored and unchallenged, while others are frustrated and struggle with feelings of failure. However, as homeschoolers, we have a lot of freedom to develop individual programs for our kids."

"But that's what I don't get!" Cassy exclaimed. "How do you keep up with so many different programs and everyone working on different workbooks and texts and all needing your help? I think it would drive me crazy!"

"It would drive me crazy too, if that's what I was doing," Lauren admitted. "I didn't mean that we don't do anything together, and we sure don't do a pile of workbooks." At the surprise on Cassy's face, she smiled. "We do most of our science and social studies together, and a lot of our special projects. We also do a lot of reading and hands-on activities rather than workbooks."

"How can they do science and social studies together when they are in different grades?" Cassy looked at Lauren skeptically.

"How do you think they taught in one-room schoolhouses?" Lauren asked.

"I don't know; that was before my time." Cassy laughed.

"The only reason we have separate textbooks for each grade is because once they divided kids by age into separate classrooms, they had to come up with some system of progression. Yes, there is an order of progression in learning math concepts, and in learning how to read, but who says that grade twos have to learn about Australia and grade threes have to learn about magnets? And who says that reading a page out of a workbook and answering twenty questions about what you read is the best way to learn about a topic? It's certainly not very exciting, but it gives teachers something to mark to come up with grades."

"So how do you teach social studies for example?" David questioned.

"Well, I'm teaching the kids all together. We started with the Bible and have been working through history in one continuous timeline."

"You can do that?" David asked.

"Why not? It sure makes more sense and fits everything together. It's neat to see how God worked throughout history. Right now we are studying the Reformation, and the kids love it. We read a lot of novels about the time period, read biographies of key people, and work on a timeline together. Then we make maps of the countries involved in our stories, or act out different events. Even the little ones like to listen to the stories and get involved. The older kids pick people or events they are particularly interested in to study further or write about. Melissa has been writing about the Huguenots."

"The who?" Cassy asked in disbelief. "How do you know all this stuff?"

"I'm learning it with them as I read the stories and learn the beliefs and struggles of those involved. It makes history so much more interesting than a bunch of isolated facts and dates! The Huguenots were the Protestant Christians in France who were persecuted for their faith. Many were massacred or fled their country."

Cassy was amazed. She had never imagined approaching school this way and realized that she knew very little about history as a whole. What would it have been like to learn it as the Andrews were doing? "I wouldn't know where to begin," Cassy declared emphatically.

"I didn't come up with it all by myself, don't worry. There are some very good teacher's guides with timelines, lots of good ideas, and lists of great books for different time periods. It's not as hard as it sounds. I could bring you some books about homeschooling next time I'm out," Lauren offered.

Cassy reluctantly agreed. Her stomach had started to twist in knots at the thought of doing all the things Lauren had mentioned. Rising from her seat, Cassy started to clear the table, seeking a diversion and a means to shift the topic of conversation. As the ladies put away the food and did the dishes, they chatted together, and soon Cassy began to feel as if she'd known this woman for years.

It was a pleasant afternoon, but when the Andrews left a few hours later, the talk about homeschooling was what kept playing over and over in Cassy's mind. She was starting to get a headache.

⌘ ⌘ ⌘

That night, after the kids were in bed, David broached the subject once again.

"I liked what Richard and Lauren said about homeschooling—it really made me think. Their philosophy of training their kids up before sending them out makes sense. I never heard the contaminated salt argument used that way before, but it's true. I think to send them out before they are ready is backwards to how God intended."

"I guess so, but they could get a solid foundation at the Christian school too. It doesn't mean we'd have to homeschool." Cassy couldn't quite hide the agitation in her voice. She was beginning to regret having asked Lauren about homeschooling at all.

David studied his wife. "What's bugging you? I thought you were interested in what they had to say."

Cassy sighed heavily as tears burned her eyes. "I was, sort of. I don't know..." She began to massage her temples. "I just wanted to understand what it was about, and it sounded neat and all, but I couldn't do it." A tear landed silently in her lap, and David came to take a seat on the couch beside his wife.

"I didn't say we were going to do it, but what scares you so much about the idea of teaching the kids at home?" David laid a comforting hand on Cassy's knee. "I thought you liked having the kids around and hate the rush to get them out the door every morning."

"I do!" Cassy snapped more forcefully than she'd intended. "But having them at home is a lot different than taking on the responsibility to teach them everything they need to know; I'm not a teacher. Besides, how would I be able to do all that and still keep up with the housework and everything that needs to get done around here, let alone having time for some of the things I like to do? What about my activities at the church, or my getting a part-time job, or just being able to go grocery shopping and stuff without having to take four kids with me everywhere? I'd have no time to myself!" Cassy felt so mixed-up.

"Look, I'm not trying to stress you out or put a lot of pressure on you or anything, I'm just trying to look at options. You said that you don't feel comfortable keeping the kids in the public school, and I've come to agree with you," David reasoned.

"I know, I know." Cassy wiped her eyes and looked up at her husband. "In theory I think the idea sounds great, and it would be nice to have the kids at home more, but at the same time I feel scared to death. I don't know what to think."

"Well," David continued, "as far as I can see, we have two options—the Christian school or homeschooling. I feel we need to look into both options to make an informed decision. If we put the kids in the Christian school and you went back to work, you'd still lose a fair bit of your spare time, and we wouldn't be much ahead financially by the time we paid tuition for four kids. I know homeschooling would be a big commitment and it would affect you a lot more than me, but can we commit to pray about it and study what the Bible says about training our children? I don't feel we've ever really sought God's direction in this before, and I think it is important and we should have."

Cassy nodded. "I want to talk to Cory and Trish and find out about the tuition costs and what they think of the Christian school as a whole. With Trish working there, she should be well informed about how things are run and everything. I'll take a look at the homeschooling books Lauren brings over and try to see what the Bible says, but I just need some time to work through it."

"Fair enough. I'll study as well and we can compare notes and pray about it together—starting now." With that David placed his arm around his wife and led her in prayer before turning out the light and heading for bed.

5

Weighing the Options

Trish was the secretary of the Red Deer Christian School where her children attended, but Cassy was reluctant to call her at work. She felt she would much rather sit down and have a chat with both her brother and his wife together, so she put off calling for a few days. When Lauren popped in quickly on Tuesday afternoon to drop off the books she had promised, Cassy made a mental note to call her brother that evening.

She wanted to discuss the Christian school option before pursuing the homeschool idea any further. It was better to consider all options equally, she reasoned with herself, as she took the homeschooling books to her bedroom and set them on her nightstand. Cassy wavered with her hand still on the books. Yes, she had agreed to read them, but after battling the recurring thoughts that kept popping into her mind since her conversation with David on Sunday, Cassy was feeling afraid. She was afraid that reading the books would convict her or make her feel guilty for not homeschooling. In the back of her mind she knew she was hoping that a talk with Cory and Trish would settle the matter, and she could put homeschooling out of her mind. Though Cassy didn't like some aspects of dealing with the school system and knew that Jeremy was struggling, she tried to convince herself that everything would be better if they just switched to the Christian school.

The last couple of days Cassy had been using her concordance to make a list of Bible verses dealing with parents training their children, and she decided that now would be as good a time as any to start looking them up. As Cassy couldn't remember ever coming across a verse that dealt with the formal education of children, she felt she was safe. She had concluded that the Bible must be silent on the matter. *It's not like there's an eleventh commandment that states, "Thou shalt not send thy children to school,"* she mused.

Anika was busy coloring at the kitchen table, so Cassy picked up her Bible from the nightstand, propped up several pillows against the headboard, and took a seat on her bed. The first verse on her list was found in Genesis chapter 18 and was set in the context of God having chosen Abraham to make a great nation of his descendants, that all nations would be blessed through him. Verse 19 read, "For I have chosen him, so that he will direct his children and his household after him to keep the way of the Lord by doing what is right and just, so that the Lord will bring about for Abraham what he has promised him."

"Hmm," Cassy said quietly to herself. "Could David and I direct our children to keep the way of the Lord and still send them to school?" Cassy thought so and looked up the next set of verses on her list, Deuteronomy 6:5-9:

> Love the LORD your God with all your heart and with all your soul and with all your strength. These commandments that I give you today are to be upon your hearts. Impress them on your children. Talk about them when you sit at home and when you walk along the road, when you lie down and when you get up. Tie them as symbols on your hands and bind them on your foreheads. Write them on the doorframes of your houses and on your gates.

It was a very familiar passage, though Cassy hadn't analyzed the verses in light of her children's schooling before. She realized that the verses admonished parents to teach the commands of the Lord to their children throughout the different events of their day, and this would be a bit harder if they were gone for a good portion of the day, but in a Christian school they would still be learning biblical teachings and she and David could supplement that at home. *Would that still accomplish the intention of the passage?* Cassy decided to read more before making up her mind. She read a few more passages in Deuteronomy, which reinforced the passage in chapter six, before moving on to Psalm 78:1-7:

O my people, hear my teaching; listen to the words of my mouth.
I will open my mouth in parables, I will utter hidden things, things from of old—what we have heard and known, what our fathers have told us. We will not hide them from their children; we will tell the next generation the praiseworthy deeds of the LORD, his power, and the wonders he has done. He decreed statutes for Jacob and established the law in Israel, which he commanded our forefathers to teach their children, so the next generation would know them, even the children yet to be born, and they in turn would tell their children. Then they would put their trust in God and would not forget his deeds but would keep his commands.

Cassy let her Bible rest in her lap as she contemplated the words. Scripture sure seemed to clearly instruct parents, especially fathers, to teach their children. Cassy felt no doubt that she and David were ultimately responsible for the godly instruction of their own children, but was it okay to delegate the bulk of their formal education to another? Feeling uncomfortable with the path her thoughts were taking, Cassy closed her Bible. She placed it on top of the homeschool books on her nightstand and went to check on her daughter.

Pondering the verses in Psalms, Cassy entered the kitchen, where Anika was still busy coloring at the table. Peeking over her daughter's shoulder, Cassy admired the picture. "That looks very pretty, Anika."

"Thanks, Mommy!" Anika turned to give her a pleased smile. "I'm a'most done, see? I just have to cower this wittle fish over here." She pointed to the spot with her tiny finger.

"Oooh, and what color is he going to be?" Cassy questioned.

"It's a she, and I'm going to make her...umm...pink." Anika grabbed a pink crayon from those scattered on the table. She bent intently over her picture once again as she carefully colored the fish. Cassy moved to the sink to fix some potatoes to go with their roast for supper.

"Wook, Mommy, I wrote my name!"

Cassy crossed the room once again to see her daughter's work. There, in big uneven letters across the top of her page was Anika's name. The "K" was tilted at an odd angle; it was the letter her daughter always struggled with. Cassy smiled. "Good job," she encouraged.

"What does this say?" Anika pointed to the bold words at the bottom of the page.

"Tell me the sounds of the letters first." It was their little game.

The little girl screwed up her face in concentration as she carefully named each of the letters followed by the sound it made. When she got to the *L,* Anika frowned. "I can't say that one." She looked at her mom.

Carefully Cassy made an *L* sound, opening her mouth wider to emphasize the position of her tongue for her daughter. Desperately Anika tried to mimic her mother. After the third try, Anika let out a heavy sigh.

"It's too hard."

Cassy didn't press her. "You'll get it, don't worry." Cassy tapped the end of Anika's nose with her finger and the little girl giggled.

"So what does it say?" Anika persisted.

"A-n-g-e-l F-i-s-h," Cassy pronounced slowly, emphasizing each sound.

"That's a pretty name, I wike it! Do they have Angel Fish in Heaven?" she questioned sweetly.

Cassy laughed. "I don't know, honey. You'll have to ask Jesus when you get there."

"I know why they're caw'ed Angel Fish. 'Cause they wook wike they have wings. They're very pretty, and I'm sure Jesus wou'd have them in Heaven!"

Just then the back door burst open and Anika jumped from her chair with a squeal to run and meet her siblings. After a quick snack, Kimberleigh and Anika disappeared to their room, Nicole settled at the kitchen table with her math book, and Jeremy made a dash for the door.

"Jeremy, do you have any homework?" Cassy called, stopping him with the door half open. Cassy listened for a response, and after a moment she heard a moan, followed by the banging of the door. Dejectedly Jeremy dragged his backpack to the kitchen.

"Aw, Mom, do I have to?" he questioned, already knowing his mother's answer.

Cassy was tired of arguing with her son about homework, but at the same time she felt a measure of sympathy. After seven hours of sitting in a desk at school, her energetic boy was dying to get outside. Cassy relented. "Okay, you have half an hour outside and then your homework, with no complaints!"

With a look of shock Jeremy ran from the room, Shasta close on his heels. He made his escape before his mother could change her mind.

"Don't slam the...door." With a bang her son was off and running. "I can't imagine trying to get him to sit all day and do schoolwork!" Cassy muttered to herself as she went back to scrubbing potatoes.

⌘ ⌘ ⌘

Following supper that night, Cassy made her call to Trish. Kimberleigh's birthday was on Friday, and she was hoping Cory's family could join them for supper and birthday cake. After a short chat, the ladies agreed on a time, and Cassy hung up the phone. Kimberleigh had requested pizza and chocolate cake for her birthday dinner—her favorite and a combination all the kids would love. This was the year Kimberleigh would be getting her first Bible. The Knights had made it a tradition to give each child a Bible of their own the year they learned to read, and Kimberleigh was looking forward to getting hers.

That evening David was still in the bathroom brushing his teeth when Cassy slid beneath her covers, so she reached once again for her Bible to read a few more verses on her list before bed. As she lifted it from her nightstand, the homeschooling books, which had been sitting beneath it, seemed to glare back at her. Annoyed, she flipped them over and found where she'd left off on her list. She leafed through her Bible, stopping at Proverbs 1:7-9. Glancing quickly at the previous verses for context Cassy began to read.

The fear of the LORD is the beginning of knowledge, but fools despise wisdom and discipline. Listen, my son, to your father's instruction and do not forsake your mother's teaching. They will be a garland to grace your head and a chain to adorn your neck.

"Solomon would have to mention 'your mother's teaching' in there, wouldn't he?" Cassy muttered to herself. "Well, I have taught my kids some things, but it doesn't mean I have to teach them everything!" Even as she said the words, Cassy felt reproved in her heart for taking offense at God's Word. It was as if the truths from Scripture echoed within her asking, *Why are you angry? I have entrusted these children into your care and ask that you raise them for Me, both for their sakes and for My glory. They are all you have that is eternal, and I am not asking you to do the impossible. Remember, I will go with you!*

Cassy sucked in her breath and looked around the room as if expecting to see someone standing beside her bed, but no one was there. With a shock she realized that the words she'd heard in her heart were true. To train her children for God's glory was the most awesome task God could ever give her. Was she willing to give it her best effort? Suddenly this whole dilemma was not just about the public school vs. the Christian school or homeschooling, but about obedience to what God may be directing her to do. How could she best honor God and train up her children for Him, and was she willing to do it? It was a tough question, and the thought troubled her.

"You look deep in thought."

Cassy jumped at her husband's words. She hadn't seen him come into the room. "I was just thinking through a verse I read," Cassy answered seriously.

"About training up our children?" David nodded. "I've been thinking a lot about that too."

"And what have you come up with?"

"Well." David sat on the edge of the bed and looked thoughtfully at his wife. "I definitely see lots of commands for fathers to teach their children the things of the Lord, and I'm not sure I've taken that responsibility as seriously as I should." David reached for his Bible from off his dresser. "I also found a few verses that really hit me when I read them with the kids in mind." He flipped through his Bible until he found the verse. "Have you read Luke 6:40 recently?"

"I don't think so," Cassy admitted.

"It says, 'A student is not above his teacher, but everyone who is fully trained will be like his teacher.' I realize that the kids have a lot of different teachers in school, but it does raise the question of a teacher's influence on their students."

David turned to another passage in his Bible. "First Corinthians 15:33 says, 'Do not be misled: "Bad company corrupts good character."' I guess between that verse, and the passage in 2 Corinthians about being unequally yoked, calling us to come out and be separate and to purify ourselves from anything that contaminates our body or spirit, I have to question the wisdom of surrounding our kids with non-Christian friends and secular teaching all day." David closed his Bible, his brows knit in thought.

"I guess it's what we grew up with, and when the kids started school we never gave it a second thought." Cassy paused, debating whether to ask her next question. She felt she was being drawn down a road she was not ready to travel, yet she couldn't turn back. Cassy had to find answers; she had to know what God wanted from her. "So, have you come to any conclusions about what we should do? Do we have to homeschool in order to train the kids for God, or can we do that alongside of the Christian school?"

"Well, I don't feel there's any doubt they would get good teaching at the Christian school, and we could supplement that at home. I'm just not sure yet what God would have us do and which method would be best for our family. You said that Cory and Trish are coming on Friday. Let's see what they have to say about the Christian school. In the meantime, let's continue to pray about it." David grasped his wife's hand, leading them in prayer for their children and the decision they were facing.

Long after the light went out and David began breathing in the even rhythm of sleep, Cassy's mind was still going. She wasn't sure how to express the conviction she'd felt earlier. Had it been her imagination, or was God trying to soften her heart toward what He wanted her to do? She would continue to seek.

Finally, she drifted off to sleep.

Cassie was tired the next morning when her alarm went off. She dragged herself from bed to wake up the kids. David was already in the shower, and their morning race had begun.

The next couple of days flew by. By Friday afternoon Cassy had Kimberleigh's presents wrapped, a cake made, and balloons strung around the kitchen with Anika's help. By the time the kids came home from school, Cassy was busy getting everything ready to make the pizza. Anika was seated on the counter beside her, sneaking bites of pepperoni. Bounding into the room, the excited birthday girl came to check on the progress.

"I know aw your presents, but I can't te'w. It's a secret!" Anika announced.

"How was school?" Cassy asked as Nicole and Jeremy joined them.

"Good!" Kimberleigh announced. "I got to sit in the special birthday chair by Mrs. Jenkins' desk and she let me lead everyone outside at recess!"

"I got an *A* on my math test," Nicole chimed in as she reached for the cookie jar.

Cassy glanced at her son, but he was sitting sullenly at the table eating his cookie. "How about you, Jeremy?" she prodded gently.

"It was okay," Jeremy answered with little enthusiasm, his eyes fixed on the cookie in his hands.

"Doesn't sound okay."

"Everybody thinks I'm stupid!" Jeremy dropped his cookie on the table and turned with angry, hurt-filled eyes. "I hate reading out loud; some of the kids laugh when I can't pronounce a word right." Tears stung the little boy's eyes, and he fought to hold them in check.

Cassy crossed the room to put a hand on her son's shoulder. She had always excelled in school growing up, but she knew kids in her classes down through the years who had been picked on mercilessly. She was now experiencing some of that for the first time through her son, and her heart ached. Kids could be vicious at times, and she hated to see her son face the taunts of others.

"You are definitely not stupid, Jeremy! Not everyone learns to read at the same time; it just takes practice. I wish I could keep the kids from picking on you, but I can't. And neither can you. What you can control is how you respond to them." Cassy wished she could wipe the hurt from her son's eyes.

"Here, Jeremy, why don't you come read to me, and I'll help you," Nicole offered sympathetically. "I've got a great adventure story; you'll like it." She ran to her room to get the book from her shelf. In a moment she was back, settled herself on the couch, and patted the cushion beside her invitingly.

Reluctantly Jeremy picked up his discarded cookie and headed to the living room to join his sister. Soon Cassy could hear the drone of her son reading. When he got stuck on a word, Cassy watched as her daughter patiently helped him sound it out, sometimes explaining little rules to help him remember. Nicole was not always so patient with her boisterous brother, but witnessing Jeremy's pain over being laughed at brought out the best in her, and Cassy was touched. Smiling, she returned to her pizza making with the added help of an excited birthday girl.

Shortly after David got home, Trish and Cory arrived with their three kids—Kiera, who was twelve, Daniel nine, and Justin seven. When the kids were all settled with their supper at the table, Cassy joined the adults who were eating in the living room. She had always felt closest to her brother, Cory, and Cassy was glad that he and Trish lived nearby—unlike the rest of her family.

"So Cory, are you staying out of trouble?" Cassy nudged her brother on her way by.

"As always!"

"Maybe I should ask Trish about that," Cassy teased.

"Oh, I've given up on trying to make him behave," Trish declared. "It's Daniel I wish I could do something with. I think he just stuffed half a piece of pizza into his mouth at once!" Trish gave an exasperated sigh and left to go speak with her nine-year-old.

"Like father, like son." Cassy laughed. "Remember when you stuffed ten marshmallows into your mouth at once and nearly choked?"

"Twelve," Cory corrected, "but don't tell Trish."

"Too late," Trish called from the kitchen. "Besides, I knew he didn't get it from me!"

"Getting me in trouble." Cory whipped a carrot stick at his sister, and she laughed as she caught it.

When Trish returned, Cassy broached the subject. "So, how do you guys like the Christian school?"

Trish raised her eyebrows in surprise. "You thinking of switching schools?"

"We want to get the kids out of the public school," David confirmed. "We're just checking our options.

"We like it and think the teachers are great," Cory said. "I especially like the secretary they have there." He winked at his wife, a silly smirk on his face.

"You do that too often, and your face will stay that way," Trish retorted. Turning back to Cassy, she continued. "We have a great bunch of teachers, and I'm glad I can be so involved with what's going on with the kids. Of course, most of the parents are involved to some extent. I like their chapel time and the fact that they are being taught the Bible in school, and they have a strict Bible memorization program. It sure challenges me just trying to help the kids with their Scripture memory at home."

"How much is the tuition?" David asked.

"Not cheap," Cory admitted, "but we feel it's worth it to have our kids there, and having Trish on staff sure helps."

When Cory named the cost, Cassy winced. The tuition was a little higher than she'd anticipated. Cassy knew that if they really cut back and adjusted their budget, they could probably do it, but with a fourth child entering school in a year, she'd for sure be looking for part-time work outside the home. "What about the books?" she asked.

"What do you mean?" Trish narrowed her brows.

"I mean, do they use Christian books, or the same books as the public school? How do they teach from a Christian perspective?"

"Oh," Trish nodded. "Some of the books come from a Christian distributor, but we follow the government guidelines so we use a lot of their curriculum, especially in the upper grades. The teachers still have the ability to supplement that and to bring Christ into classroom discussion, though."

"So you're pretty pleased with the general atmosphere and what the kids are getting there?" David asked.

"Oh yeah, it's great having all Christian staff and the spiritual emphasis and all. Of course, it's not without any troubles," Cory admitted, "but for the most part they have a good bunch of students. The school enforces a higher standard of behavior than the public school, but kids will be kids. You're always going to have some issues to deal with when you get that many of them together in one place."

"Is there anything you don't like?" Cassy asked.

Trish thought for a minute. "The main thing I struggle with is the amount of homework they have sometimes, but you get that in any school. I just wish it didn't have to cut into family time at home, and it will only get worse when they get into the upper grades. Plus then you'll have to tack on all the afterschool activities if they get involved with sports or drama or anything. I guess that's just the way life is nowadays and you can't avoid it." Trish shrugged.

Cassy thought of her son and frowned. She knew what the homework battle was like. It would be nice if, after spending all day in school, the kids could be done when they got home.

"If you're thinking about registering, let me know and I'll bring you the forms," Trish offered. "We're working on registrations for next year right now."

"Thanks, we'll let you know," David agreed.

By then the kids had finished their pizza and were ready for cake and ice cream. There was little time for further discussion as the attention shifted to Kimberleigh. Following cake came the presents, and the excited cousins piled into the living room and found spots on the floor encircling the birthday girl. Kiera eagerly held out the present they had brought for her to open first.

"Oh cool!" Kimberleigh exclaimed when she unwrapped the game she'd been asking for. "Thanks."

Opening her Bible next, Kimberleigh smiled. She carefully lifted it from the box and flipped through the pages before setting it gently on the floor beside her. The next gift was a china tea party set, which brought a squeal of delight. Kimberleigh carefully studied the collection of miniature cups, saucers, plates, and accessories with their dainty rose pattern.

"I he'ped pick it out," Anika bragged as she peered over her sister's arm. "Now we don't have to use Mommy's big cups for our tea parties anymore." It was clear that Anika was anxious to try them out as well.

Upon unwrapping the last present, Kimberleigh discovered a bundle of fancy dress-up clothes. She proceeded to place the sequined hat on her head at a jaunty angle, pulled on the long white gloves, slipped her feet into the sparkly, high-heeled shoes, and flung the feather boa around her neck with a flourish. With a dramatic air she turned and curtsied to each guest and announced primly, "Thank you. Thank you so much for attending my affair and for all your wonderful presents. They were lovely."

"They were lovely," Daniel mimicked perfectly in a high voice, complete with fluttering eyelids and a flick of his wrist. Everyone laughed, and Kimberleigh glared at her ornery cousin.

"You, Sir Daniel, can be replaced!" Kimberleigh said and, with a huff of arrogance, she left to get her treat bags and pass them out. She made sure to give Daniel his last.

"Just think what she'll be like at sixteen!" Cory teased his sister. Cassy just rolled her eyes.

It was late by the time her brother's family left and the kids headed to bed. As Cassy was finishing up the last of the dishes, David came in to sneak a second helping of birthday cake and took a seat at the table.

"Jeremy had a rough time at school again today," Cassy informed him. "He said the kids laughed at him while he was reading, and it's really getting to him."

"Poor guy. I'm not sure why he struggles so much—whether he just gets too uptight when he feels under pressure to perform. I don't want him feeling like he's a failure; he'll just get more and more discouraged and not want to try at all." David set his fork down on the side of his plate. "Unfortunately, he probably won't get away from some of that even if we switch schools."

"So you don't think we should put the kids in the Christian school?" Cassy felt her body tense as she waited for the answer.

"I didn't say that; it's just something to think about. I'm not sure yet what we should do."

Cassy let out her breath and wiped down the counter. It was time for bed, and she was too tired to think about it more tonight.

6

The Decision

Saturday morning, as Cassy slipped from her bed, her eyes fell on the neglected homeschool books resting on her nightstand. A twinge of guilt fluttered through her over the fact that she hadn't even opened the cover of either one to look inside. She had to admit that she had still been hoping the talk with Cory and Trish would give her a sense of peace about sending the kids to the Christian school, but, if she were honest with herself, she knew it hadn't. There was no doubt that the Christian school would offer a Christian environment and some Bible teaching, but Cassy hadn't felt settled since the other night following her Scripture reading. God clearly expected parents to disciple their children in biblical truth and godly character. Was she merely trying to transfer the bulk of that responsibility to someone else for her own convenience? Thoughts of training her children at home kept resurfacing, and Cassy made up her mind that she would take some time later that day to check out the homeschooling books and see what they were about.

It wasn't until just after lunch that Cassy finally retrieved the books and curled up in her favorite chair to read. The kids were all outside playing and David was at work, so she had the house to herself. After eyeing both book covers and skimming the chapter titles, Cassy settled on one and began to read.

When the kids bounded noisily into the house awhile later, Cassy was astonished to discover that it was almost 5:00. She'd been so engrossed in what she had been reading, she'd lost all track of time. The approach to homeschooling presented in the book varied so greatly from the familiar structure of a traditional classroom that it challenged

Cassy's concept of education as she had experienced it. At the same time, what the author said seemed to make sense and appealed to her heart. Could it really work?

Better yet, could she, Cassy Knight, effectively teach her children at home? It seemed a daunting task, yet her heart had been opening up to the idea through her ongoing reading of Scripture, and the biblical principles presented in the book started to take root in Cassy's heart and mind. Though she still had lots of questions, she felt her resistance slowly melting away. Closing the book, Cassy hurried to the kitchen to prepare supper. David would be home soon, and she couldn't wait to share with him what she'd read.

⌘ ⌘ ⌘

Throughout the following weeks the Knights continued to discuss the sense of God's calling, which seemed to tug on both of their hearts. They searched through the Scriptures some more, read through the books about homeschooling, and prayed together for God's direction for their family. Finally, just before the end of the school year, the couple reached a decision and felt a sense of peace. They were sure that God was asking them to homeschool. The final step was to see what their children thought of the idea and to notify the school that the kids would not be returning next year.

That Wednesday after supper, the Knights called their children into the living room to discuss the matter.

At the call, Jeremy appeared in the living room doorway, his face apprehensive. "Whatever it is, I didn't do it!" he announced firmly.

David and Cassy laughed and motioned their son into the room. "Nobody's in trouble. We just want to talk to you," Cassy clarified.

"Whew!" Jeremy let out his breath in obvious relief and entered the room. "Usually when you want to talk, it's because somebody's in trouble, and usually that somebody's me!" he declared emphatically.

Anika climbed up on Cassy's lap, while the others settled on the floor at their parents' feet. Over the last few weeks the kids had heard bits and pieces of their parents' conversations, enough to know that there was talk of change, but they had yet to understand what it was all about.

Clearing his throat, David began. "Your mother and I have decided that we want to make sure you're learning things that help you to follow God and develop the attitudes He wants you to have, so next year you will not be going back to school—"

"Whoo-hoo!" Jeremy interrupted, jumping up from the floor in excitement. "No more school!"

"I'm not finished." David eyed his son in an attempt to cool his enthusiasm. Jeremy plopped back on the floor, but he couldn't wipe the huge smile off his face. "You're still going to have to do school, but we've decided to teach you at home."

"Like the Andrews?" Nicole asked with interest.

"Yes, like the Andrews," Cassy affirmed.

"Can I do schoo' at home too?" Anika turned to look in her mother's eyes. It was clear she thought the idea a good one.

"Yes, you too."

"Melissa was telling me about homeschooling, and I think it sounds cool." Nicole smiled.

"Will I still have to take spelling tests?" Jeremy looked a little skeptical.

"We haven't figured that all out yet, but we'll do things differently from what you're used to," Cassy explained, and that seemed to appease her son. She looked at Kimberleigh, who was sitting quietly, her head down. "What do you think, Kimmy?"

"What about my friends?" she asked forlornly.

Cassy should have guessed that for her social butterfly, her daughter's friends would be an issue. "You'll still get to see some of your friends in church, or maybe have them over sometime, but you'll get to spend a lot more time with your sisters and Jeremy. Mrs. Andrews also said that the homeschool families get together a lot for activities and fieldtrips, so you'll get to make some new friends too," she encouraged. "Won't you like that?"

Kimberleigh nodded unconvincingly.

Anika hopped off her mother's lap and stooped to give her sister a hug. "I'm your friend, Kimmy!" she declared, bringing a lopsided smile to her sister's face.

The family discussed the reasons for choosing homeschooling and what it might look like for most of the evening, and Cassy and David did their best to answer all the questions thrown at them. In the end, they all agreed that they would like to give it a try, though Cassy still sensed that, for Kimberleigh, the decision was a little tougher. Jeremy, however, was elated at the idea of spending a little less time sitting in a desk, and having more time to be outside. Nicole's eyes lit up at the prospect of reading stories together, and Anika, who had never experienced the classroom, was just thrilled to get her siblings home and to be able to be a part of it all.

That Friday, the last day of classes, Cassy made her way into the school office to notify the head secretary of their decision. She was not prepared for the cool response she would receive.

"Are you a certified teacher, Mrs. Knight?" the middle-aged woman asked haughtily.

"Why, no, I'm not," Cassy admitted, surprised.

"It never ceases to amaze me how parents think they can provide the quality of education their children receive from professional teachers in the school system! How do you suppose you're going to do that without the training and resources we possess?" she huffed.

Taken aback, Cassy just stared at the woman across the desk from her, unsure how to respond. "I think we'll manage," was all she said before turning for the door. She stopped when she heard the secretary mumble something derogatory under her breath, then bit her tongue and exited the room before she was tempted to say something she might regret. Anika was waiting outside the office door and, grasping her hand, Cassy went to find her children. The wind had been sucked from her sails. Now Cassy really wondered what she was getting herself in for.

⌘ ⌘ ⌘

That summer David and Cassy gradually told friends and family of their decision. They were met with mixed reactions, ranging from polite acceptance to being battered with pointed questions that left Cassy feeling frustrated and defensive. Cory and Trish seemed a little disappointed that the kids would not be joining their cousins at the Christian school, but they said that they understood and hoped it worked well for them. Throughout their decision-making struggles, David had talked often with Anthony at work, so his brother was well aware of what was going on and seemed supportive. Cassy still felt awkward discussing their choice to leave the public school with Sarah, however, as Timothy, their eldest, would be starting grade one at the public school this fall. David and Cassy's parents and other family members seemed surprised at their decision. Some voiced numerous concerns ranging from the kids' need to interact with their peers, to worry over the high demands that would be placed on Cassy to ensure they got a thorough education. Others said very little, but the looks on their faces left Cassy wondering what they were really thinking. Few, Cassy felt, understood the heart of their struggle or viewed their decision to be a wise one.

Her older brother, Don, was the most outspoken. As a public school teacher, he took their announcement most personally and voiced concerns of where the school system would end up if all the Christian kids were removed. Though they understood his frustration, David and Cassy could hardly justify keeping their children in an ungodly system based on those grounds. It was a gamble to predict whether the Christian kids would have more effect on the system or vice versa, a gamble they were unprepared to take. After all, they had all gone through the public school system as Christian youth and Cassy ventured that, if anything, the system was less tolerant to Christian values now than it was a dozen years ago. She also knew a number of her peers from youth group who were no longer walking with the Lord, and it made her wonder.

Don advised them that they would have to be diligent to make sure their children didn't fall behind so that when they put them back into school for junior high and high school, they would not be held back. Cassy was not yet sure what the future held, or if their children would return to school down the road, but she didn't feel prepared to tackle that issue with her brother just yet.

Cassy found encouragement over the summer through her many visits with Lauren. Whenever she felt discouraged or full of doubt, she called Lauren, who patiently answered her questions and lifted her spirits. Lauren also helped Cassy get the kids registered with a homeschool board and spent a whole day with her at a homeschool curriculum store. Making their way systematically through the store, Lauren pointed out many good books her family had enjoyed and explained to Cassy the different types of curriculum, helping her pick out books she felt suited her family. Cassy found the selection overwhelming and voiced her appreciation to her new friend so many times that Lauren accused her of sounding like a broken record.

At the end of the summer, Cassy sat down with all of her newly purchased books sprawled across the kitchen table and wondered for the hundredth time what she'd gotten herself into. She leafed through teacher's manuals and lesson books, checking the number of pages and calculating how many she'd need to cover every week to complete each one. Taking notes as she went, she developed a schedule, breaking the days into segments designated for each subject. She allotted an hour for each period, figuring that should give her the necessary time to complete the required work. Her days were filling up fast, and she sighed.

Putting her schedule aside, Cassy picked up the guide book she had purchased for teaching the Bible alongside the history of ancient civilizations. This book was the one that she found the most exciting, and she fingered the novels Lauren had helped her pick out to go along with the study of Ancient Egypt. She knew very little about Ancient Egypt and wondered how difficult it would be to teach her children anything on the subject, but reading the backs of the novels and glancing once again through the well-illustrated book telling about life in the ancient civilization, Cassy felt certain her children would enjoy them.

At the sound of the doorbell, Cassy rose from the table. She was pleased to see Lauren and the kids greet her when she opened the door.

"We were out running errands and thought we'd stop in and see how you were doing," Lauren offered cheerily. "I hope we're not interrupting anything."

"No, come in," Cassy welcomed. "I was just looking through my curriculum, trying to make some order of it all. I'd appreciate your input!"

Cassy's kids came scrambling down the hall, thrilled with the unexpected company. They were quickly making friends with the Andrews' gang, and in no time the boys were following Jeremy outside, while the girls disappeared to Nicole's room. Cassy led her visitor to the table and offered her a cup of coffee.

"I was working on a schedule," Cassy held the paper out to her friend. "What do you think?"

Lauren took the paper and smiled. "Looks very school-like," she teased.

"When do you find time to do any housework or prepare meals is what I'd like to know!" Cassy demanded.

"Well, you start by assigning each of the kids a few chores to help out."

"But what about their schooltime? Their day looks pretty full. And besides, the younger ones are much better at making messes than cleaning them up!" Cassy insisted.

"It's called 'home economics,' and they'll learn." Lauren countered.

"They don't do home economics until junior high," Cassy tried to rationalize.

"Says who? School curriculum is chock-full of classes trying to teach about family, community, co-operation, responsibility and life skills—all taught from behind a desk or in a classroom setting. You'll be living it in reality. How much better can you get than to learn life skills and home economics in a real home! Novel idea, eh?"

Cassy laughed in spite of herself. "I guess I never thought of it like that."

"They'll discover what it really means to work together as a family and what running a home is all about, that everyone is responsible to help out, and it comes naturally. I know at first you may feel like pulling your hair out, or that it takes you twice as long to get everything done, but even Kegan has a few jobs to do. They learn that life's easier if everyone helps out and it makes a big difference."

"Your kids sound perfect!" Cassy was amazed.

Lauren laughed, "They're certainly not perfect; I didn't mean that. I still have to remind them sometimes to get their jobs done, but I think it's good for them and I think all kids need to learn responsibility and to be a valued member of the family. And about your concern for time, I think you'll find that it doesn't take near as long as you've scheduled to get most of their work done."

"Really?" Cassy was relieved.

"I know it's hard to know what to expect at first, but I'd encourage you to be flexible. If they're in the middle of a project and they're excited about it, don't stop them just because the schedule says it's time to move on. And in the same manner, if they are done with their math pages in fifteen minutes, let them move on to the next thing. You have to find what works for you, but don't just copy the school time clock just because that's what you think has to happen." Lauren handed the schedule back to Cassy.

"I guess this can go in the garbage." Cassy tossed the paper aside, not at all offended by the notion. She liked what Lauren had to say and it obviously worked for their family. Cassy had come to value Lauren's experience and realized that her mindset was still bound by the traditional school approach. It was going to take some time to break free of that she could tell.

When Lauren and the kids left awhile later, Cassy felt a little more ready to begin her adventure.

7

Family Outing

L abor Day Monday the Knights packed up a picnic lunch and headed to Sylvan Lake for the day. It was a warm, sunny morning, and they wanted to take advantage of the nice weather. Living in central Alberta, Canada, one never knew when the weather would shift to usher in the first snow, so the beach was already crowded with families enjoying the late summer holiday—the last day before the start of the school year. The Knights had arrived at the beach early, but they still had to walk along the beachside path a ways before locating an unoccupied spot along the narrow strip of sand. They spread out their blankets, parked their cooler, towels and beach toys, and headed for the water.

Cassy waded in the shallow, cool water with Anika and Kimberleigh, while David headed out a little deeper with Jeremy and Nicole, both of whom could swim like fish. Cassy smiled. It was good to have David off work for the day after the busy building season. That was one thing Cassy enjoyed about winter. She didn't care much for the snow and cold, but it was good to have David home more on Saturdays and during some of the coldest spurts. She watched her husband now as he took turns tossing their two oldest into the air to land with shrieks and giggles into the lake with a splash. She could hear Jeremy coaxing his dad to toss him higher and higher.

A few small boats could be seen making their way lazily across the lake in the distance, and Cassy noticed a couple of Sea-Doos zipping along the water's surface near the middle of the lake, leaving trails of white spray in their wake. She wondered how long it would take before Jeremy would see them and start begging his dad to rent one for an hour and take him for a spin. He had only been on one twice before, but he loved it, especially when David placed him in front and allowed him to drive.

Suddenly Cassy was bombarded with cold water splashing down the front of her swimsuit and legs, drawing her attention back to her two mischievous daughters who were ganging up on her.

"Ooh, you think so, do you," she laughed as Kimberleigh paused, gauging her mother with an expectant grin. She was poised to make a run for it, but Cassy was too quick. Stooping, Cassy swooshed both hands through the water in one quick thrust, sending a wave of water over Kimberleigh's head.

"Me too, me too," Anika chimed in, still trying her best to splash her mother with small handfuls of water.

"Take that!" Cassy gently flipped water onto her four-year-old with one hand, while continuing her onslaught of Kimberleigh with the other. Kimberleigh danced around her mother giggling and splashing, trying to avoid Cassy's retaliation. Anika now had her eyes scrunched tightly closed to avoid getting water in them as she flicked water aimlessly in all directions. Cassy laughed again.

When the battle was over, the girls decided to build a sand castle, so they all headed to their spot on the beach. After patting themselves dry, the girls flung their towels down, gathered pails and shovels, and headed back to the water's edge. They stopped just out of reach of their mother who had settled on her large, brightly striped blanket. For the next hour Cassy watched as the two of them squatted in the sand side by side, packing their pails with the wet compound and tipping them over in a series of mounds. They dug a moat around their castle and then darted back and forth into the lake, filling their pails and running to dump them into the trenches, watching as the water pooled and trickled back to where it belonged.

By the time David made his way to shore with the older two, everyone was starving for lunch. Anika had to go to the bathroom, so Cassy sent the three girls over to the washroom while she got lunch organized. Jeremy was talking a mile a minute as Cassy pulled food from the cooler, telling of all their morning escapades.

Wrapping himself in a towel, he plopped down on the blanket and announced excitedly, "Dad said we can maybe rent a Sea-Doo!"

Cassy turned to her husband, who popped a chip into his mouth and gave her a sheepish grin. "And whose idea was it?" she teased.

"Totally his." David raised his hands in defense. "Right, bud?" He turned to Jeremy.

Jeremy nodded. "Can we, Mom?" he pleaded.

"I don't care, though I know how much your dad hates it," she added sarcastically.

Jeremy looked shocked at his mom's comment. "No, he doesn't! I know he doesn't, do you, Dad?" He looked to his dad for affirmation. When both his parents laughed, a relieved grin spread across Jeremy's face.

After the girls came back, David prayed for the food and everyone helped themselves to paper plates and loaded them with tuna sandwiches, chips, and carrot sticks. Jeremy fidgeted with excitement and stuffed his food in his mouth as fast as he could go.

"Slow down, Jeremy; you're not in a race," Cassy admonished, and her son did his best to comply.

"Did you see our sand castle, Daddy?" Anika pointed to their creation a few feet away.

"Looks cool! And who's the queen of the castle?" David asked his youngest daughter.

"That would be me!" Kimberleigh chimed in before her sister could answer.

Anika threw her sibling a frown and crossed her arms in front of her chest with a humph.

"I'm Queen Annabel, and she's Princess Leah," Kimberleigh quickly amended, hoping to appease her little sister. It worked. Being allotted the position of princess seemed just fine to Anika, and her frown disappeared.

"You don't always have to be the queen," Cassy admonished her daughter, wanting to curb her tendency to control every situation and become too bossy.

"But I'm the oldest," Kimberleigh said stubbornly.

"Even with Nicole, you want to be in charge. I don't want you to become selfish. You have to take turns, or it's not much fun for everyone else," Cassy corrected her daughter gently.

"Sorry, Anika," Kimberleigh apologized reluctantly.

"That's okay," the easygoing preschooler offered. "Being a princess is much better than being your maid. A princess doesn't have to w'isten to a queen!"

Cassy decided that now was not the time to explain that the queen is a princess's mother and let the matter drop.

Nicole had been watching a seagull inching its way toward her, eying her sandwich. On a whim, she broke off a crust of bread and held it out to the aggressive bird. The seagull paused only a second before rushing forward to grab the bread from her hand.

"Look, Mommy." Nicole grabbed another piece of her sandwich and offered it to the bird. Instantly, every seagull in the vicinity honed in on their picnic site.

"Uh, I don't think that was a good idea, Nicole," Cassy cautioned. The words were no sooner out of her mouth, when Cassy felt something plop on her head. Reaching her hand up to investigate, she felt a warm, gooey mess that had been deposited by the gull that had just flown over. "Oh, yuck! Nicole, stop that!"

Nicole's hand flew to her mouth in shock when she realized what had happened. "Oops, sorry, Mom," she mumbled.

David started shooing away the pesky birds, trying desperately not to laugh. Cassy wiped her hand on a napkin and grabbed a towel as she headed to the bathroom to rinse out her hair in the sink.

"It's not funny!" Cassy flung back at him, causing her husband to lose control.

By the time Cassy returned, everyone was done with lunch and Jeremy was squirming and anxious to get going. None of the girls wanted to go on the Sea-Doo, so David and Jeremy headed down the beach in the direction of the boat rental building. Cassy sprawled on her blanket in the warm sunshine as she watched the girls playing in the water. Tomorrow she would be starting school at home, and she was still a bit apprehensive over the whole thing, but at the same time she felt sure God was leading them down this path. As Cassy watched her girls romping and splashing in the shallow water, she wondered what changes the year would bring and what the future held for each of her children. Most of all, she wondered how she'd survive her first week of teaching her rambunctious son.

A little over an hour later, the two wanderers were seen headed their way. The girls were once again huddled in towels on the blanket, munching on some cookies. Cassy could see her son's beaming face long before they were in audible range. Walking hand-in-hand along the beach with his father, Jeremy stared up at the tall man beside him, talking animatedly all the way. Cassy smiled at the picture they made, anxious to hear about their adventure. When they were almost to the blanket, Jeremy finally turned and saw his sisters. He broke away and ran over to them.

"You should have seen us," he declared excitedly. "Dad went so fast! We whipped around like this and made a big wave and the Sea-Doo leaned way over so we almost flipped!" Jeremy swung his arm in a big arc, curving his hand to demonstrate their sharp turn. "I got to drive too, and I went almost as fast as Dad," he bragged.

"I don't like to go that fast," Nicole announced unimpressed.

Nicole had been on a Sea-Doo once, and ever since she'd been afraid to go again. Her fear had been enough to keep her sisters from trying it, but Cassy felt they were plenty young anyway and didn't want them out so far when they couldn't swim—lifejacket or no lifejacket.

Nicole's comment did little to dampen her brother's enthusiasm. If anything, it seemed to make him all the more proud for being so daring and he continued to fill them in on all the details. He told them how they had gone all over the whole lake, "way across to the other side just like that," and he snapped his fingers for emphasis. Cassy could tell that her husband had enjoyed it just as much as Jeremy had.

By late afternoon it was starting to cool off, and the beach was beginning to clear. The Knights packed up their belongings and headed for home. They had all enjoyed the day at the beach, and Cassy could only hope that Jeremy would show a fraction of the enthusiasm he'd shown today once she got out his language arts workbook tomorrow.

8

Getting Started

Tuesday morning Cassy was up early, encouraging her sleepy children from their warm beds and to the kitchen table for breakfast. David had already eaten and was ready to head to work, but he stopped to speak to his children before leaving.

"You guys listen to your mom today, or she'll have to send you to the principal's office!" he admonished.

"Who's the principal?" questioned wide-eyed Kimberleigh.

"Me!" announced her father, displaying his sternest expression. The kids laughed, even though none of them would think it funny if they were to face their father for misbehavior. Yet the idea of him as their principal was a new one.

"Have a good day." David winked at his wife and gave her a kiss.

Cassy could tell he was hoping to alleviate her anxiety. "Thanks, you, too." She smiled at him before he left.

Cassy turned and glanced around the kitchen, feeling like she was forgetting something. There were no backpacks lined up and no lunch boxes waiting to be filled. It felt strange. With a sigh, Cassy sat at the table and ate breakfast with her children. It felt good not to be rushing or telling them to hurry. Moments later when she heard the school bus rumble past their drive, Cassy glanced around the table at each of her children as they chatted together, leisurely finishing their breakfast. She sure wasn't going to miss the morning rush.

When everyone was done eating, Cassy encouraged them to put their dishes in the dishwasher and take care of the jobs she had assigned, while she finished cleaning up the kitchen and got their books ready. Taking Lauren up on her suggestion of getting all the kids to help, Cassy had developed a chore chart with age appropriate chores for each child to complete every morning. They were each to make their own bed plus do their individually assigned chore for the day. Nicole was to help with vacuuming, scouring the bathroom sinks, and folding laundry. Jeremy was to empty the garbage cans, straighten up the shoes and coats in the entrance way, and empty the dishwasher. Kimberleigh was to sweep the kitchen floor, dust, and sort the clothes in the laundry room into baskets, while Anika was to pick up her toys and feed Shasta.

One day last week, Cassy had explained the chart and what was expected for each chore before hanging the chart on the fridge. After checking the sheet again, the kids dispersed to complete their various jobs. As Cassy collected cereal boxes from the table, she watched as Anika went to the cupboard under the sink to get the dog food. Filling the scoop to overflowing, she began carrying it across the kitchen toward Shasta's dish in the corner, dropping nuggets of food in a trail as she went.

"Don't fill the scoop so full, sweetie," she advised her young daughter.

"I didn't." Anika turned to show her mom, tipping the scoop as she did so and spilling more dog food in a pile beside her feet. "Oops!" Anika straightened the scoop and looked at the mess. "Shasta, here Shasta," she called. Shasta came running and started to gobble up the spilled food. "It's okay, Mom, see? Shasta wikes it this way!"

"Well, I would prefer if it were in Shasta's dish and not all over the floor, okay?" Cassy went to help her daughter empty what was left into the dog dish. Luckily Kimberleigh hadn't swept the floor yet, she reasoned to herself, but this chore thing was going to take some more training, she was sure.

By the time Cassy had the schoolbooks all organized on the table, the kids were about done and ready to join her. She decided to start with their math books. Situating Anika in her chair with an alphabet activity book to keep her occupied, Cassy explained to the other kids that they needed to finish four pages of math a day. They each proceeded to open their book to the first page, looked it over, then one-by-one they looked up at Cassy and waited. Going from child to child, Cassy glanced at the directions and carefully explained what to do, making sure they were set to work before going on to the next child. By the time Cassy was finished getting Kimberleigh started, she glanced up to find Nicole quietly watching her.

"Do you have a question, Nicole?" Cassy moved around the table to stand beside her daughter.

"No, I'm done and waiting to go on to the next page," she answered simply.

"Well, you can keep going."

"You mean, I don't have to wait for everyone to finish?" Nicole seemed surprised.

"No, you keep going until you've finished four pages. You can ask me to help if you have any questions."

"Cool." Nicole flipped the page and bent over her math book.

"Mom, I don't get this," Jeremy moaned in frustration.

Cassy stepped behind her son to peer over his shoulder. He was pointing to some fractions that were to be reduced. Lauren had warned her that this math curriculum was more advanced than the public school, so she might need to explain new concepts a little more at first.

"Do you know what fractions are?" she questioned her son.

"Sort of." Jeremy shrugged as if unsure.

"Well, fractions are talking about pieces of something." Cassy tried to think how to explain the concept of fractions more clearly. "The top number tells you how many pieces you have, and the bottom number tells you how many pieces are in the whole object. So if you have two-fourths, that tells you that you have two pieces out of four."

"Out of four what?"

"Out of the four pieces that it takes to make a whole," Cassy explained awkwardly.

"A whole what?" Jeremy huffed.

"A whole of whatever you have." Cassy glanced up and saw the bowl of apples on the table and grabbed one. "A whole apple," she declared spontaneously, crossing the kitchen to get a knife.

"Why don't they just say you have two pieces of apple, then!" Jeremy shook his head in annoyance.

"Because, it could be two pieces of anything, and it wouldn't tell you how big the pieces were or how much of the apple you had. They just want you to understand what a fraction means, but I'll show you." Cassy deftly cut the apple into quarters for her son. "Okay, first it's important that you always cut the pieces the same size so that they are equal portions of apple."

"Well, that piece is a little bigger than this one." Jeremy pointed out the discrepancy as he carefully compared the pieces Cassy had cut.

Cassy looked at the apple wedges and clenched her teeth in exasperation. "It doesn't matter right now."

"But you just said…"

"I know what I just said, and it does matter for a real fraction, but the pieces are pretty close. Can you pretend they're the same size for a minute?" Cassy glared at her son.

"I guess so," Jeremy agreed.

"Good! So, how many pieces of apple does it take to make a whole apple?" Cassy asked more calmly.

"Four," piped up Kimberleigh who had been listening to Jeremy's lesson.

"Right, Kimmy. Do you see that it takes four pieces to make up a whole apple, Jeremy?" Cassy held the pieces back together to form the apple. At Jeremy's nod, she continued. "Now, if I take two of those pieces, I have two out of four, or two-fourths. Right?"

"Yeah, two-fourths of a whole apple!" Jeremy declared triumphantly.

"Can I have two-four's of an apple? I'm hungry." Anika eyed the apple in her mother's hand.

"When I'm done showing Jeremy," Cassy agreed. "Now, they want you to write that fraction using different numbers, but showing that you are still talking about the same amount of apple. So, if I put two pieces together, what do I have now?"

"A half!" Jeremy brightened.

"Right, and how would you write that?"

Jeremy proceeded to write the fraction on the corner of his page.

"Okay, so now you have one piece out of two, so by making fewer pieces, the numbers change, but we still have the same amount of apple. One-half is equal to two-fourths." Cassy proceeded to show how she could cut the apple into more pieces and what the fractions would look like, then explained to Jeremy how to change those fractions on paper by multiplying or dividing the numerators and denominators by the same number to get equivalent fractions. Using the apple to demonstrate helped Jeremy visualize what was happening, and he got excited as he computed each of the problems on the page.

"Can I have my apple now?" Anika gave a big sigh. She had been watching as the apple kept getting cut into more and more pieces.

"Yes you may," Cassy scooted the pieces across the table beside Anika's book with satisfaction.

After the math pages were finished, Cassy took out the language arts workbooks and got each child started on their first lesson. By now Anika had tired of her book and had gotten some toys to play with on the kitchen floor. At one point, Cassy paused to skim through her teacher's manual so she could explain prepositional phrases to Nicole. She was so focused on what she was doing that she failed to notice Kimberleigh squirming impatiently on her chair, hand raised.

"Mommy," Kimberleigh finally exclaimed, "I've been waiting for, like, hours for you to come help me!"

Cassy raised her eyebrows at her daughter. "That's a slight exaggeration, Kimmy. I've been helping Nicole for five minutes, and I can only help one person at a time. You're just going to have to be patient."

"Well, it seems like hours to me," Kimberleigh mumbled as she stopped her wiggling and planted her elbows on her workbook, her chin in her hands.

"Why don't you hop down and play with Anika for a few minutes while you wait," Cassy suggested, hoping to curb her daughter's restlessness so she could concentrate on remembering what a preposition was.

Kimberleigh was more than happy to comply and was soon on the floor beside Anika, helping her arrange the furniture in her small dollhouse.

"That's no fair! Can I go play too?" Jeremy complained.

"No, you can finish the page you're working on."

Jeremy opened his mouth as if to protest, but at the look Cassy gave him, he turned away with a frown. Cassy missed the haughty smirk Kimberleigh threw in Jeremy's direction, as well as the scowl he returned the minute her attention was focused back on Nicole's book. It was only a matter of minutes, however, before Nicole was back at work locating and circling the prepositions on her page and underlining the nouns at the end of each phrase. When Kimberleigh's break was called to an end, she reluctantly climbed back on her chair to finish her work. Overall, Cassy was pleasantly surprised at how quickly the assigned pages were completed, in spite of her need to call Jeremy's attention back to his work a few times.

To practice penmanship, Cassy gave the kids a Bible verse to look up and copy in their neatest handwriting, informing them that they would take turns hanging their verses on the small bulletin board by the kitchen phone. While they were working, Cassy sat down to check their math pages. She circled their mistakes for them to correct before they could continue the next day.

Nicole and Jeremy finished their verses before Cassy was done marking, so she sent them to get some colored pencils to decorate their pages. Glancing at Kimberleigh's paper to see how she was doing, Cassy watched as her daughter carefully added little curly-cues to the tips of the letter she had just written to match the rest of her writing. She was only halfway through her verse.

"What are you doing, Kimberleigh?"

"I'm making my verse really fancy, see!" Kimberleigh smiled as she held up her paper to show her mother.

"Just don't overdo it; I want to be able to read it when you're finished."

By 10:30 everyone had completed their morning assignments, so Cassy called them into the living room to read together. They were starting with creation, and would be working through key stories and events in the Bible, as well as discussing what life was like in Bible times. As Cassy read from the Bible, each of the kids drew a picture of the creation week to put in a binder. Cassy hoped to get them to add something to their binder to go with each story or lesson—a picture, poem, notes, maps, whatever they could come up with for the day. Even Anika lay on her belly on the floor, coloring a piece of paper and listening to the true beginning of history.

While they were reading, Cassy was surprised by the questions and comments her children had to share. Then they took turns showing and explaining their pictures. Jeremy had drawn a dinosaur standing beside a stick figure of Adam. He was obviously still intrigued by his newly discovered knowledge concerning dinosaurs being created on day six. Nicole had divided her page into seven squares, each filled with a picture representative of the different days of creation, and Kimberleigh had colored a picture of trees and flowers and had written *Garden of Eden* across the top of her page. When it was her turn, Anika proudly showed off her picture and explained what all the colorful lines and circles were to the "oohs" and "ahhs" of her siblings. She seemed quite pleased with herself and wanted a binder for her pictures as well. By then it was lunch time, and Cassy headed to the kitchen to make some sandwiches.

She was pleased with how their day had gone so far and that she had accomplished more than what she had hoped for the morning. Her plans were to do math and language arts every morning, and then alternate in the afternoons with social studies two days a week and science two days a week. Friday afternoons would be left open so they could get involved in some of the homeschool activities planned by the local support group. Lauren had let her know about the first meeting scheduled for this Friday evening, which would provide an opportunity for new homeschoolers to meet everyone and learn more about the support group and their plans for the year. Cassy wasn't sure just what to expect, but she was looking forward to getting involved with the other families. Next week Nicole and Jeremy would be starting piano lessons on Monday afternoons with Mrs. Watkins from church. Nicole was excited about the prospect and Cassy hoped that once Jeremy started, he would enjoy it as well.

After lunch, Cassy again brought the kids into the living room to read a couple of chapters from a book she had picked up on Canadian history. It started with the landing of John Cabot in Newfoundland in 1497 and went through the history of Canada in story format. She felt it would be good to work through Canadian history as well as her Bible history program, reading a little each week. When she was done, Cassy sent Kimberleigh to the computer room to retrieve the globe so that she could show them the path of John Cabot's voyage from England to the newly discovered North American continent. Jeremy especially liked the adventure of his voyage across the ocean in search of a new route to China and his discovery of land for England. He thought it sounded great to be an explorer and was full of questions. Cassy couldn't answer them all, but thought she could probably find some more books at the library and promised to try.

With that, Cassy had finished her plans for the day. She glanced at her watch. It was a full two hours before the kids would have gotten home on the bus, and Cassy wondered if she'd forgotten something. Doublechecking her schedule, she couldn't find anything she'd skipped. What if she hadn't planned enough to do, and she was missing something? Cassy suddenly panicked, but then remembered Lauren had told her she should get through things faster than in school. She wasn't sure if Lauren had meant two hours faster, but since she didn't have anything else planned anyway, she dismissed the kids.

Jeremy was ecstatic! It was a gorgeous day and in a flash he grabbed his jacket, called Shasta, and was out the door. With no homework to worry about, Jeremy's sisters decided to join him. They spent the afternoon acting out an adventure of their own, crossing the Atlantic Ocean with none other but Captain Jeremy at the helm.

While they played, Cassy looked through a few things, making sure she was prepared for their science lesson the next day. Thankfully she only had one lesson to study, as the kids would be doing science together. Her teacher's manual went step-by-step through the lesson and then gave detailed instructions for completing the activity pages. The curriculum covered many aspects of earth and life science, all from a Christian perspective, and the kids workbooks looked like lots of fun. For each lesson they would complete special activities involving lots of coloring, charting, cutting and pasting, to create all kinds of unique pages to be compiled in their science binders. She thought Jeremy would especially enjoy the study of nature and the hands on activities. When she was done, Cassy collected the books and stacked them neatly on the small shelf they had moved into the corner of the kitchen for that purpose.

With the table cleared, Cassy went to throw in a load of laundry before starting on supper. She could watch the kids from the kitchen window while she worked, and when supper was about ready, she went to the back door to call them in to get cleaned up and set the table. Bounding noisily into the house, four rosy cheeked children made a dash for the bathroom to wash up, racing to see who would get there first.

"We were sai'wing in a boat!" Anika announced as she fled by the kitchen in an attempt to keep up.

"Sounds like fun," Cassy called after her. She could hear the kids vying for space at the sink.

"Don't make such a big mess, Jeremy," Nicole scolded. "I just cleaned that sink this morning! You wipe that up!"

Cassy laughed to herself in the kitchen. Maybe the extra chores were making a difference already. If nothing else, it might teach them to appreciate the effort that goes into the work, and to be more conscientious.

By the time David came in, the table was set and supper was ready. During the meal, David asked how their day had gone, and everyone started talking at once. Kimberleigh pointed out her Scripture verse hanging up on the bulletin board, and Anika slid from her chair to get her new binder to show her dad the picture she'd drawn. Jeremy told him about John Cabot and their adventures outside, while Nicole told him how much fun it had been to read together. Cassy added a few words here and there when she got a chance.

"I got to eat Jeremy's math wesson," Anika announced with a grin.

David gave his daughter a puzzled look. When Jeremy explained about the apple, David laughed. "I thought that was the homeschool version of 'the dog ate my homework.' It sounds like you had way too much fun. Maybe I should stay home and go to school," he teased, triggering the kids' laughter.

When David announced awhile later that he had picked up a children's devotional book to read to them each night before bed, he got an enthusiastic response. Cassy wasn't sure if Jeremy was more excited about the devotional or the prolonged bedtime, but Cassy was pleased nonetheless.

Once they were all ready for bed, David ushered the kids into Nicole's room to read and pray together. Cassy soon realized that this new bedtime ritual would give her some extra moments of peace each evening, and she made sure to show David her appreciation when he joined her later on the couch.

"So, everything really went okay today?" David asked as Cassy lifted his feet into her lap to give him a foot rub.

"Yeah, it really did," Cassy responded in surprise. "I'm not sure if I covered everything I should have, though. I got done at 2:00."

"I'm sure you did fine, and the kids seemed to enjoy it," David encouraged.

"Well, if every day goes as smoothly as today did, it won't be near as bad as I thought," Cassy admitted. "I guess time will tell."

9

Learning Flexibility

Early Wednesday morning, Cassy again called the kids for breakfast, feeling enthusiastic about the day. Yesterday had gone well, and her new schedule seemed to leave ample time for the kids to complete their work. She had looked through the lessons for today and felt prepared. Following breakfast, Cassy once again sent the kids to complete their chores while she cleaned off the table and got their books ready.

Just as she headed for the small bookshelf, the phone rang. Cassy turned to answer the call. It was her mother from British Columbia. She had just gotten off the phone with Cassy's sister in Africa who was asking for prayer for their son DJ. Rob and Debbie had received a call from the missionary boarding school that their twelve-year-old son was sick. After the dorm parents had taken him to the hospital, they discovered that DJ had been diagnosed with malaria. Cassy talked with her mother for some time, getting more information on her sister's family and asking how things were going at her father's church in BC, math books far from her mind. By the time she got off the phone, she had to go in search of the kids, who had all disappeared to their rooms when they saw that their mother was busy.

Nicole was lying on her neatly made bed reading a book. When she saw her mother in the doorway, she reluctantly set it aside to come to the table. Kimberleigh and Anika were playing with their stuffed animals, and if they had cleaned any of their room, Cassy couldn't tell. She told them to quickly pick up their toys and head to the kitchen while she went in search of Jeremy. He was sitting on the floor in his room playing ball with Shasta, and glancing to see how he had done with making his bed, Cassy thought it resembled a stormy sea.

"Jeremy, is that any way to make a bed?"

"I didn't have to make it because I slept on top of the covers," her son announced, obviously pleased with himself.

"That's not the point, it looks a mess. The idea isn't that you try to get out of work, but that you do a good job of what I ask you to do. From now on you sleep in the bed and make it properly, is that understood?" Cassy pointed to the offending covers.

"Okay." Jeremy rose slowly from the floor and went to straighten the covers while his mother watched.

When he was done, they headed to the kitchen together. The girls were chatting at the table, waiting for their mother.

"That was Grandma Harris calling," Cassy explained. "DJ is sick with malaria, and we need to pray for him."

"What's malaria?" Concern edged Nicole's voice.

"It's a disease that is more common in tropical countries, and it is spread by mosquitoes. I know it causes a fever and that it can keep coming back, but I don't know too much more about it," Cassy admitted.

"How serious is it?" Nicole wanted to know.

"I'm not sure. Why don't we pray for DJ before we get to work, and while you guys do your math, I'll see if I can find out more about it on the internet," Cassy offered.

The young family took turns praying for their cousin as they sat around the table. When they were done, Cassy got them going on their math for the day. Once they were all busy, she headed to the computer room. Skimming through several websites, she discovered that southern Africa was especially at high risk for the type of malaria that could cause kidney failure or result in death if left untreated too long. She was shocked at the number of deaths attributed to the disease each year on that continent. Almost a million people died from malaria in Africa alone in 1995. That would be equivalent to 2700 people dying each day. Cassy felt an even deeper level of concern for her sister and for DJ than she had felt initially. She was relieved that DJ was in a well equipped missionary hospital and that he had been diagnosed so quickly. However, Cassy also realized that DJ's recovery from the troublesome parasite that was invading his bloodstream could be a lengthy one. Carefully Cassy jotted down some information and stats to share with her children, though she would try not to emphasize the fatality rate caused by the infection.

When the young mom returned to the kitchen, she sat down to share about the cause, symptoms and treatment of malaria. This prompted a barrage of questions about the risk of mosquitoes in Canada, what the parasites look like, how they could live inside of you, and whether Uncle Rob and Aunt Debbie would get sick too. Cassy did her best to answer the questions and alleviate their fears. She was conscious of their morning slipping away, but at the same time she felt that it was important to help them understand their cousin's condition.

By the time Cassy got out the language arts books, it was almost time to get lunch. Hurriedly she explained their assignments and went to prepare some soup. She was pelted with questions as she worked at the stove and found herself alternating between reading off lists of spelling words, explaining the difference between synonyms and homonyms and doing her best to review the rules of capitalization while stirring the soup and slicing cheese. She felt harried trying to do so many things at once, and finally told the kids to stop and set the table, though none of them had finished their lesson. Carefully Cassy stacked their work at one end of the table so they could finish it after lunch.

Following the meal, Cassy cleared the dishes and helped her children finish their grammar. Nicole especially found it hard to focus, as her mind was still on her sick cousin in Africa.

"Could I write DJ a letter?" Nicole asked when she had finally completed her workbook pages.

Cassy glanced at her watch and thought of her science lesson planned for the afternoon. They were already running much later than the day before, but thinking of her sick nephew, Cassy reluctantly nodded. She sighed and tried to ignore the twinge of guilt over the abandoned lesson. "You can all write letters, he'd like that," she conceded.

"Do I have to?" Jeremy looked less than thrilled about the extra writing.

"Well, I can't very well do our science lesson if some of you are writing letters, and it would mean a lot to DJ, so yes you have to."

Jeremy threw Nicole a look of disgust. "Thanks a lot!"

Nicole wrinkled her nose at him and joined Kimberleigh, who had left the table to go get some paper.

"Can I write a wetter too?" Anika chimed in.

"How about you color DJ a picture to cheer him up," Cassy suggested.

"Okay." The preschooler scrambled off her chair to get her coloring book and crayons.

Soon all four were busy at the table, heads bent over their papers. Cassy admired Anika's picture and spelled an occasional word for the older kids. When Kimberleigh was finished, she brought her letter for her mom to inspect. Her page was about half full of uneven printing with the occasional dark erasure mark blurring a word. The only period Cassy saw was one placed at the very end of the letter. Gently Cassy helped her daughter neaten up her work while explaining the importance of periods and adding them where appropriate. Carefully she erased misspelled words and spelled them correctly for Kimberleigh to rewrite.

The young girl stood at her mother's elbow, staring up at her with large brown eyes. Her shoulders heaved with an exaggerated sigh of frustration, and Cassy wondered if she was expecting too much from her second grader. She was surprised by her lack of punctuation and tried to remember what was expected at that age, but realized that she had no idea. At the same time, Cassy wanted her daughter to learn proper writing skills.

In turn, Cassy reviewed Jeremy and Nicole's letters. Nicole's needed a few corrections, and Cassy made a mental note to explain paragraphs to her daughter. For now she settled on correcting a few spelling errors and her overuse of commas, which seemed to be inappropriately thrown in at regular intervals.

Jeremy's spelling was atrocious, and Cassy grimaced. How was she ever going to teach him to spell? By the time Cassy had finished with their letters, it was midafternoon and she was tired. She still had to correct their math books, so she sent the kids outside with some cookies while she finished up. She knew the kids were ready for a break, and Cassy didn't have the patience for science yet today.

As she checked page after page of math problems, Cassy felt a wave of frustration over how their day had gone. Why had it taken so long to accomplish so little? By the time she had looked over twelve pages of math, she was bleary eyed as she returned the books to their shelf.

Cassy decided to go lay down for a few minutes before she had to fix supper, but as she walked past the bathroom in the hall, she noticed water all over the floor. Upon further investigation, she discovered that the toilet had been stuffed with what looked like at least half a roll of toilet paper, and it had overflowed. "Anika!" Cassy cried out in exasperation as she went in search of a plunger and mop. By the time the bathroom was put back in order, it was time to fix supper. She would have to hurry to have it ready on time.

Cassy prepared some chicken breasts and stuck them into the oven, racking her brain for something quick and easy she could fix to go with them. Just then the phone rang.

"Hello," Cassy answered as she opened the freezer to rummage through, looking for vegetables.

"Hi, Cassy, this is Bonnie."

"Oh, hi," Cassy greeted. This phone call could take awhile.

"Yeah, I was just calling because I missed you at the young moms' Bible study this morning. I was hoping that you hadn't forgotten it started this week or that you weren't sick or anything. You're always so faithful in coming." Bonnie paused expectantly.

"Uh, no, I didn't forget." Cassy balanced the phone on her shoulder as she pulled a bag of corn from the freezer and shut the door. "I'm afraid I won't be able to come to Bible study this year. It doesn't work out with my schedule." She hoped that Bonnie would be content to leave it at that for now.

"Oh, how come?" her caller prodded, causing Cassy to grimace as she thought of what to say.

"Well, I don't know if you heard or not, but I'm homeschooling the kids this year and my days are pretty full. I don't think it would work to take every Wednesday morning off. Besides, I don't think the babysitters are really prepared to watch my older children." Cassy was met with silence on the other end, and she shifted uneasily as she waited for a response.

"Homeschooling! What made you decide to do that? I mean, what about your commitment to the ladies' group and Bible study and all that? Are you really going to quit everything and just stay at home all day with your kids?"

"For now, yes," Cassy answered, trying to hide her annoyance. "This is a decision that David and I made together and we feel it's what God wants us to do right now. I can't do it all, so I'm going to have to say no to some things."

"So you don't feel God wants you to be involved in church ministry? I thought that was always a priority for you."

"It was a priority, but right now my kids come first. I think God will honor that." Cassy's shoulders slumped as she went back to the fridge and started pulling out the fixings to make a salad.

"So you're really set on this homeschooling thing." It was more of a statement than a question. "I hope you know what you're doing!" When Cassy didn't respond, Bonnie cut the call short. "Guess I'd better go."

Cassy mumbled a good-bye and hung up. "I hope I know what I'm doing, too." Blinking back tears, she returned the phone to its cradle and started on her salad.

When David came in a moment later, he crossed the kitchen to give his wife a hug. "How'd your day go?"

"Okay, I guess." Cassy turned back to the counter, busying herself with the lettuce she was preparing.

"Did the kids misbehave?"

"No, I just didn't get much done today. Mom called, and DJ has malaria."

"Is he okay?"

"I don't know. Mom didn't know much yet; he'd just been diagnosed and was starting treatment. The kids were full of questions, so we spent a fair bit of time talking about malaria and mosquitoes, and they all wrote letters to DJ this afternoon." Cassy tossed the carrots she'd chopped into the salad and carried the bowl to the table. "We never even got to science."

"Sounds to me like you did," David stated matter-of-factly.

"What do you mean?" Cassy threw her husband a disgruntled look as she crossed to the stove.

"Learning about malaria and mosquitoes sounds like science to me, and writing letters is educational. Besides, they were both practical considering your news about DJ, and I'm glad you could take time to do that."

Cassy stopped with her spoon midair above her simmering pot of corn. "I guess you're right. Except you should see your children's spelling and punctuation skills," she countered after a pause. "They're horrible!"

David laughed now.

"What!" Cassy looked indignant. "They are!"

"Precisely why they are learning, Cassy. You can't expect them to be perfect." He crossed the room to place his hands on his wife's shoulders.

Cassy slumped. "But that's just it! How do I know what to expect from them? What's normal for grade four? I don't remember."

"You're getting too uptight, and it's only your second day," David gently warned. "As you work with them, you'll discover where they're at and be able to help them improve. That's what it's all about. Just don't expect it all to happen in the first week, okay?"

Cassy was grateful for her husband's attempt to cheer her up, but her heart still felt heavy. She threw him a wobbly smile. "I'll try to wait until next week for perfection," she responded softly, but David could see the presence of tears in her eyes.

"Aw, Cassy, I know you're upset, but you have to realize that everything is not always going to go according to plan and not let it get to you so much. I'm sure it doesn't help that you're worried about DJ."

"That and I got a call from Bonnie while I was getting supper—questioning my priorities," Cassy finally admitted.

"Ah-ha!" David turned her around to face him. "That explains it. So what edifying little tidbit did she have to share?"

Cassy smirked in spite of her injured feelings. "She wanted to know why I missed Bible study. When I told her I wouldn't be coming and why, she implied that I was crazy to want to stay at home all day with my kids, that my priority should be church ministry, and then she said that she hoped I knew what I was doing!"

David clamped his lips together and pulled his wife into his arms. "We're doing this to please God, not man—least of all to please Bonnie Sorenson! We already know that not everyone agrees with what we're doing, and we're just going to have to come to terms with that."

"I know." Cassy sniffled into her husband's shirt. "It just hit me at the wrong time."

"Are you upset about missing the Bible study?" David pulled Cassy away from him enough to look into her eyes.

"Sort of," she admitted. "I always enjoyed getting together with the ladies and having a morning out, but for now I think it is best. Maybe when the kids are older, I can be more involved again. But if I'm going to do a good job of teaching the kids, I feel I need to be home. I have enough on my plate right now."

"I know that this is going to be a big adjustment for you, and I'll try to help where I can. Just remember, you're not giving up your chance to minister. You have four impressionable little souls right here that God has entrusted us with, and they come first."

"I know." Cassy brushed at her tears. "I feel better just talking about it. Supper is ready; you want to call the kids?" She turned to pull the chicken from the oven and finish dishing up. "Nicole is in her room, and the others are still outside."

The kids were laughing as they raced to the house at their father's call, hurrying to wash their hands and come to the table. By then, all traces of Cassy's tears had vanished. After David led in prayer, Anika turned to him and announced, "DJ has some sites, and we prayed for him today!"

"Some 'sites'?" David raised his eyebrows in confusion.

"Yeah, two of 'em," Anika explained authoritatively.

"You mean 'parasites', sweetie," Cassy corrected.

"Yeah, two sites, that's what I said!" Anika shook her head in exasperation.

Cassy and David both caught their daughter's misunderstanding of the word at the same time and started laughing. Anika just stared wide-eyed at her parents as if they'd lost their minds.

"They're called 'parasites,' Anika, not a pair of sites," Cassy explained.

"Oh, that's funny." Anika laughed at her own joke and was joined by her siblings.

Throughout supper the kids shared what they'd learned about malaria with their father. Cassy was pleasantly surprised at how much they remembered and were able to explain about the disease. Maybe she had accomplished more than she'd thought; she felt encouraged. Suddenly Cassy realized what Lauren had meant when she had warned her to keep her schedule flexible. It was good advice, she decided, though she would have to remind herself of it many times over the coming year.

10

Support Group

Cassy had kept Friday afternoons open on her schedule for group activities, but as nothing had started yet, it was the perfect time to make up her missed science lesson. Pulling her teacher's manual and three activity books from the shelf, she called the kids to the table. At the mention of the word *science,* Jeremy's eyes lit up, and he started to fidget in anticipation.

"Do we get to mix some chemicals together and make an explosion?" he asked.

"No, that's not the type of science we're doing," Cassy informed her exuberant son. "But you can go get some scissors, glue, and colored pencils."

"Oh, man, science is supposed to be fun!" Jeremy mumbled as he went to do as he was told. He looked deflated, but Cassy just rolled her eyes.

The first lesson was on God's creation of the universe, and the kids were each supposed to color pictures of the sun, moon, and the earth. Then, as Cassy read interesting facts about each, they were to cut out squares containing the information and match them to the corresponding picture. By stacking the squares on top of one another and gluing the left edges together, they formed a little book to glue in place beside each celestial body. Included was a collection of facts about the size and unique features of each object, as well as their distance from each other. The lesson went on to describe how the earth, its atmosphere, and the oceans were created perfectly to maintain life. Cassy's teacher notes explained why the intricate design of the universe made it impossible for everything to have fallen into place by pure chance or as the result of an explosion.

"See, even God didn't use an explosion for science." Cassy laughed and nudged her son.

"But He would have been allowed if He'd wanted to!" Jeremy defended with a smirk.

"Maybe, but He wouldn't have been doing it inside my house."

"I could do it outside…"

"No! When you're thirty-five, you can make an explosion in your own backyard." At his mother's words, Jeremy crossed his arms in defeat.

To finish off, Cassy had the kids take turns reading the Bible verses that accompanied the lesson. They had all been attentive while she taught and had genuinely seemed to enjoy putting together their little booklets—even Jeremy. Too late, however, Cassy realized her mistake in not getting an activity book for Anika as well. She desperately wanted a book to work on, and Cassy had to promise to get her one at the first opportunity. During the summer when she'd gotten them, Cassy had never dreamed of buying a science book for her four-year-old.

Once the books were put away, Cassy quickly mixed up a pan of brownies to take for the fellowship time following the homeschool meeting to be held at their church that evening. She had planned a simple supper of chili and buns so that they would be ready to leave on time. At least half a dozen times over the last couple of days Kimberleigh had reminded her of the meeting. She knew the kids were anxious to meet the other homeschoolers, though she could tell that Nicole was a little nervous about the prospect. Her eldest usually found it the most difficult to step out and make new friends. Cassy was glad that Melissa Andrews would be there to introduce her to the others.

⌘ ⌘ ⌘

That night Cassy walked into the church alongside her husband and children, feeling a mix of anticipation and apprehension at the same time. What if her children found it hard to fit in? What if she was not readily accepted by the other mothers who were well established and all knew one another? As she hung up her coat in the foyer, Cassy suddenly felt a twinge of insecurity.

The minute Cassy took Kimberleigh's jacket, her giddy daughter was off with a powerful stride, barely controlled under what could be classified as running, which she knew her parents forbade her to do in the usually crowded church foyer. Cassy chuckled at her daughter's enthusiasm to get to the fellowship hall.

Nicole helped hang up Anika's jacket. As her siblings rushed ahead, Nicole stuck close to her mother, her face mirroring the apprehension Cassy had felt a moment earlier. Cassy smiled at her daughter, at once recognizing the quiet uncertainty she had often felt herself when growing up, and which she still struggled with at times.

"Shall we see if Melissa's here yet?" she offered encouragingly.

David had already retrieved the plate of brownies Cassy had set on top of the coat rack. Falling in behind his wife, he sneaked one from underneath the plastic wrap and quietly shoved the whole thing into his mouth.

"I heard that!" Cassy reprimanded good-naturedly without turning around.

David nearly choked. "I don't know how you do that," he sputtered with his mouth full.

"She knows you, Dad," Nicole said.

In no time the three were entering the fellowship hall, David quickly swallowing any evidence that he had pilfered the refreshments ahead of time. Cassy could see a dozen couples standing about visiting, and kids seemed to be scattered everywhere, grouped in clusters. What struck Cassy immediately was the fact that they were not congregating according to age, but rather seemed to mix freely together, youngsters and teens side-by-side. Several teens toted young siblings in their arms as they chatted with friends. From the corner of the room, Lauren waved to Cassy and, excusing herself, made her way in their direction.

"I'll go put these on the table," David indicated with a lift of his plate of brownies toward the refreshment table on the far side of the room.

"Maybe I should take that; I don't trust you over there," Cassy teased.

"I'll be good." David winked at his wife just as Lauren reached them. He greeted her before sauntering off with the brownies.

"Melissa's just over there." Lauren directed Nicole's gaze to a group of kids not far away. "You want to join them?"

With one last hesitant glance towards her mother, Nicole nodded and headed slowly in Melissa's direction.

"Thanks; she's a bit shy in new situations," Cassy watched her daughter a moment to make sure she was settled and then scanned the room. It wasn't hard to spot Jeremy stationed in the midst of half-a-dozen boys huddled by the refreshment table, while Kimberleigh and Anika seemed at ease mingling with Brianne and a number of children Cassy didn't recognize. More families had come in the door behind them, and the room was filling up. "There are a lot of people here," Cassy acknowledged in surprise.

"Homeschooling is really growing in Alberta," Lauren informed her. "We usually have about fifty families involved in our group, though they don't all come to everything."

Cassy's eyebrows shot up. She hadn't realized there were so many. She'd recognized Teresa Henderson from church, but so far she hadn't seen any other familiar faces. Lauren introduced her to a few ladies in their vicinity, but soon it was time for the meeting to begin. Rounding up her children, Cassy followed David to a row of seats about halfway down the aisle.

After a fellow named Rick Kauffman opened with prayer, his wife, Carol, introduced their family of five. She had been homeschooling for nine years, and was the president of the local association. In turn, she went around the room and had each family stand and introduce themselves, tell the ages of their children, as well as how long they had been homeschooling. Cassy was amazed to hear a number of moms claim ten to fifteen years' experience in teaching their children, carrying some right through to graduation. The prospect seemed daunting, and she was relieved to hear that she was not the only first-timer in the room. Even so, Cassy felt timid when it was their turn to stand. She wondered how long it would take for her to get to know some of these ladies or even to remember all their names. The Brysons, a new family to town who had joined their congregation over the summer, had come in late and were now seated in the back row. They were the last to introduce their family, and it was encouraging to see a few more familiar faces in the crowd.

Following introductions, Carol passed out thick handouts containing information about the association and how to sign up for their monthly email newsletter. There was more interaction from the group as Carol went through the schedule of upcoming events, encouraging a few moms to stand and explain activities or fieldtrips they were organizing, as well as opening the floor for additional suggestions. It was clear that anyone was welcome to plan events for the group, though Cassy noted that half-a-dozen key moms seemed responsible for most of the planning.

As Cassy followed along on her handout, she saw that most months had at least one fieldtrip—including heritage sites, the zoo, the Philharmonic Orchestra, a radio station, cheese factory, and an assortment of other interesting places. Then there were a number of weekly activities or special functions to sign up for throughout the year, from swimming lessons to writing seminars. Kimberleigh, who was peering over Cassy's arm, nudged her suddenly. She pointed to an item near the bottom of the page telling about a six-week Reader's Theater drama class to be held at a small community theater. Cassy glanced down at her daughter's animated face and smiled.

"I'll check into it," she whispered, making her daughter squirm with excitement.

When the business part of the meeting was complete, Carol introduced the special speaker for the evening. Vanessa Jackson was from southern Alberta, and had authored a couple of books on classical home education. She had started homeschooling when there were few families choosing that option and the idea of teaching your children at home was not generally understood or well received. All four of her children had since graduated through homeschooling and were doing well in a variety of fields. Her eldest son was married and working as a chartered accountant, her daughter was married and starting a family of her own, her second son was in Bible school finishing up his pastoral degree, and her youngest had just entered university in the field of journalism.

Vanessa shared how homeschooling had molded her children's lives and character and that it had been a blessing for their whole family. With humor she told of their fears in teaching through high school and their first experience walking into a university registrar's office to seek admittance for their son without a high school diploma.

"I don't think the poor man had ever seen a homeschooler before, and he looked at Josh like he had two heads. When we said he didn't have a government diploma, I thought the man's eyes were going to pop right out of his head. It took a lot of persistence to get the university to look at Josh's qualifications on their own merit, and he had to take a series of entrance exams, but I'm happy to say that the process is getting progressively easier. Enough homeschoolers have gone through the system now that they are not so scared of us anymore. When Josh graduated at the top of his class, the registrar was totally astonished. He hunted Josh out personally to congratulate him, making it considerably easier for my youngest son when he showed up at the registrar's office with an application last spring!

"So hang in there, and don't give up," Vanessa encouraged. "There were years when I felt discouraged that I hadn't gotten everything done I had planned. In fact, I don't know if I ever got everything done I planned," she added and everyone laughed, many moms nodding knowingly. "That's not the point. I was doing what I felt God had called me to do and I could see that it was a good thing. I could see the strong foundation of faith that my children were developing, and watch their love of learning grow. I could help them pursue specific areas of interest, and build on their strengths.

"Yes, I had my doubts at times whether I was covering everything they needed to learn. I felt the pressure and disapproval of friends and family when they learned that my kids were not following Alberta curriculum and would not get their diplomas. I was afraid that they were right, and I was ruining their lives. Now, as I look back, I know I did the right thing and I have no regrets, but it wasn't easy at the time.

"Sometimes you may feel very alone, or like those around you don't understand what you're doing. It's enough that you know why you're doing what you do, but you are not alone. That's why groups like yours are important. Not just so that you can convince others that your kids are really getting 'socialized'—that horrible word that is supposed to make homeschoolers cringe and believe their kids will grow up to become hermits! No, you folks are here to encourage one another along when it gets tough, to set an example and to help the new families who are just starting to homeschool. The world may never fully understand us, but eventually they'll have to admit that our children turned out all right. Besides, the average homeschool family tends to have more children, so in a few generations maybe we'll outnumber them. Then they'll be the weird ones."

Again laughter rippled through the room. Vanessa wrapped up her talk, and the group was dismissed for refreshments and to visit with one another. Anika had crawled up on Cassy's lap during the program and had fallen asleep. Gently Cassy shifted her young daughter onto her shoulder and stood up.

"Can you grab my purse and those papers, Nicole?" She nodded toward the items by her feet and Nicole bent to pick them up, following her mom down the row of chairs. Jeremy had wasted no time in reaching the refreshment table and was happily stuffing his mouth and laughing with the Andrews' boys. Cassy was relieved to see that at least he hadn't attempted to overload his plate with sweets when she wasn't looking. Glancing around the room, she spotted Kimberleigh nibbling on a cookie next to Brianne. There were a few older girls chatting with them, and Cassy could see that her daughter was enthralled by their attention. David was headed for the coffee table, and Cassy was following more slowly, when she was intercepted by Teresa Henderson.

"I didn't know you were homeschooling this year; that's great!" The petite woman with long, dark hair smiled warmly.

"Yeah, we just decided to switch the end of last school year. Lauren's been coaching me through the summer. She's been a great help but I still feel a bit overwhelmed, especially in a room full of families who have been doing it for years!" Cassy admitted.

"Don't worry," the woman before her encouraged, "we all had to start where you are, so I know how you feel. It's not so scary once you get going. Boy, when I think back to my first year and what I put my kids through, I have to shake my head," Teresa said. "I tried to make a minischool at home, complete with desks and a chalkboard, and I worked them to death. I was afraid everyone would think I wasn't doing enough so I went overboard bigtime. I took all the fun out of learning. Luckily, I met a couple of good friends in the group who helped me along before I had a mutiny, and we all love it now."

Cassy laughed, "Well, I haven't seen any signs of a mutiny yet, but I could see myself falling into that trap. You should have seen my first schedule I made before Lauren redirected me. I guess the formal school setting and mentality is hard to break away from—it's so ingrained. I don't know what I'd be doing without all Lauren's help!" Cassy shifted the weight of her sleeping daughter to her other shoulder.

"So how do you like it so far? Is your mom too tough?" Teresa turned to quiz Nicole, who was standing quietly at her mother's elbow.

Nicole giggled shyly. "It's fun; I like having Mom teach, and we get to read lots."

"Good! You can be glad you didn't have to come to my school the first year then. I was really bad." Her teasing brought more giggles from Nicole.

About then David returned with a cup of coffee for his wife, and he relieved her of the weight of carrying their sleeping daughter. With Anika cradled in his arms, he moved off toward a group of fathers who were involved in boisterous conversation. The women chatted awhile longer, and Cassy was introduced to a few more moms before the evening was over.

By the time it was done, Cassy was tired, but she realized she no longer felt so alone in her endeavor. And by the looks of the first newsletter, there would be no shortage of opportunities to interact with these families on a regular basis. As they were leaving, Lauren warned her to be careful not to think they had to be involved in everything. She suggested they look over the list carefully and pick only those events they were most interested in.

"I've seen too many new homeschool families try to do it all. They spend their whole year running and get burned out. You need to guard your family time together and not set a hectic pace for your studies," she cautioned.

"That's good advice," Cassy agreed, and she promised to keep it in mind.

While being buckled into her booster seat, Anika stirred and rubbed her eyes sleepily. "Is it snack time yet?" she mumbled before closing her eyes once again, bringing snickers from her siblings.

The kids chattered all the way home. From the sounds of it, they had all enjoyed the evening as well. Cassy sighed. She had survived the first week!

11

Pursuing Interests

The following week seemed to fly by for Cassy. Nicole and Jeremy started piano lessons on Monday, so Cassy penciled their practice times into her daily schedule. Her days were full, but Cassy found herself looking forward to the afternoons when she could sit on the couch and read to her children. Sometimes the kids might snuggle around her and listen while she read. At other times Cassy would assign them a project to go along with her reading, and they would sprawl with their binders on the hardwood floor to work at her feet. They all seemed to like this informal time of learning together.

On Thursday Cassy helped her kids work on a timeline to put into their notebooks, tracing the genealogy listed in Genesis from Adam to Abraham. Once their life spans were marked out on graph paper, Cassy was surprised to realize that Adam was still alive when Noah's father was born and that Abraham's life overlapped Noah's. It was also interesting to discover that Enoch preached judgment on the people and that his son, Methuselah's, name meant "after me, it comes." As their timelines were completed, it became evident that Methuselah died the same year the flood occurred. Truly, God's judgment followed Methuselah's life.

Anika had been playing while the older children made their timelines, and Cassy didn't think she had been paying attention to what was going on, but when Jeremy exclaimed over the fact that Methuselah had lived 969 years, the little girl looked up incredulously.

"Wow, he was even o'der than Mom!" Anika said seriously, causing an outburst of laughter from her siblings.

"Thanks a lot!" Cassy huffed.

"You're we'come." Anika shrugged and went back to her play.

Cassy had usually skimmed over genealogies in the Bible, considering them boring. She was surprised at how much fun her children had charting out the lives of the biblical characters and labeling them. Somehow it made their lives seem more real. It was hard to fathom how the world could have gotten so corrupt by Noah's day, when Adam—the first man who had walked in the garden with God—had lived until just before Noah's birth.

The incredibility that only a family of eight remained on the earth that was deemed worthy by God to escape destruction seemed to shock the kids, though they had heard the story of Noah and the flood many times before. How could almost all of Enoch's descendants, even Noah's brothers and sisters, have forsaken God, considering their godly heritage? The children grew serious over their timelines as they discussed the devastation of sin and God's judgment. Suddenly the life of Noah was not just a cool story involving a boat full of animals. When they were finished, each child proudly placed a timeline into their binders, a reminder of their lesson and something to show Dad when he got home.

Along with the lesson on Noah, Cassy included a brief overview of fossils and the evidence in geology of a worldwide flood. She had borrowed a book from Lauren from Foundations in Truth that was geared for kids on the topic. It explained about fossils of sea creatures found on the tops of mountains, dinosaur fossils, and interesting facts about the layers of sediment found in the Grand Canyon. Jeremy found the book particularly interesting, and when they were finished, he asked if he could take it to his room to look at later.

"Are you feeling okay?" Cassy felt her son's forehead as she gave him a teasing smile.

"Aw Mom, this is cool!" he said as he reached for the colorful book.

Cassy breathed a prayer of thanks that her son had found something to study that interested him. Books had always been a source of frustration for Jeremy; he'd much rather spend his time outside or creating things with his hands. She'd often thought that her son might follow in his father's footsteps in the construction business someday, but to do so, he would have to learn to apply himself to his studies—

especially math.

That afternoon as Cassy was fixing supper, she glanced out the kitchen window to see Jeremy digging a hole in the backyard with their garden spade.

"What's your brother doing?" she asked Kimberleigh, who had just come inside for a drink of milk.

"He's looking for fossils. He thinks there's a dinosaur buried in our backyard!" She rolled her eyes and plopped onto a kitchen chair.

"Well, finish your milk and go tell him to dig in the garden, please. I don't want the lawn all torn up!" Cassy shook her head and went back to her meal preparations.

When her dirt-smudged boy finally came in for dinner, Cassy noticed him quietly sneak a pail of rocks to his bedroom before going to wash up. She laughed to herself, relieved that at least she couldn't see anything crawling amongst the rocks. She didn't think he had much chance of finding any fossils in the garden, but at least fossils of bugs were better than the real thing!

⌘ ⌘ ⌘

The next morning, while Jeremy was working in his language arts workbook, he plopped his pencil down with a heavy sigh. Cassy had been struggling for the past half hour to get her restless son to sit still and concentrate, but without much luck.

"What's the matter now?" Cassy asked in exasperation as she leaned over from helping Kimberleigh to peek at her son's book.

"Do I have to write a paragraph about fall leaves changing colors?" Jeremy propped his cheek in his hand, misery on his face.

"It's important that you learn how to write, Jeremy, even if it's not your favorite thing to do," Cassy insisted. "It wouldn't take so long if you would just apply yourself and do it."

"But it's so boring! Who wants to write about leaves? Can't I write about something else?"

Cassy opened her mouth to exhort her son to do his lesson without complaining, but she stopped short. Was it so important that he write about leaves just because the book suggested it? As long as he was writing, what did it matter if he chose his own topic sometimes? "What would you like to write about?" Cassy inquired instead.

Jeremy sat up from his hunched position, a light in his eyes. "Could I write about fossils?"

"I guess so. When you're done, you can put it in your binder after your timeline. It can go along with our study of the flood." Cassy smiled at his change in attitude as he ran to his room to get the book on geology and his history binder. If letting him choose his own topic to write about could get him motivated to do his language arts, it would be well worth it, and her frazzled nerves would get a break. She wondered what he would come up with from their lesson the day before.

Moments later Jeremy was leaning diligently over a clean sheet of paper, the book about fossils open beside him for reference. Cassy went back to work helping Kimberleigh with her lesson on contractions. Nicole sat at the end of the table, silently working through her assigned pages. She seemed quite capable of working independently for short spurts, making the demands for Cassy's attention a little easier to handle. Situated to Cassy's other side, Anika sat carefully printing her alphabet in wobbly rows on some wide-spaced writing paper. Occasionally the little girl would tap her mother's elbow to point out a finished row, or to seek help with a difficult letter.

"I'm a'most done with my writing," Anika announced proudly, as she slowly printed a capital *X, Y,* and *Z.* Kneeling on her chair, her tiny frame was hunched over her paper in fixed concentration, the tip of her tongue protruding from between her teeth.

Cassy smiled and praised her daughter's work. "Very nice, Anika. You'll have to hang that on the bulletin board beside Nicole's verse for Daddy to see."

Excited, the little girl hopped off her chair and ran to the bulletin board in the corner. "I can't reach." Anika lifted her paper as far as she could while she danced on tiptoes beneath the board above her head.

"Here." Nicole crossed the room to give her little sister a boost. "How's that?"

"Great, thanks." Anika grasped a tack and awkwardly stuck it into the top of her paper. "I wike having you home." Nicole smiled and gave her little sister a hug before gently placing her feet back on the floor.

As Cassy reached for the kids' completed math books to check them, she noticed Jeremy was still busy writing. She was astonished to see that he had completed a whole page and was halfway down another. Leaning across the table, she bent down to look into his face. "Okay, who are you, and what did you do with Jeremy?" she questioned suspiciously.

Jeremy glanced up in surprise. "What?"

Cassy chuckled and the girls joined in, while Jeremy looked from one to the other in confusion. "Is this the same boy who hates to write?" She nodded toward his notebook.

Jeremy glanced down and seemed surprised at the amount he had written. "Well, fossils are more interesting than leaves," he admitted with a sheepish grin.

"Keep it up!" Cassy tousled her son's hair and sat down to complete her marking before lunch. If Jeremy was so interested in fossils and paleontology, she would have to talk to David and see if they could take the family to the Badlands in Drumheller on the weekend before the weather got too cool. He would love walking through the rugged terrain where so many real dinosaur fossils had been found.

While Cassy was getting lunch, her mother called to inform her that DJ was responding well to his malaria treatment. It was good news, and when she got off the phone, she shared the answer to prayer with her children.

"So DJ's all better?" Kimberleigh clapped her hands enthusiastically. Though she had hardly ever seen her twelve-year-old cousin, she was proud of her missionary relatives and prayed for them often.

"Not all better," Cassy corrected. "DJ will be recovering for quite a while yet, but the medicine is helping, which is good. We still need to remember to pray for him."

"Can we pray right now?" Anika inquired.

So as they sat down around the table to eat lunch, they joined hands and prayed again for their cousin so far away—thanking God for hearing their prayers and interceding for DJ's ongoing recovery.

Following lunch Cassy again ushered her children into the living room to read some more from their book on Canadian history. By now her young family was getting used to the schedule and their story time together. Next month Friday afternoons would be filled with ice skating and the Reader's Theater class she'd signed the kids up for, but for now Cassy was glad to have the extra time at home.

"This is so much better than school!" Nicole stated with satisfaction as she huddled against her mother's arm in anticipation. Anika climbed up onto her mother's lap so that they could all fit on the couch and see the pictures.

"Stop squirming!" Kimberleigh jabbed her brother with her elbow.

"I'm not squirming; I'm just trying to get comfortable. If you weren't taking up the whole cushion, I'd have more room," Jeremy snapped back.

"That's enough. Kimberleigh, give your brother some more room, and Jeremy sit still. And no more poking with elbows, young lady, I expect you to treat your brother kindly."

Kimberleigh looked sheepishly at her mother and scooted over. Jeremy did his best not to fidget, and soon Cassy opened her book and found where she had left off. Everyone seemed settled, so Cassy cleared her throat and began.

Cassy read of the French fishermen who came to take advantage of the abundant fish along the shores of Newfoundland. Among them was a fellow by the name of Jacques Cartier, an explorer commissioned by the king to sail up the River of Canada in search of a passage to the Spice Islands of the Pacific Ocean. Cartier named the river the St. Lawrence. The kids giggled when they heard of the Indians along the shore who anxiously traded all the furs they had, including the ones they were wearing, for the brass buttons the Frenchmen cut off their coats.

"Wow! A beaver skin for one button?" Jeremy was incredulous.

"What did the Frenchmen do with the furs?" Kimberleigh wanted to know.

"They sold them, right?" Nicole reasoned.

"That's right. They could take the furs back to France and get a lot of money for them. People in Europe were glad to get furs for making hats and coats and things, and beavers were pretty scarce there," Cassy explained.

"Poor beavers," Anika sympathized. "They would have been co'd without their fur!" Everyone laughed, and Anika crossed her arms in front of herself. With furrowed brows she glared at her siblings. "It's not funny, they would be," she insisted.

"They wouldn't be cold, they'd be dead!" Jeremy announced with satisfaction, and his little sister gasped in horror.

"Jeremy!" Cassy scolded, struggling to hide her smile.

"Well, they would be!"

Cassy decided to change the subject and sent Jeremy to get the globe. When he returned, she pointed out France, as well as the St. Lawrence River, for the kids.

"The Frenchmen couldn't sail all the way across Canada on the St. Lawrence River," Kimberleigh pointed out, tracing the river with her finger.

"No, they sure couldn't, but they didn't know how big Canada was when they started. It took them a long time to explore and discover that and to finally make it across to the Pacific Ocean," Cassy acknowledged.

Anika was still stewing on her mother's lap. Later, when the others left to go outside, she shifted to look into her mother's eyes. "Were the beavers rea'wy dead?" she inquired with tears in her eyes.

"Yes, Anika," Cassy soothed gently, "but the men used the furs to keep warm in winter. They weren't just killing the beavers to be mean. God had to kill an animal to make clothes for Adam and Eve after they sinned too, and it was a sad thing. It's not the way God intended the world to be. We do have laws now to protect the animals so that people don't kill too many, though."

That seemed to satisfy the little girl, and with a nod, she slid from her mother's lap to go join her siblings.

When David came home later, Cassy asked him about the possibility of going to Drumheller the next day for a picnic. David agreed that it was a good idea and, as he and Anthony were ahead of schedule on the house they were building, it would not be a big deal to take Saturday off.

After supper he called Anthony to let him know, and before he was done, the plans had been made for Anthony, Sarah, and the kids to join them.

⌘ ⌘ ⌘

Promptly at 9:30 the next morning, Anthony's van pulled up the drive. David was just stowing the cooler into the back of their minivan. With a shout Jeremy came bounding out the door, followed closely by his three sisters and Cassy, who was carrying the jacket Jeremy had left behind, a blanket, and her camera. The air felt a bit cool, but the sky was clear and the day held the potential of turning out quite nice for being mid-September. Waving to their cousins, the kids scrambled into the van and they were off.

About two hours later, the families pulled up at their destination. They located an empty picnic table close to the head of the interpretive trail. As all the kids were "starving," the consensus was to eat lunch first and then hike the trail. Cassy spread her blanket on the ground beside the table for the kids to eat on, and in no time everyone was happily visiting over sandwiches, fruit and cookies. Six-month-old Samantha had been nursed and now jabbered amiably from her seat in the umbrella stroller.

"So how's the schooling going?" Sarah inquired.

"Very busy, but I'm enjoying it more than I thought I would," Cassy admitted. When she shared the story of Anika and the beaver furs from the day before, David and Anthony had a good chuckle.

"Leave it to Jeremy to be painfully blunt," David exclaimed. "No tact in that boy!"

"He's starting to enjoy his studies a bit more, though, which is a welcome change. You should have seen him writing yesterday when he got to write about fossils. He needs to work on spelling and grammar, mind you, but he was enjoying it, and the content was good." Cassy's tone revealed her pleasant surprise.

"Hence the trip to a paleontologist's paradise." Sarah indicated the rugged, fossil rich landscape surrounding them.

"Precisely! It was either this, or let Jeremy dig up our whole backyard searching for dinosaur bones," Cassy pronounced emphatically, bringing more laughter.

By now most of the youngsters had finished their meal and were waiting impatiently along the edge of the trail, anxious to begin. Only Anika and Lissy were still seated on the blanket, quietly exchanging secrets. Quickly the adults cleared away the remains of lunch and then joined the children. The sun felt wonderfully warm in the Drumheller valley and everyone shed their jackets before heading around the 1.4 km loop.

It was a lazy afternoon as the two families meandered slowly along the trail. The now six-year-old Timmy had caught Jeremy's enthusiasm for the possibility of finding a real dinosaur fossil, and the two scanned the terrain meticulously. They stopped occasionally to kneel and brush away loose debris at the edge of the path in hopes of discovering a treasure. The girls skipped back and forth along the trail, admiring the rugged, multi-colored, sandstone and shale cliffs, reading the information on the signs along the way, and generally making fun of their brother's and cousin's antics.

"Oh look, Nicole, it's a real live dinosaur leg bone." Kimberleigh dramatically held out her hands, a small stick cradled in them for her sister to inspect.

"Ooh!" Nicole marveled with exaggerated awe. "Can I touch it?"

"How can you have a 'live' leg bone?" Jeremy snorted with laughter. "Shows how much you know about fossils!" His sisters' teasing did little to dampen his spirit of adventure. And even though Jeremy had not discovered a valuable fossil by the end of their leisurely walk, he was thrilled just to know that many dinosaur fossils had been recovered from the area.

Afterwards, the group headed to the Royal Tyrrell Museum, and the couples decided to take the kids through it. Although Nicole had been there last spring, she enjoyed it much more this time. The kids made a game of pointing out as many false evolutionary claims as possible. Anthony and Sarah were impressed with their knowledge and had a few questions of their own.

The large, reconstructed dinosaur skeletons were, of course, a highlight for all the kids, though Anika and Lissy found them a bit intimidating and kept as much distance as possible between themselves and the monstrous beasts. When they had finally completed the circuit and returned to the gift shop, it was late afternoon. Jeremy was eying the selection of books on dinosaurs and fossils, but his father convinced him to wait and they would order him some books from Foundations in Truth instead. There was no point in buying books that would present everything from an evolutionist's perspective, and Jeremy agreed it would be worth the wait.

It was cooling off by the time the two families returned to their vans. As the older children clamored into the vehicles, Sarah and Cassy buckled the youngest family members into their respective car seats. David and Anthony quickly chose a spot to stop for supper before heading home. They didn't tarry long over their meal, as it was a bit of a drive back to Red Deer, and neither set of parents wanted to get back real late.

It was dusk before the two loaded vans were finally on their way, and it wasn't long before Anika nodded off in her seat. Jeremy babbled most of the way home about all he had seen that day, and Cassy shot several smiles David's way, glad they had come. She could only hope that the excursion would satisfy Jeremy for now and that there would be no more digging in the backyard.

12

Learning Together

One Friday the end of September, the Knights joined some other homeschool families on a fieldtrip to the Reynolds-Alberta Museum in Wetaskiwin, about an hour away. The kids all enjoyed walking the "highway through time," beginning with a horse drawn carriage from the late 1800s and progressing through the vast collection of restored electric, steam, and gas-powered vehicles and farm equipment invented over the years. There were a number of themed displays where the kids could pretend to work an assembly line in a factory from 1911, check out the inner workings of a 1920s grain elevator, pump gas at a 1930s service station, or check out what was playing at a 1950s drive-in. It was with enormous difficulty that Cassy managed to convince her son to leave the aviation hangar, which housed seventy vintage aircraft, including a full-scale replica of the Avro Arrow fighter jet—Jeremy's favorite.

Just past noon, the families all found a spot outside to eat their picnic lunches. It was a cool day, and Cassy pulled her coat tightly around herself as she sat on one of several wooden benches alongside of Lauren, Teresa, and half-a-dozen other moms. For the most part Cassy sat quietly and listened as the ladies discussed an assortment of curriculum, good books they were reading, or simply shared struggles they were going through. The group represented children from various age groups with a variety of approaches to their homeschooling. Cassy was soaking it all up—gleaning insight and encouragement, while filing away choice bits of wisdom gained from years of experience.

"I feel like I haven't accomplished anything yet this month," moaned a young mom named Wendy. "My mom has not been feeling well. She's been in and out of the hospital for numerous tests, and I've been spending a lot of time running between the hospital and taking meals to my dad. I've hardly touched the boys' schoolbooks in weeks!"

"It sounds like you've had enough to worry about right now without giving yourself guilt trips over school," Teresa empathized. "We all have times like that for one reason or another—that's life. God would be pleased by your dedication to teach your children, as well as your commitment to help your parents."

"She's right," Lauren encouraged, "and a missed month or so in the whole scheme of things makes little difference in the long run. Ethan and Evan are too young to work much on their own, but you'll be surprised how quickly they'll catch up. In the meantime, they are learning valuable life lessons and what it means to serve others."

Wendy sighed in frustration. "I wish Ron's parents could see it that way. The boys have been staying with them a lot while I run to the hospital, and they've been dropping some not-so-subtle hints that Ethan and Evan should be in school. They feel I have too many commitments right now and it's not good for the boys."

"It's hard when others don't understand what you're doing, especially family," Diana consoled. "I know; I've been there. My family has never been very supportive and it's been hard. A couple of years ago, when we built our house, it was really tough. We were doing almost all the work ourselves, and we didn't get a lot of formal school in for four months. The kids all helped with everything from framing, to sanding drywall and painting. They worked hard and learned a lot about the trades, bank loans, making accurate measurements—you name it. My family gave us a pretty hard time about it, though." Diana patted Wendy's shoulder sympathetically.

"An education should give your kids the foundations for life, help them develop godly character, and show them how to live out their faith. What better way to learn that than through life's experiences?" Lauren interjected again. "You have to pray about it and do what you feel is right for your family, but I know it's hard to swim against the current sometimes."

Cassy nodded thoughtfully. Though she was coming to realize that each homeschool scenario was unique in itself, she felt a growing affinity with and commitment to the underlying philosophy of life, family, and faith that so many of them shared. Glancing around she spotted Jeremy racing around the yard with a handful of boys, his cheeks rosy from his efforts to catch one of the teen boys and a huge smile on his face. Nicole and Kimberleigh were engulfed in a huddle of girls sitting on the grass, their lunches long finished, while Anika sat on the edge of the circle watching the older girls with awe. Cassy was glad her kids were feeling a part of the group so soon and noticed that there didn't seem to be a single child who was being shunned or picked on. She hoped Jeremy would find the encouragement and friendship he needed in this environment, which was so different from his previous classroom.

With a shiver, Cassy folded her arms tightly around herself in an effort to stay warm. The dropping temperature was a keen reminder that summer was over. Noticing the other ladies collecting their things, Cassy was only too ready to round up her children and head for the van. She and Lauren had both mentioned a need to stop and pick up a few groceries on the way home, so when everyone was buckled up, Cassy pulled out behind the Andrews' van. Once back in Red Deer, the women pulled into the busy store parking lot.

"Do I have to go to the grocery store?" Jeremy moaned as if he were headed to a torture chamber.

"Do you want to eat supper?" Cassy shot back with little sympathy.

"Yes," he admitted reluctantly.

"Then that's your answer."

When Jeremy saw the Andrews' boys pile out of their van the next aisle over, he brightened somewhat. Together the ladies headed into the store with their nine kids in tow.

"What are you doing for Thanksgiving this year?" Lauren inquired as they wheeled their carts side by side into the produce section.

"We're heading to David's folks for the day Monday. My parents are coming from B.C. for Christmas, so most of my family will be at our place then—all but my sister in Africa, that is. What about you?"

"We're driving to my parents' in Medicine Hat for the weekend," Lauren responded.

The two families made their way through the store, each filling their carts with the necessary items, plus a few extras which the kids were successful in talking their mothers into buying. It wasn't long before Cassy followed her friend into a checkout line. As Lauren was paying for her groceries, Cassy heard the clerk question Lauren's children.

"No school today?" The young woman eyed the group with raised eyebrows.

Cassy quickly glanced at her watch and realized that school would not be out for twenty minutes yet.

"We homeschool," Melissa answered quietly.

"Ooh," the cashier drawled as she glanced pointedly from Lauren to Cassy and back to the kids. "What about socialization?"

"What about it?" Lauren quipped brightly.

The cashier turned to face Lauren. "Well, you know, how will they learn proper socialization if they are not in school? They are so isolated from their peers."

"Oh, I understand. You must find that difficult as well!" Lauren looked directly at the cashier and smiled.

"What do you mean?" The young woman looked confused.

"Why it must be terribly lonely working at a place like this with people all different ages than yourself—you know, no one you can socialize with."

"Why I-I—" the woman stammered as she stared, dumbfounded, at the customer across from her, forgetting momentarily Lauren's change which she still held in her hand.

Cassy had to turn away and clench her lips tightly as she continued to unload her cart to keep from laughing outright at the woman's expression of astonishment.

"I guess I never thought of it that way before," the young woman mumbled as she recovered herself and handed Lauren her change.

"There are more natural ways to socialize than to be exclusively with people your own age." Lauren smiled as she thanked the woman before pushing her cart over beside the exit door to await her friend.

"I don't believe you said that!" Cassy nudged Lauren and laughed as they exited the store a few moments later. "Did you see the look on her face?"

"I shouldn't have embarrassed her like that," Lauren admitted with a rueful laugh, "but I get so tired of the condescending looks and that stupid socialization question. I have to get creative in answering it sometimes to keep from getting annoyed. People tend to think that the best way for children to be socialized is to spend every day shut in a room full of kids exactly their own age, but that is so far from real life! Once they leave school they will never again be restricted to such a scenario. It's a shame really that so many people can't see the bigger picture."

"I guess I'm just learning that lesson myself," Cassy said, pulling her shopping cart to a halt beside her friend in the parking lot. "Not too long ago I would have asked the same question. So you get that a lot?"

"All the time, so get used to it. I usually just smile and say they're doing fine, but every once in awhile my aggravation gets the best of me. I should learn to bite my tongue!"

Cassy laughed and the two friends parted to catch up to their children who had run ahead and were waiting to get into their respective vehicles. Anika was clinging to Nicole's hand, and when Cassy unlocked the doors, she was helped into her seat by her big sister while Cassy stowed the groceries in the back.

"What's for supper?" Jeremy questioned eagerly the moment his mom was seated in the van.

"Spaghetti."

"Is it almost supper time?" he asked again.

"Not for a couple of hours yet." Cassy glanced over her shoulder at her son, waiting for what she knew was coming.

"But I'm starving," he declared with a groan.

"There were some cookies left over from lunch. Can you get them from out of the bag behind your seat?" Cassy paused before backing out of her parking stall to allow her son to find the cookies and get re-buckled. *What is he going to be like by the time he's a teenager?* She wondered.

"How many?" Jeremy questioned once he'd regained his seat.

"Two and then pass them to your sisters," Cassy was amazed that he insisted on asking that question every time, even though her answer was always the same. She heard his quiet sigh as he got his cookies and handed the tin to Nicole.

"Thanks Mom," he called, instead of voicing his usual complaints about his friends getting to eat as many cookies as they want.

Cassy glanced back at her son with a look of shock. "You're welcome." Jeremy gave his mother a crooked smirk. Cassy backed up the van and headed for home.

13

Ancient Egypt

The following week Cassy read the story of Joseph to the kids—it was one they were all familiar with. When she was done, however, she pulled out the colorful book she had picked up on life in Ancient Egypt and started reading through it with them. They all crowded onto the couch together so that everyone could see the many pictures.

"How come everyone is wearing white?" Kimberleigh pointed to the people on the page.

"Well, Egypt is very hot, and white is much cooler to wear than dark colors because it reflects the sun," Cassy explained.

"That would be boring. It would be no fun at all getting new clothes if they were all white, but I like all their fancy necklaces and gold bracelets!" she declared.

"What are aw those pointy things on top of their heads?" Anika studied the picture closely from her position on her mother's lap.

Her siblings leaned closer to see what Anika was looking at, and Cassy scanned the words to the side of the picture.

"It says they are little perfume cones the Egyptians wore around in their hair. The cones slowly melted in the hot sun and drenched their hair with sweet-smelling oils. It probably made them smell better when they were hot and sweaty," Cassy explained.

"That's funny," Anika said with a giggle.

"Cool!" Jeremy exclaimed when his mom turned the page and read of the great pyramids with their many hidden passages and piles of treasure buried with the Pharaohs. "I'm going to go to Egypt someday and explore the pyramids and find a hidden treasure!" he boasted.

"Well, I'm sure that most of the treasures have already been either stolen, or found and put into museums," Cassy cautioned her son, "but it would be neat to see the pyramids and know they were built thousands of years ago. Joseph would have seen some of those same pyramids when he was in Egypt, and they are still standing."

"Why did they worship so many crazy gods and think that they could take all their treasures with them when they died?" Nicole wanted to know as she read through the long list of things the Egyptians worshiped. "Didn't Joseph and Moses tell them about the real God?"

"I'm sure they did, and they would have seen all God's miracles when Moses came before Pharaoh. Some probably did believe. In fact, the Bible says that some other people left Egypt with the Israelites. Unfortunately, it was probably a lot like today. Some people don't want to hear about God no matter what they see around them, and many Christians just don't bother to tell their neighbors about Him.

"Oh." Nicole was thoughtful. "But I still don't see why they would have worshiped the sun and animals and things."

Cassy turned the page. "This is interesting. I never realized this before." She started to read: "The plagues brought on Egypt in Moses' time served not only to bring Pharaoh to a point of releasing the Israelites from bondage, but they were a direct attack against the Egyptian gods and a clear declaration of the power of the one true God. The first plague was against the Nile god Hapi, whom the Egyptians worshiped for his life-giving power. They believed Hapi controlled the flooding of the Nile as it overflowed its banks, depositing fertile soil for the next growing season. By turning the river into blood, God was showing His supreme power over this important god.

"The Egyptians also worshiped a frog goddess, Heqet, whom they believed aided women in childbirth. Heqet was a symbol of growth and new life. The second plague showed God's power over this goddess. If they wanted to worship frogs, then God would give them frogs."

"They actually worshiped frogs?" Kimberleigh was incredulous. "That's disgusting."

"It would have made the plague even more difficult," Cassy mused, "because if they worshiped them, they wouldn't have wanted to kill the frogs to get rid of them."

"That's just plain dumb to think a frog is a god." Jeremy shook his head in disbelief.

"But when you don't know the truth, people are willing to make up and believe anything," Cassy explained. "That's why God wanted to show them who He was and how foolish their gods were."

"Keep reading," Nicole nudged her mother.

"Plague number three was the plague of lice, followed by the plague of flies. Both of these plagues would have made it difficult, if not impossible, for the Egyptian priests to carry on the worship of their gods. They could not come before the gods if they were unclean, and an animal infected with lice or flies was unfit for sacrifice.

"With plague five, an attack on the livestock, God was proclaiming to all the land that he ruled over Apis, the bull god. This specially selected bull was considered the most important of all the sacred animals in Egypt. It was a symbol of courage and strength. The Egyptians looked to this god for the well-being of all their livestock, something God proved Apis had no power to control."

"I bet God wanted the Egyptians to quit worshiping His creation," Nicole commented.

"What would they have done with all those dead, rotting cows?" Jeremy wanted to know.

"Eew, don't be gross, Jeremy!" Kimberleigh elbowed her brother.

Cassy smiled and continued. "Next were the boils, which broke out on men and animals throughout the land. This would have affected all the remaining animals that the Egyptians worshiped, while the Israelites and the animals belonging to them remained free from harm. This fact would have again emphasized the power of the Israelite God to protect His people, while the gods of the Egyptians were powerless.

"The plagues of hail and locusts would have destroyed the crops of the Egyptians, not only leaving them desperate for food, but questioning their gods of the harvest who had failed to provide."

"Boy, I bet the Egyptians were getting angry at Moses and God!" Anika shook her head.

"Well, we know that Pharaoh was, but he still didn't want to follow God." Cassy responded before finishing the account. "At the top of the list was the sun god, Ra, their chief object of worship. Ra was considered to be the lord of the universe, yet for three days God blackened the light of the sun from Egypt. Even Ra was powerless before God.

"Finally, God declared the death of the firstborn male—the most important figure in every family. Egypt's gods had failed on all counts to provide and protect, and they were proven powerless before the Almighty God. God's reign is universal, and the protection of the Israelites on that night through the substitutionary death of a lamb, was a beautiful foreshadowing of God's redemptive plan."

"That's neat," Nicole said quietly.

"Yes it is," Cassy agreed. She continued to read awhile longer. The children seemed enthralled with the many facts about Ancient Egypt and the description of what life was like during the times of Joseph and Moses, though the girls found their process of making mummies disgusting.

On Thursday Cassy made up some yellow, green, and blue playdough using Kool-Aid powder. She wanted to find something more hands-on for Jeremy's sake than having the kids each draw a map, and she knew how much they all enjoyed playdough. Placing a map of Egypt in the center of the kitchen table, she gave each child some playdough and set them to work recreating the shape of Egypt, complete with the Nile River, Mediterranean Sea, and Red Sea.

While they worked, Cassy went to throw in some laundry and clean the bathroom. Having the kids help with chores eased some of her burden, but they still needed oversight and there always seemed to be more than enough to do. When she was done, Cassy made the rounds and had each child explain their map.

Anika had molded a conglomeration of blue snakes and yellow and green mountains that showed little resemblance to the picture, but she was thrilled with her creation nonetheless. "You wike my map?" she asked proudly.

"It looks very nice, honey." Cassy patted her blond head, making her daughter's face brighten with a huge smile.

Kimberleigh displayed her map next, pointing out the snake-like Nile River with its many fingers spreading toward the Mediterranean

Sea. She had done quite well with her proportions. With excitement she indicated her cluster of pyramids placed to the west on her map.

"Why do they call this the 'Red Sea' when it is blue?" she asked, pointing to the two fingers of blue setting off the Sinai Peninsula.

"I'm not sure how it got its name," Cassy admitted. "I'll have to see if I can find out. Your map looks great, though!"

Jeremy was next, and after he'd identified all of his landmarks, Cassy looked at the irregular green-shaped lumps all along the Nile River with puzzlement. "Are these the fertile fields along the Nile?"

"No, they are the crocodiles!" Jeremy declared.

"Oh yeah, I see." Cassy recognized now the slender shape of the reptile body.

"Aw, neat! I'm gonna add crocodiles to mine." Kimberleigh reached for a bit of green playdough and returned to her spot to work on her map. Jeremy beamed with pleasure.

Nicole's map was intricately formed and included pyramids, a small statue representing the Sphinx, as well as pencil point indentations she identified as Thebes, Memphis, and Giza. To the north, along the Mediterranean coast, was a patch of green showing the fertile planes of Goshen where Joseph's family had settled. Cassy was completely amazed at what they had created with playdough, and they'd had such fun doing it.

"You guys all did an awesome job," she announced when Nicole had finished explaining her map.

"Can we leave them to show Daddy?" Nicole asked.

It would be a few hours before David would be home, but Cassy instructed them to cover their maps with plastic wrap to keep them from drying out too much, then sent them to play.

Next week she would start on the novel Lauren had loaned her, which was set in the time period of Ancient Egypt. Lauren had assured her that it was full of intrigue in Pharaoh's courts and that it gave a great picture of the lifestyle and customs of the period. Cassy was looking forward to it and was sure the kids would enjoy it as well.

For now, however, Cassy focused on finishing her review of the children's work from the morning and preparation for the next day. She wouldn't have to plan anything for the afternoon with the start-up of skating at the arena from one o'clock to two o'clock and Reader's Theater shortly after. Kimberleigh had been counting the days, and Cassy hoped she wouldn't be disappointed.

When David came home, all four kids met him at the door, anxious to be the first to show off their maps.

"Don't tell me you made a map too." David picked up Anika, who was dancing excitedly in front of him.

"Yep, I did!" she said with a big grin.

"But you're not old enough for school yet," he teased.

Anika grabbed David's chin with both hands as she stared intently into his eyes. "But Daddy, it's just schoo' here with Mommy, so I'm a'wowed!" she explained indignantly.

"Oh, I see." David laughed and Anika's smile returned. "So what did you make a map of?" he inquired further.

"Um…" Anika screwed up her face. "I forget what it's ca'wed, but it has rivers and pointy mountains and Jeremy's has crocodi'os!" Anika's eyes got huge as she spoke.

"Wow! I've never seen a map with crocodiles before."

"Mommy didn't know what they were," she explained conspiratorially in a whisper loud enough for Cassy to hear from the kitchen.

"Well, you'd better hurry and show your maps to Daddy so we can get the table cleaned off and set, or Daddy's going to think all he's having for supper tonight is playdough." Cassy poked her head around the corner.

They were all sorry to take their maps apart when they were done, but finally all traces of Egypt had disappeared and the Knights were able to sit down to supper.

The next morning the kids could hardly concentrate on their studies; their thoughts kept drifting to the afternoon's activities. Jeremy loved skating, but he wasn't so keen about the Reader's Theater class.

"Do I have to read out loud?" he moaned.

"That is the idea," Cassy replied. "It will be good practice for you, Jeremy, and it sounds like lots of fun. I want you to give it a try," she encouraged her reluctant son.

Nicole and Kimberleigh added their enthusiastic prodding and

Jeremy finally agreed to give it a chance. With all the chatting going on, not many math problems were being completed, and Cassy tried to get her distracted children to focus on their work. An hour later she finally gave up, tucked the books away, and fixed an early lunch.

At one they were joined at the arena by a few dozen kids of all ages, and for the next hour they chased one another around the ice.

Cassy spent the first half hour supporting Anika as she took baby steps along the ice, doing her best to look like she was actually skating. Lauren struggled alongside her friend, holding onto three-year-old Kegan with both hands, while four-year-old James clung to her arm and wobbled unsteadily beside her.

"Wook at me go, Mrs. Andrews," Anika boasted.

"Wow, you're so fast I can hardly keep up," Lauren teased playfully.

Anika giggled and gave an excited jump—cracking her mother, who was leaning over her, under the chin with her head. Taken by surprise, Cassy jumped back, lost her balance, and flailed her arms wildly before falling soundly on her behind on the cold, hard surface.

Anika looked with shock at her mother, turned to Lauren and, shaking her head, stated matter-of-factly, "My mommy isn't very good at this." This brought an outburst of laughter from Lauren as Cassy rolled her eyes and struggled to her feet, rubbing her bruised tail bone and wiggling her sore jaw.

"At least I didn't bite my tongue," Cassy said ruefully, "but I think my jaw is broken. Good grief, you have a hard head!" she told her daughter. Anika just stared at her mother innocently.

They managed to "skate" for a while longer, but Cassy was relieved when Anika decided she was cold and wanted to get off the ice. Cassy's back was getting tired from bending over supporting her daughter's weight, and she was more than glad to join the other moms sitting on the bleachers visiting while they watched their children skate.

Later, when Cassy dropped the three older kids off at the small theater, she stuck around long enough to see them settled in with the ten other children taking part. The drama teacher introduced herself and gave them each a paper with a few lines to read in order to help her choose which parts she would have them play. Jeremy looked miserable as he stared at his sheet. Knowing how much he had struggled with reading in school, Cassy felt guilty for pressuring him to come. Maybe she should have waited until he felt more confident. If it didn't go well, she determined she would talk to the instructor and pull him out. When it was his turn to read, Cassy saw him glance hesitantly at the kids around him before carefully reading the words on his page.

"Good, you sound like you have a very strong voice. With a little practice, you should be able to project real well," the teacher encouraged, causing Jeremy to look up with obvious surprise.

When it was Kimberleigh's turn, she stepped forward with an air of confidence and looked at her paper. She read with all the enthusiasm she was capable of, following her short audition with a low bow.

"Wow, I think I have just the part for you—one that needs lots of expression," the teacher responded with a smile.

Cassy listened to a few more kids read while she waited to see how Nicole would do. She had to strain to hear her older daughter's quiet voice from across the room, but she was sure that as Nicole got to know the other kids a little better, she wouldn't feel so nervous. It was too bad none of the Andrews' kids had come. Looking at her watch, Cassy figured she'd better get going. She needed to run to the grocery store while the kids were in class. She gave them a little wave and, taking Anika's hand, walked quietly out.

Returning to the theater a few minutes before class ended, Cassy immediately looked for Jeremy among the children scattered about the room, reading through their scripts in small clusters. It only took a moment to locate her son amidst three other kids in the far corner of the room. He seemed to be doing all right, she noticed with relief.

"So, what did you think of it?" she asked the moment Jeremy reached her when he was finished.

"It was okay," he answered with a shrug.

"Do you think you're going to enjoy it?"

Jeremy shrugged again. "I get to play the Big, Bad Wolf; it's not too hard." This time Cassy detected a slight lift in his countenance.

"I decided if you really don't want to stay, I'll talk to your teacher and see if it would be okay for you to drop out."

Jeremy's eyebrows shot up and he paused a moment as if debating.

"I'll stay. You can't do a play of The Three Little Pigs without a wolf," he said simply.

"You're sure?"

Jeremy nodded and turned to wave good-bye to one of the other boys who had been in his group.

Cassy wasn't sure what his name was. "Who's that?" she asked.

"That's a very smart pig," Jeremy said with a smirk. "His name is Austin." And with those few words Jeremy headed out the door and in the direction of the van.

On the way home the girls filled their mother in on how the class had gone. They had been divided into smaller groups and assigned parts in different skits based on popular children's stories. Nicole was pleased with her role as Little Red Riding Hood, while Kimberleigh had been given the part of Baby Bear from Goldilocks and the Three Bears. There would be a performance for the parents on the last day of class. All the way home, Jeremy noisily practiced his lines in a gruff voice from the backseat.

By the time Cassy pulled into the garage, she had the beginnings of a headache. Wearily she lugged her groceries into the house and sighed at the sight of dirty dishes still piled in the sink from lunch. The dishwasher needed to be unloaded and it was time to start on supper, but she was suddenly very tired and needed a few moments to put her feet up. Cassy made herself a cup of coffee and took it into the living room where she could relax in the recliner. Cupping the mug in her hands, she leaned her head back and closed her eyes.

It was Friday; tomorrow would be catch-up day. After a busy week, she was ready for a break. Though Cassy found that she was enjoying many aspects of homeschooling, she still found it overwhelming keeping ahead of organizing lessons, marking workbooks and keeping up with the housework. With the kids home all day every day, the clutter seemed to accumulate more quickly, and by evening Cassy was often either too tired to pick it all up, or preoccupied making plans for the next day.

Taking a sip of her coffee, Cassy tried to shut out the noise of the kids talking down the hall as she poured out her heart to God. While she prayed, reassurance once again filled her heart that she was doing what God had asked of her, and with it came peace. Even once her mug was empty, Cassy sat for a moment longer before finally rising, and with a deep breath, she headed to the kitchen. Supper would be late tonight, but it had been time well spent.

14

Thanksgiving

The following Tuesday afternoon, Cassy gathered the kids around her on the couch to start reading the novel about Ancient Egypt. The storyline was captivating, and it didn't take long before they were each caught up in the intrigue of Pharaoh's court. By midafternoon, when Cassy started to close the book, Jeremy let out a loud groan. Nicole and Kimberleigh grabbed their mother's arm and pleaded with her to keep reading.

"You can't stop there," Nicole insisted, "we have to find out what happens to the slave girl, and Samoset is still in danger!"

"Keep reading, Mom, p-l-e-a-s-e." Kimberleigh looked at her mother with imploring eyes.

"Do you want me to keep going?" Cassy tilted her head to look into Anika's face. Snuggled on her mother's lap, Anika gave a sleepy nod. "Okay, but somebody needs to get me a drink of water first," Cassy bargained.

Nicole dashed to the kitchen and soon returned with a glass of ice water. In no time she was snuggled back against her mother's shoulder and the story was resumed. The afternoon flew by as together they navigated the Nile River in a boat full of slaves, walked the courts of the Egyptian Palace, and trekked across scorching sand to hide in the Valley of the Dead. When the back door opened and David walked in, Cassy looked up in shock. Shifting the sleeping Anika to check her watch, she was surprised to discover that it was almost six o'clock.

"Wow, I lost all track of time, I haven't even started supper," Cassy apologized as she closed the book and gently shook Anika to wake her.

"Aw Mom, you can't stop now, it's at the best part!" Jeremy

exclaimed.

"That must be some book if you'd rather read than eat!" David stared at his son with astonishment.

"We've only got one chapter left. Can't we finish it?" Nicole pleaded.

"How about I order some pizza and go pick it up while you finish your book," David suggested. He smiled at his wife, who was still surrounded by their children on the couch and was rewarded by her appreciative nod and a cheer from all but the half-awake Anika, who stirred and gave a tired yawn.

"Now that you mention it, I am starving," Jeremy admitted with a grin.

"Daddy!" Anika exclaimed when she noticed her father. "I'm hungry too," she said as she reached to be picked up in his strong arms.

"Ahh, at least someone is glad to see me," he teased. "Were you enjoying the story?"

"Uh-huh." The little girl nodded.

"How about you come help me order some pizza? We'll get some double pepperoni for us and some with cottage cheese and pickles for them!" David nodded toward the couch with his head bringing a giggle from his youngest.

"Get ham and pineapple," Jeremy called after them as they headed towards the kitchen.

Cassy was able to finish the story and get the table set just in time for David to arrive with the pizza, and the family enjoyed a lively dinner. The children tried to fill their father in on the story they had read, but Cassy was sure that David was thoroughly confused by the time they kept interrupting one another to fill in parts the other missed.

Later that evening, once the kids were settled in bed, David came back to the living room and took a place on the couch beside his wife. "My time to snuggle with the teacher," he announced, causing Cassy to smile.

"Thanks for bailing me out for supper," she responded as she leaned against David's shoulder. "I still can't believe that Jeremy sat while I read all afternoon. They were really into the story."

"I hadn't noticed!" Cassy elbowed her husband and he laughed. "It was a nice sight to come home to, even though supper wasn't on the table. So how have you been enjoying homeschooling, now that you've had awhile to adjust?"

"It's really tiring some days, but it's been good too. I feel like I'm learning almost as much as they are, and I'm starting to connect with the kids on a different level than I was before." Cassy thought a moment. "I've noticed the biggest change in Jeremy and his attitude about school. Not that he loves all of it, mind you, but it's not the battle I thought it would be."

"I think he seems more content, and I know he's enjoying having more time to be outside. He's always full of stories about his adventures at bedtime," David agreed.

"It's the math I wish I could add some variety to. The workbooks just seem so repetitive. I guess the kids are used to that, but it's driving me nuts by the time I correct twelve pages of it every day!"

"Does Lauren have any suggestions?" David asked.

"I don't know; I'll have to ask her. I just don't want to wear out my welcome, or she'll begin to dread seeing me coming. I feel like I'm always asking her questions."

"Why don't you try setting up a bit of a store and let the kids buy things from each other and practice making change?" David suggested.

Cassy sat up and looked at her husband. "That's a great idea! I could do that one day a week for a while to give us all a break from workbooks. Though they probably wouldn't get their books finished by the end of the year unless we went longer," she added as an afterthought.

"They'd still be doing their math," David reasoned. "Does it matter if they don't finish their books?"

"I don't know." Cassy shrugged. "I could ask Lauren, but I have a feeling she'd say no."

⌘ ⌘ ⌘

Over the next couple of days Cassy collected spare change and bills in preparation for their trial store. Friday morning she had everything

126

ready when the kids came to the kitchen to start on their schoolwork. On the table was a divided bin Cassy had made into a cash drawer of sorts. Next to it was a stack of the kids' language arts books, pencils, erasers, and notebooks, as well as Anika's coloring book and crayons.

"Instead of working in your math books today, we're going to try playing store," she informed them. "You're going to take turns being the shop keeper throughout the day, selling different things to each other and making change."

"Cool!" Jeremy was the first to respond. "Can I go first?"

"I thought Nicole would go first, since the first batch is the hardest, but you can have a turn later and sell lunch to your sisters."

"All right," Jeremy agreed with a grin.

"What do I have to do?" Nicole questioned.

"You're going to sell the others their language arts books, pencils, and everything you see on the table. Each item has a price marked on it," Cassy indicated the little pieces of masking tape stuck on the make-shift merchandise. "Your sisters and brother will each have a different amount of money to give you, and you'll have to add up their purchases and make change."

"Sure." Nicole nodded and took a seat at the table behind the money bin with a look of importance.

Cassy handed Kimberleigh a twenty-dollar bill and told her to go first.

Kimberleigh strutted up to the table and cleared her throat. "Excuse me, but I would like to see what you have available for language arts books," she said primly.

"Let's see." Nicole pulled her sister's book from the pile and held it out to her. "How do you like this one?"

"Hmm." Kimberleigh studied the book for a moment as if debating whether to take it before giving her assent. "That one will be fine, but I need a notebook and pencil to go with that," she added.

"Okay." Nicole carefully checked the price on each item and added them in her head. Spotting the erasers, she picked one up and asked her sister if she would like to add one to her list.

"I rarely make mistakes," Kimberleigh said with a smirk, "but I'll take one anyway."

Adding the cost of the eraser to the list of purchases, Nicole announced confidently, "That will be $17.25." Kimberleigh handed over the twenty-dollar bill, and Nicole deftly made change.

"Can I keep it?" Kimmy asked her mother hopefully.

"Nope, sorry, we'll need it for later. Just hand it back to Nicole, and it's Jeremy's turn." While Kimberleigh deposited her change back in the bin, Cassy handed her son two twenty-dollar bills.

Jeremy eyed the money and looked mischievously at his mother. "What if I don't want to buy my language arts book?"

"Too bad." Cassy pushed her son forward.

Again Nicole went through the procedure of selecting Jeremy's purchases for him and checking the prices. Cassy had placed a scrap of paper and a pencil beside the money bin to aid in adding the more difficult, odd figures, so Nicole carefully wrote the prices down and added up the columns. "That will be $24.73," she informed him.

"Hey, how come my book is more expensive than Kimberleigh's?" Jeremy wanted to know.

"Because you have more money, and I didn't want everything to be exactly the same," Cassy explained.

"Oh." Jeremy paid for his purchases and, after receiving his change, counted it out to doublecheck Nicole's accuracy before dutifully placing it back in the bin. When he was done, Jeremy found a seat at the table.

"Can I have a turn?" Anika had been watching the whole affair and was now dancing excitedly beside her mother.

"Yep." Cassy handed her youngest a ten-dollar bill. "You get to buy a coloring book and some crayons."

Anika stepped proudly forward, waving her money in the air. "I get to pway, too, Nico'e!"

Nicole smiled at her little sister and held out her favorite coloring book and a much used box of crayons. "How do you like these?"

"Yeah, those are just wike the ones I have at home," she declared, and Nicole snickered.

At lunch time, Jeremy had even more fun selling each of his sisters a sandwich, dish of oriental noodles, carrot sticks, and a glass of milk. He carefully added up their different totals and counted out the right amount of change. Then, after getting home from their afternoon activities, it was Kimberleigh's turn. She sold each of her siblings a snack from an assortment of differently priced items, including granola bars, cookies, and little dishes of dried fruit and nuts. The store theme was such a hit that they had to come up with one more set of items for Anika to sell. When Kimberleigh gave her little sister two dollars for a glass of water, Anika gave her back a five-dollar bill for change, causing everyone to laugh again. Anika laughed right along with them.

At supper that evening, the kids all had fun recounting their marketing adventures to their father. Cassy just looked at her husband and smiled at the obvious success of his idea. She hadn't realized just how successful it was, however, until Jeremy's final comment.

"The best part of it was, we didn't even have to do any math today!" he declared with a grin of satisfaction.

"What do you think adding up prices and making change is called?" David challenged his son.

A startled look crossed Jeremy's face. "Oh yeah, I forgot. It was so much fun it didn't feel like math!"

⌘ ⌘ ⌘

The Knights had a peaceful weekend, but the kids were waiting anxiously for Monday and a chance to spend the holiday with their cousins. Thanksgiving morning, they loaded the van with kids, snacks, and fresh pumpkin pies and headed northwest of the city to Grandma and Grandpa Knight's farm for the day. The tantalizing aroma of roasting turkey greeted them as they climbed the steps of the wide veranda running the length of the old farmhouse. David's father, Paul, welcomed them at the door. After greeting her father-in-law, Cassy made her way to the kitchen with the pies. David's mother, Jean, left what she was doing at the stove to greet her daughter-in-law and admire the baking, before setting about the task of rearranging her fridge to make room for the pies. Andrew's wife, Laura, was at the counter making salad, while Sarah was seated at the table looking after baby Samantha.

The kids gave their grandparents a hug before running back

outside in search of their cousins, who were playing on the straw bales beside the barn. Lissy had wasted no time in hunting out the new kittens, and she eagerly held a gray and white ball of fluff out to Anika when she arrived. Eight-year-old Mark gave his older sister, Mandy, a shove off the top of the stack of square bales, causing her to squeal as she tumbled into the mound of loose straw at the base of the stack. Timmy was struggling to climb the wood fence beside the bales in an effort to gain the top. Loose straw stuck out from his hair and clothes at all angles; it was easy to see that he had tumbled down the makeshift slide many times already. Jeremy dashed to join them with Kimberleigh and Nicole close on his heels.

By the time the children were called in to wash up for dinner, they were rosy cheeked from laughter and exertion. Sarah stopped them all at the door and made them pick the straw off each other before letting them inside. Once washed up, the hungry children flocked to the long tables loaded with turkey, dressing, mashed potatoes, and an impressive assortment of vegetables and salads. It was a hearty meal, and the kids chatted noisily at one table while the adults visited around another.

The housing market was booming right now, and the three brothers discussed the trend from their varying perspectives. Andrew worked as an architect, and he was under pressure from his firm to put in longer and longer hours to keep up with the demand.

"My boss isn't too pleased with me right now because I've put a limit on the number of overtime hours I'm willing to put in, but I'm already gone from home more than I'd like to be," he admitted.

"Yeah, there's a lot of building going on and everyone wants their house finished immediately. A guy could sure keep as busy as he wanted to," David agreed. "That's the nice thing about being your own boss—you can accept the number of jobs you want to handle and turn down the rest."

"It's a real battle for some men out there to keep work and home life in balance," Anthony commented. "With the abundance of work, you can see why so many become workaholics. It's often expected." The men continued to visit over coffee while the women moved to the kitchen to put the food away and get dessert.

"So how does Mandy like the change to the Middle School?" Cassy asked Laura as they dished up pumpkin pie.

"Oh, I think she likes it okay." Laura glanced at her sister-in-law. "Of course it is always a little hard to go from being the oldest in your school to being the youngest, but she seems to be adjusting fine. She has some pretty good friends in her class and she likes her teacher. Parent-teacher conferences aren't until the end of this month, so I guess I'll find out how she's doing then. What about you? Is the homeschooling thing going okay?"

"Yeah, we're getting into the routine, and I like it."

"So, do you have a teacher or someone who checks their work and makes sure they're keeping up, or how does that work?"

"Not really. I have a facilitator who will be coming next week, but from what I understand, he just wants to see what books we are using, ask how the kids are doing, and see if we have any questions." Cassy tried her best to explain from what Lauren had told her.

"How often do they come to see you?" Laura wanted to know.

"Just twice—once at the beginning of the year and once at the end, but we can call them if we're having problems or have a question or anything."

Laura looked over in surprise. "That's all? Doesn't the school have to monitor more closely or test the kids or something? How do you know if they pass?"

"Well, I monitor their work. We just keep progressing and when they understand the concepts, we move on. I won't let them keep going if they aren't getting it," Cassy tried to explain.

"How do you know if you're covering everything they do in school and that you're not missing something? I could never do that; I couldn't offer them everything the school offers. I wouldn't feel qualified to teach them all the subjects." Laura handed the last two plates of dessert to Sarah, who was transferring them to the tables.

"Maybe I can offer my kids something their teachers can't," Cassy responded quietly, feeling a bit intimidated. Visions of their afternoon curled up on the couch enthralled with a story about Ancient Egypt floated through her mind, but how could she explain that to her sister-in-law? Would Laura even view reading a book on the couch to be legitimate schooling, or would that just reinforce her opinion that she was not a trained teacher, and therefore inferior?

"I don't know, maybe," Laura amended. "I just know that I couldn't do it. I think I'll stick to my nursing." Laura turned to find her place at the table while Cassy followed more slowly.

Was this what they were all thinking, that she wasn't qualified to teach her children? Cassy wondered to herself. She had struggled enough with feelings of doubt and inadequacy leading up to their decision to homeschool. She had done her best to give those fears over to God, but suddenly she felt a heaviness settle over her as she sat down beside David and pulled her dessert plate a little closer. Cassy fiddled with her fork in the whipped cream for several minutes before finally cutting off a small bite and lifting it toward her mouth. Glancing up, she caught Sarah watching her from across the table. With an encouraging smile and an almost imperceptible nod, Sarah gave her a knowing look.

"Good pie, Cassy," was all she said, but Cassy could tell she meant more. There was no doubt that Sarah had heard at least a good portion of the conversation between her two sisters-in-law, and Cassy knew her well enough to understand what she was trying to do.

With a shaky smile Cassy nodded back. "Thanks."

After dessert, the children quickly made their departure back outside. Sarah laid Samantha down for a nap in the crib Jean kept in the spare room and came to help with the dishes. It wasn't long before the mess was cleaned up and some games were brought out. Cassy tried her best to block out Laura's words and enjoy the afternoon, and the day passed with no more questions about homeschooling, for which she was grateful.

It was late by the time they climbed into the van and headed for home. One by one the exhausted kids succumbed to the rhythmic motion of the van rocking them to sleep. In the dark silence that ensued, Cassy laid her head back as thoughts of doubt once again assailed her. *What makes you think you can teach your children everything they need to know? You're not a teacher. Your kids are going to fail in life—they'll never qualify to get into college or be able to get a decent job. They'll be misfits in society....*

Cassy's thoughts tumbled over and over in her mind. Lies, it was all lies. She knew this in her heart, had felt God's leading and had seen the process working over the last month and a half. She had witnessed a spark of enthusiasm in her son and a change in his countenance.

Oh God, why do I feel so intimidated because of a few questions? Cassy prayed silently. *I asked some of those same questions just a few months ago because I didn't understand either. I know You have called me to do this and that You have promised to go with me. I can't do it without You, Lord. I know that I'll make mistakes; I wasn't taught this way and I have so much to learn. God, You know I'm scared of the future. I don't know how long I am to teach my children, or how I'm going to handle it, but I pray that You will give me direction and help me take one day at a time. My kids could attain the highest educational degrees in the world and the best paying jobs, but if they lose You in the process, they'll have lost everything. So help me first and foremost to give them a solid foundation in Your Word. Take away my fears and doubts, God, and when it gets tough, help me to be willing to keep going.*

Cassy's prayer trailed off as she stared up at the stars twinkling down at her from the clear October night. She imagined the Almighty God staring back at her through the darkness. She felt overwhelmed by the thought. As she reflected on God's love, Cassy's heart was filled with peace and her fears slowly melted away. She would carry on, and she would not be alone.

15

The Experiment

Cassy had registered with the same private board as Lauren and had been assigned to the same facilitator. Lauren had done her best to encourage Cassy to relax as she prepared for his visit, but Cassy was still a bundle of nerves. Absently she flipped through the small stack of papers containing her list of resources she was using, as well as the goals she and David had written up. Neatly stacked on the kitchen table were all the kids' schoolbooks, including their binders they had been working on during their study of history together and their binders for science. As Cassy eyed the stack, she fretted over whether it would look like they had gotten enough accomplished. Quickly she crossed to the bookcase and grabbed the small pile of papers with all the Bible verses the kids had written out so far to add to the growing mound.

Before she could think of anything else to show her facilitator the doorbell rang, and with a nervous sigh, she went to open the front door. Lee Hanson was a tall, well-dressed man who appeared to be in his early forties. He greeted the young family with a warm smile, and after shaking Cassy's hand, he turned to Jeremy.

"Who is this young man?" He held out his hand, and Jeremy clasped it with a grin.

"I'm Jeremy," he announced, "and these are my sisters!" He introduced them one by one as they crowded into the entrance way, curious to meet the new arrival. Only Nicole hung back, peeking from around the corner, but she smiled and said hello when Jeremy introduced her.

Slowly Cassy ushered her children to the kitchen table, where she offered Mr. Hanson a seat and a cup of coffee. He smiled at the huge stack of books before him and then proceeded to ask each of the kids how they liked working at home so far, allowing them to show pages from their binders that they were especially proud of. Jeremy showed him his report about fossils, and Lee nodded in approval as he read it. Cassy was glad that she had made him correct his spelling. Nicole told him about all the books they had read so far, while Kimberleigh told him about their play coming up and showed him her science binder.

"I have a binder too!" Anika informed him proudly. "Wanna see it?"

"Of course I do." Lee smiled at her.

Anika located her binder on the table, brought it to Lee's side, and plopped it in his lap. "I'm not s'posed to be in schoo' yet, but Mommy wets me anyway. I'm on'wy four, but I can write aw my wetters and count, and I'm studying history too! Science is kind of hard, but my sisters help me sometimes."

Lee chuckled at the wide-eyed little girl by his side. "Wow, you must be a genius!" he told her.

"Rea'wy?" Anika asked in obvious delight. Then after a moment she pulled on Lee's sleeve and whispered, "What's a genius?"

With a smothered laugh he whispered back, "It means you're really smart."

"Oh." Anika nodded with a look of pleasure.

When Lee was done talking with the kids, he took a look at Cassy's lists of goals and resources and smiled in approval. "Can I keep a copy of these for my files?" he asked before placing them in his briefcase. He asked Cassy a few more questions about how things were going and assured her that it looked like she was off to a great start.

"Am I fulfilling all the requirements they should have for school?" she asked tentatively.

"You're doing just fine. You are covering all the necessary basics, and I like what you are doing for social and science. We don't have to copy the public school curriculum; we just need to be teaching the concepts of science and things about our world and history. We can do that in a lot of ways and your choice of material certainly accomplishes that. I'm a homeschooling father myself with six children, and I fully believe in the parents' right to pick and choose what and how they teach their children. God has given that authority to you, not the government—though the government would like to think they have authority over our children. Your children obviously enjoy what they're learning and it looks like you're doing a great job. Keep it up! It often takes new homeschool families a couple of years before they feel free enough to set their own course of studies apart from the government curriculum guide, so it's good that you've been able to adjust to some of your family's interests so quickly."

"I had a lot of coaching from Lauren," Cassy admitted. She couldn't believe the two-hour visit was already over, and Cassy thanked Mr. Hanson kindly as she walked him to the door. Lauren was right; she needn't have gotten so worked up about the visit. Encouragement mixed with relief washed over her as she waved to her facilitator from the front step. He was not at all the cool, rigid administrator type that she had expected.

⌘ ⌘ ⌘

That Friday, after skating and Reader's Theater class, Cassy stopped at the grocery store for a few items. As they got out of the van, Jeremy tugged on his mother's arm.

"Can I get a couple of things for a science experiment?" he worded carefully.

"What kind of experiment?" Cassy turned to her son absentmindedly while she tried to think what she was going to fix for supper when she got home.

"Josh told me at skating how to make a volcano with pop and mints." Jeremy waited eagerly for his mother's response, afraid she would say no.

"That's all you need?" Cassy was surprised, but the items seemed harmless enough.

"Yep, that's what Josh said." The energetic boy squirmed anxiously at his mother's elbow as she entered the store and pulled a cart from the line.

"Okay," Cassy agreed, "but hurry and get what you need because I'm not going to be long."

In a flash Jeremy darted through the store in the direction of the pop aisle. He selected a two-liter bottle of Diet Coke and then headed for the candy counter at the front of the store. Scanning the tiers of gum and candy bars, Jeremy finally located a pack of Mentos and headed in search of his mom. Cassy hardly noticed as he placed his items into the cart, and soon they were headed for the checkout counter.

When they got home Cassy quickly unloaded the groceries, stuck a package of hamburger in a frying pan to start browning, and headed to the laundry room to put another load of clothes into the washer before supper. Anxious to try out the "experiment" Josh had told him about, Jeremy grabbed a large bowl to set under the bottle of pop and opened his package of Mentos. Josh had warned him to put the Mentos into the bottle as quickly as possible, so he grabbed as many as he could hold in one hand and centered them over the open neck of the bottle. All at once Jeremy released the mints, then jumped back with a look of shock at the immediate, explosive results. The Diet Coke erupted with such force that it shot straight up like a huge geyser, hitting the kitchen ceiling and from there shooting out in every direction.

"Cool!" he exclaimed as he stared with wide eyes as the two-liter bottle nearly emptied its contents over every possible surface in the kitchen.

When Cassy flew around the corner to investigate the unexplainable sound emanating from that direction, the full force of what had just happened seemed to hit him, and Jeremy looked cautiously around the kitchen.

With horror, Cassy stopped and stared incredulously as the disaster unfolded before her eyes. "Jeremy David Knight!" she bellowed as the last of the Coke ran down her walls. She was so dumbfounded she could hardly speak. "What in the world do you think you were doing?" she demanded as she marched over to her astonished son.

When Cassy felt a drip on her head, she looked up just in time to catch the next drop as it fell from the ceiling and landed with a plop on the end of her nose. At the smothered chuckle from her son, Cassy leveled a menacing glare in his direction. Immediately Jeremy lost the humor of the situation and stiffened to attention before his mother. Hearing the commotion, three young girls flew from their rooms and stopped dead in their tracks, eying the huge mess before them.

"He's dead!" stated Nicole under her breath as she shook her head in disbelief.

"I put a bowl under it," was all Jeremy could say in his defense. "Josh said it makes a great volcano."

"Did the thought ever occur to you to wait until I could help you, or that maybe you should try it outside?" Cassy stared at the rivulets of sticky pop making their way down the front of every cupboard and appliance, dripping from the ceiling and collecting in little pools all over the counters and floor. Shasta had come running and was already licking up some of the puddles.

Jeremy tentatively looked around at the mess and shook his head dejectedly. "I didn't think it would do that," he mumbled.

"Nicole, can you stir the hamburger on the stove and keep an eye on it while I get a mop and bucket for Jeremy to start mopping the floor?" Jeremy's shoulders slumped as his mother left the room and Nicole tiptoed gingerly over to the stove.

"Wait 'til Daddy gets home!" Anika shook her finger at her big brother.

"I'll help you clean it up," Nicole soothed sympathetically.

"I don't know what you did," Kimberleigh said with a smirk, "but I wish I'd seen it!" She crossed to the sink and grabbed the dishrag to start wiping down the cupboards.

When Cassy returned, she demonstrated to Jeremy how to wring out the mop and set him to work on the floor, while she went for a step ladder and some rags to start on the ceiling. Between the four of them they somehow managed to get the kitchen relatively free of Diet Coke and supper on the table by the time David got home. After they were seated and David had asked the blessing, he turned to his kids.

"So what'd you learn today?" he asked as he helped himself to a flour tortilla and passed the plate.

"Well, we learned what not to do." Kimberleigh giggled and looked at her brother, who slunk a little lower in his chair.

"Oh?" David raised his eyebrows suspiciously at his son. "And what was that?"

"Jeremy made a vo'cano with pop and it expwoded aw over the who'e kitchen!" Anika explained as she swung her arms out wide to demonstrate.

"So, what'd ya do, bud?" David quizzed his son as he filled the taco on his plate.

"Well, Josh Henderson told me today at skating that you can make a great volcano by putting Mentos into a bottle of Diet Coke, so I wanted to try it," Jeremy tried to explain.

"I take it, it works?" David guessed.

"Did it ever!" Jeremy exclaimed. "It flew all the way to the ceiling!"

"Really?" David let out a surprised laugh before Cassy punched his leg under the table and glared at him.

"Yes, really!" Cassy went on to explain to her husband. "And the whole two-liter bottle of pop shot all across the ceiling and covered everything in the kitchen. We spent an hour cleaning it up before you got home, and my shoes still stick to the floor," she added for emphasis.

"Sounds like something my brothers and I would have tried if we had known about it," David added with a smirk. "Did I ever tell you about the time when we almost burned down the garage?"

Cassy elbowed her husband to cut him off. "I don't think he needs any more ideas." She looked at her husband pointedly.

"Well, it wasn't a very good idea anyway," David declared more sternly, but Cassy could still see the twinkle in his eyes. "And setting off 'volcanoes' in the kitchen probably wasn't a good idea either, right?" Now David looked seriously at his young son with a gentle reprimand.

"Yes, sir," Jeremy answered solemnly. "I didn't mean to make such a mess."

David gave his son a little smile. "I know," he simply said, and with that, the matter was dropped.

On Sunday, when Cassy relayed the story to Lauren after church, her friend burst out laughing.

"You're as bad as David!" Cassie said, playfully slapping Lauren on the arm. "You didn't spend an hour cleaning up pop from your whole kitchen, or you wouldn't think it was so funny!" But Cassy had to laugh in spite of herself. "I should have told him to tell Christian to try it," she threatened.

"Too late. Now I'll know not to buy any Diet Coke and Mentos," Lauren teased. "Besides, I have three boys and you only have one—remember that!" And the two were still chuckling as they went in search of their families.

16

Medieval Feast

By the end of November, Cassy was feeling fairly settled in her routine and within the homeschool group. Though some days were more difficult than others, Cassy was slowly adjusting her expectations. The opportunity she had to interact with some of the other mothers every Friday, helped to fill the void she'd felt when she'd given up her Wednesday morning Bible study at the church. Cassy was getting to know some of the other homeschool moms a little better and was enjoying the new friendships. Not that she didn't struggle at times with her busy schedule and giving up some of the freedom she'd enjoyed, but she was learning to be content in the role God had called her to and was finding value in investing herself wholeheartedly into her family.

The last Friday of the month, Cassy joined the other parents at the small theater in Red Deer to watch the performance the kids had been working on in Reader's Theater. They used very few props and just simple items for costumes to represent their characters, but most of the children were quite enthusiastic as they threw themselves into their parts. It was obvious that Kimberleigh was having a ball, and Cassy was glad to see Nicole expressing herself with more confidence as well. Once Jeremy had started the class, he had gotten into the idea of acting and was making the most of his role as the Big, Bad Wolf. The short plays were simple enough, but Cassy thought they were cute and the parents stood and clapped when it was over. The performance was well done, and the kids seemed pleased.

⌘ ⌘ ⌘

On Saturday Cassy was greeted with the first snow fall of the year. It left a fresh blanket of white on the ground and allowed her to enjoy a peaceful afternoon reading while David and the kids had a snowball fight outside. She didn't have to worry about supper that evening, as the Andrews had invited them over for a special medieval feast, which Lauren and her kids had prepared for them. Even though the Andrews had covered the Middle Ages the year before, Lauren had informed Cassy how much her children had loved studying the era and how they had begged to do this special project. Cassy was looking forward to the event. Glancing at her watch, she decided she'd better call her family inside. They would need to get cleaned up if they were going to be ready to leave on time.

Upon arrival at the Andrews' home, they were met at the door by three young "knights" complete with silvery, hooded vests resembling chain mail, toy shields, and swords.

"Welcome, Lords and Ladies, to the Andrews' Castle," Christian heralded, as he bowed low to the women and was copied by his two younger brothers. "Watch your footing on the drawbridge," he cautioned, as he pointed with his sword to the large square of cardboard lying on the top step outside their door. Two ropes were knotted through the outer corners of the board and anchored to the upper edge of the doorframe to complete the effect. "It can be slippery when wet," he explained.

When David and Jeremy reached the door, the boys all stood to attention. Three-year-old Kegan eagerly whipped his sword from its scabbard to show Jeremy and nearly whacked James in the face with it. Jumping to the side to avoid getting clobbered, James landed right on Christian's toe.

"Ouch!" Christian gave his brother a light shove and glared at him before continuing. "May I introduce myself—I am Sir Christian and these are my two squires, James and Kegan," Christian recited, obviously enjoying his role.

"It's an honor, Sir Christian!" David shook the young boy's hand.

"What fine squires you have here," he added.

Melissa and Brianne were waiting inside to greet their guests. Each wore a long skirt and blouse, and atop their heads were colorful, cone-shaped hats with long, sheer veils flowing from behind.

"Aw, cool hats! Can I try one on?" Kimberleigh wanted to know, as she admired the shimmering veils. Melissa lifted hers off and placed it on her friend's head. Immediately Kimberleigh started to spin in circles to make the veil float and dance behind her.

"Me too, me too!" Anika declared in delight.

Brianne gave Anika a turn with her hat until they were called to the table a few moments later. In the dining room the Knights discovered a long, candlelit table crowded with chairs so that they could all sit together. At each place was a small plate, a bowl of beef and barley soup, a spoon, and a mug of grape juice. The rest of the table was bare. Once they were all seated, "Lord Richard" asked the blessing and the meal began.

"Don't worry, there's more food," Christian informed Jeremy, who was seated beside him.

"Oh good," Jeremy whispered back with relief.

When the soup was finished, Lauren started clearing the bowls and utensils away. She gave a nod to Melissa, who rose from the table and left the room. The girl returned shortly with her violin, and Lauren introduced her as a traveling minstrel. Melissa played a short classical piece on her instrument, which suffered a slight interference when her hat started to slide off her head and she had to pause to right it again. Everyone clapped and Lauren motioned for Brianne to help her in the kitchen while her sister put away the violin.

Soon the next course—a large loaf of fresh, multigrain bread served on a wooden cutting board, a small dish of butter and a stoneware platter displaying a square block of cheese—was placed on the table. The bread and cheese were passed around and each person served themselves by slicing off the desired amount with the knives provided.

"We churned the butter ourselves in a jar using a potato masher," Melissa announced proudly.

"Yeah, we all had to take turns. It took a long time!" Brianne added.

"What did you make it out of?" Kimberleigh wanted to know.

"Cream," Brianne answered. "You just keep mixing it, and it slowly gets thicker until it turns to butter. It got my arm really tired!"

"I could do it 'cause I'm stwong!" Kegan boasted as he flexed his muscles for everyone to see.

When the second course was cleared away, Brianne rose and pulled out a folded piece of paper that had been tucked in the waist of her skirt. Making her way to stand beside her father at the head of the table, she unfolded the paper and cleared her throat.

"This evening I wish to entertain you all with a poem I wrote with Melissa's help," she announced solemnly. "It's called, 'Life in the Middle Ages.'

Life in the Middle Ages was really tough,
The work was hard, the clothes were rough.
The castles were big and built to last,
They had to withstand the enemy's blast.
The knights were brave and fought with honor,
The women cooked and churned the butter.
Some Lords were rich but not very good,
They didn't treat farmers as they should.
I'm a traveling minstrel and that's my poem,
Thanks for welcoming me into your home."

Amidst laughter and applause, Brianne curtsied and took her seat. This time Melissa departed to the kitchen to help her mother, and they returned a moment later with two platters—each laden with a whole roasted chicken. To that was added a large bowl of roasted potatoes, and a bowl of carrot sticks. Again the dishes were passed around for each guest to help themselves. Looking beside her plate, Anika was the first to comment on her missing utensils.

"Mommy, I don't have any fork or spoon," she declared.

"That's because in the Middle Ages, people just cut off a hunk of meat and ate it with their fingers!" James announced loudly.

"Rea'wy?" Anika looked to her mother for approval, and at Cassy's nod, she picked up a piece of chicken from her plate and took a large bite.

"This is fun!" Jeremy announced from across the table as he grabbed a potato in one hand and a piece of chicken in the other.

"Don't get too used to it," Cassy warned her son. "You don't live in the Middle Ages!"

Everyone laughed and visited over the meal. Following the main course, the guests were treated to a third bit of entertainment. Christian brought out a printed cardboard model of a castle their family had carefully constructed. As he pointed out the different parts of the structure, he explained what each part was used for and how the fortress was defended. His presentation was followed by some tarts and clusters of grapes for dessert. The meal was heralded a huge success by Cassy's children, and when Christian informed them that there would be a jousting tournament following supper, they were all in a hurry to finish their dessert. Finally the candles were blown out, and the group retired to the family room downstairs for the tournament.

Christian walked importantly to the center of the room to explain the rules. Each competitor would wear a silver shield on his chest, consisting of an aluminum pie plate with a string attached to the top so that it could hang around one's neck. Then he held up the lances made of newspaper rolled into long cones and covered with duct tape. The contestants had to start at opposite ends of the room, straddle a broom and gallop his "horse" toward his opponent. The first to hit the other's shield with his lance would be declared the winner.

"I challenge Sir Jeremy to a joust," Christian declared the moment he was done giving the instructions.

With one leap, Jeremy was beside his friend, donning his silver shield. Straddling broomstick horses and with lances in hand, the two paced themselves across the room and turned to face one another, ready for action. At the trumpet blast, simulated by James, the two boys charged! Both thrusts deflected off one another, and the two faced off again. This time Christian sneaked his lance under Jeremy's and succeeded in making contact with his opponent's pie plate just a second before Jeremy's lance struck home. With a cheer from the crowd, Christian strutted around on his makeshift horse and asked for another challenger.

Each of the kids took a number of turns against one another until Melissa was finally declared the overall victor. Next the boys managed to talk their fathers into a match, so with woefully mangled lances in hand, the two straddled their horses and laughingly faced off, each uttering threats to knock the other off their respective steed. After six charges, they still had not managed to determine a victor. Each man had successfully blocked and maneuvered to avoid the other's thrusts. The ladies and kids were laughing so hard at their wild antics that the men just kept hamming it up.

As David and Richard faced off once again, a nearly hoarse trumpeter gave the signal and they both lunged forward. This time David made as if he were going to whack his opponent on the head, and when Richard ducked and raised his lance to block him, David made a quick jab for Richard's shield and was rewarded with a sound strike. David raised his lance in victory, and Richard gave his opponent a good-natured whack on the side of the head in retaliation.

"Yeah Dad!" Jeremy ran to congratulate his father, who hopped off his horse and gave a low bow.

"I hope you realize that I've just won your horse," he threw over his shoulder at Richard, who dismounted and handed David his broom.

"That's no fair. I had to fight a real Knight," Richard said.

"Just remember to call me Sir David from now on!" David shot back.

It was late, and the Knights graciously thanked their hosts for the wonderful evening as they took their leave. The kids couldn't stop talking about the fun they'd had and recounting the play-by-play of various matches all the way home.

Finally, when the kids were all tucked into bed, Cassy and David headed to their room. As Cassy brushed out her long hair, she remarked to David how enjoyable it had been to interact all together as families.

"I think families should do more of that," David responded thoughtfully.

Cassy climbed into bed beside her husband. "Good-night, Sir David, my Knight in shining armor." She planted a kiss on David's lips.

"Good-night Fair Lady," David responded with a laugh as he flicked out the light on his nightstand.

17

Family Christmas

By now Cassy had worked through the story of Moses, the years in the wilderness, and the many battles led by Joshua in conquering the Promised Land. She had discussed the numerous warnings that God had given His people to rid the land of the pagans and their idols, in order to avoid compromising with the many false beliefs and practices around them.

"Do you think we have false beliefs around us that we need to be careful of?" she asked her children to see what they would say.

"Yep," Nicole responded after a moment, "evolution."

"Right. What other kinds of beliefs?" Cassy pressed further.

"Beliefs about other gods?" Jeremy asked with uncertainty.

"Yeah, there are a lot of religions that don't believe in the true God, did you know that?"

"Sort of, but I don't know much about them," Jeremy admitted.

"If we aren't following God, then who are we really following?"

"Satan!" Kimberleigh piped up confidently.

"So how do we know what is true?" Cassy asked once again.

"The Bible," Nicole answered. "But Mom, the Bible said that Joshua was to wipe out all the people—is that right? I mean, in school, Mrs. Owen told us that we're to be tolerant and that there are people from many different cultures and religions and they are all equal. She said that we aren't to judge them."

"Hmm." Cassy thought for a moment. "She was right that we are all created equal and that we are to respect others and treat them with love, but that is different from accepting their beliefs as being right and equal with the Bible. God wants us to love people but also to know what the Bible says and to judge right from wrong. He doesn't want us to accept their beliefs or to compromise with them, because that would lead us away from Him. We still need to take a strong stand on what is right and be obedient to God. Does that make sense?"

"Yeah, I think so, but I don't think that's what Mrs. Owen meant," Nicole responded thoughtfully.

"No, I'm sure she didn't, and that's the danger. That's why God didn't want the Jewish people to mix with the pagan people because He knew they would start to accept their idols and to act like they did. Then the Hebrew nation would no longer be an example to show the world around them the truth. Sometimes I think Christians forget that we need to be careful not to accept wrong ideas and start to act like those around us too. We just want to fit in. Then people can no longer see Jesus in us either and learn the truth."

When Cassy got to the story of King David, she helped the kids keep a running list in their binders of what character traits David displayed throughout his life that made him a "man after God's own heart," as well as a list of his sins and their consequences.

"David was blessed and used by God because he loved the Lord and humbled himself and sought forgiveness when he did wrong. But sin has consequences and he still had to pay a huge price for some of his choices, didn't he?" Cassy asked the kids when they had finished reading his story from Scripture.

"Yeah, his baby died," Kimberleigh said solemnly as she looked at her list.

"And his kids fought and hurt each other and some were killed," Nicole added.

"Right," Cassy continued. "That's why our character and choices are so important. What character traits off your lists do you think you could work on to become good followers of God?" Each of the kids studied their lists for a moment.

"I could be brave!" Jeremy declared.

"Be a good friend, and forgive when someone wants to hurt you," added Nicole.

"We can trust God," was Kimberleigh's reply.

"Okay, we can trust God even when things don't look like they're

148

going very well, right? Like when King Saul was trying to kill David," Cassy agreed. "What about you, Anika? Can you think of some ways that David showed he loved God by what he did?"

Anika, sprawled on the floor, coloring in her binder, looked up. "Um, he talked to God wots!" she answered enthusiastically, bringing a smile from her mother.

"He sure did! How about for the next three weeks leading up to Christmas, we show God how much we love Him by practicing good character. We can start right here by doing little things to be kind or to help each other," Cassy suggested. "Just like Jonathan was loyal and helped David out when it would have been easy for him to hate David for taking his place, and then David helped out Jonathan's crippled son. They were kind to each other when they didn't have to be and treated each other more like brothers. Did you know that pleases God and shows you love Him when you are kind to each other?"

The kids nodded and agreed that it would be fun to try and come up with ways to help their family members. Cassy had come to cherish this time together when she could read with her children and discuss godly principles with them. She realized this hadn't happened very often when they were all in school, but she found it becoming more and more natural as they sat together in the afternoons. Cassy felt blessed to be able to interact with her children on this level.

That month, amidst preparations for Christmas, decorating the tree and working together on all the Christmas baking, Cassy noticed the many giggles and stealthy movements of her youngsters as they secretly sneaked behind each others' backs, looking for little things they could do without their siblings catching them. One morning when Anika came to the kitchen, she headed for the bin of dog food under the sink. Filling the scoop, she carefully carried it across the room, only to discover that someone had already filled the dishes for her.

"Hey you guys!" she exclaimed in astonishment and then she started to giggle. "Somebody awready fed Shasta," and she headed back to the sink to replace her load. A blond-headed boy scooted back from where he had been peeking around the corner and scampered unnoticed down the hall.

Another morning, Jeremy had forgotten to make his bed and left his math book to hurry back to his room, only to discover it had been made for him. He marched back to the kitchen and eyed his sisters quizzically, but only when Cassy looked real close could she detect the slight grin on Nicole's face as she studiously stared at her math book.

While getting ready for bed late one evening, Cassy found a carefully penned note, thanking her for being such a good mom, balanced atop a small mound of pennies on her pillow. She wiped a tear from her eye as she read it. The David and Jonathan plan was obviously working. The grateful mom tiptoed back to the kitchen, found a bag of candy on the top shelf of the pantry and carefully hid a piece in each of her children's math books, where they'd be sure to discover it the next day.

Another afternoon the kids all worked together to pack a large basket full of Christmas baking and little gifts to take to their hurting neighbor family. Anika lovingly helped wrap a beautiful doll for her friend Amy, hoping it would cheer the little girl who was still desperately missing her father. Carefully they loaded the heavy basket into their van and Cassy drove them up the lane and into the neighboring drive. The kids giggled and shushed one another as they awkwardly maneuvered their Christmas offering up the front steps, each clinging to one edge of the gift basket. When it was safely deposited just outside the door, Nicole adjusted their handmade card so that it was clearly visible. Inside the card, each family member had written a few simple words of encouragement or blessing. Once the gift was in place, the kids darted back to the van, hoping they hadn't been spotted, and Cassy drove them home.

Even David got snared into the game. Early one morning, before heading out to work, he sneaked into the living room and hung little gifts on the Christmas tree labeled with each child's name. The kids were thoroughly enjoying their character building project, and little did Cassy know when she had spontaneously suggested it while reading on the couch one day, that years later her kids would still talk with fond memories of their David and Jonathan Christmas.

⌘ ⌘ ⌘

The day before Christmas Eve, Cassy's parents arrived from British Columbia. The house was in an uproar as the kids greeted their grandparents and showed them to the guest room. Mike and Joyce would be staying with them for a few days before moving on to stay a little while with both Cory's and Don's families. Christmas dinner would be shared with the whole family at Cassy and David's. The kids could hardly contain their excitement as they helped their grandparents place the presents they had brought under the already loaded Christmas tree. They would get to open their family presents the following night before all the Christmas Day celebrations with their cousins.

David and Anthony had booked a whole week off work over Christmas, and it was good to have him home. Over supper the kids shared with their grandparents, whom they hadn't seen in many months, how their school was going. Cassy wasn't sure if her parents fully understood what they were doing but they seemed supportive, for which she was thankful. After the meal they visited long into the evening, discussing a few issues Rev. Harris was facing in his church on the coast, but mostly just catching up on general news and sampling some of the many goodies Cassy had spent weeks making.

The next evening Mike and Joyce joined their daughter's family as they read the Christmas story from Luke chapter two. Once the story was read, the kids helped pass out the presents and took turns opening them. It was a special time together. When the wrappings had been cleared away, Cassy just sat back and enjoyed the familiar Christmas songs playing in the background. She watched her children playing with their new toys under the soft glow of the Christmas lights twinkling on the tree. Gazing at the tiny manger scene below the pine branches, she wondered what that first Christmas had been like when the best gift of all had been given to man.

With a contented sigh, Cassy looked at her watch. "Time for bed, kids," she announced. "Tomorrow will be another big day."

Jeremy let out a quiet groan but joined his sisters as they stacked their presents under the tree and headed down the hall. They returned shortly, all clad in their warm pajamas, to make the rounds giving good-night hugs and kisses. One-by-one they pattered off, with David close on their heels to pray with them and tuck them into bed.

⌘ ⌘ ⌘

Christmas morning it was still dark outside when Cassy sleepily crawled out from under her covers and headed for the kitchen to prepare the Christmas turkey. The house was quiet yet, and Cassy tried not to wake anyone as she mixed up the dressing and stuffed the plump bird, before sliding the heavy roasting pan into the oven. Hearing the muffled sounds of the first early risers, Cassy washed her hands and took a peek out her kitchen window to discover a winter wonderland outside. There had been a hoar frost during the night, and everything was coated with a thick, white, crystal film that glittered in the soft glow of the rising sun, making the landscape look like it had been dipped in crushed diamonds. It was beautiful, and Cassy admired the scene. Soon family members began slowly straggling into the kitchen and Cassy started placing muffins, fruit, and cereal on the table. The strong aroma of coffee filled the kitchen and Joyce breathed it in appreciatively as she entered the room.

"Can I help with anything?" she offered.

"Sure, you want to get the milk and juice while I set the table?" Cassy answered.

"Mmm, my favorite muffins!" Jeremy proclaimed as he eyed the banana chocolate-chip muffins stacked on the large platter.

"Good, you can get the butter and put it on the table," his mother told him.

Jeremy ran to the fridge. "I can't find it," he said as he stared blankly into the open door.

"It's on the second rack in the door where it always is," Cassy directed. Sometimes she wondered if her son would be able to find something in the fridge if it had a flashing neon sign attached to it.

When breakfast was finished, Cassy had the kids clear the dishes while she started peeling potatoes for dinner. The meal was scheduled for one-thirty, but Cassy expected her siblings and their families to arrive midmorning. David set up an extra table and chairs in the living room, while Cassy and her mother chatted in the kitchen. A couple of hours later the house was full of cousins and more goodies than Cassy knew what to do with.

"I can't believe how much Connor and Christy have grown," Cassy remarked to Kathy as she entered the kitchen. Though Don and his family lived only a couple of hours away, it seemed they only saw one another for the occasional holiday or special event. Her fifteen-year-old nephew had shot up over the months since she'd seen him last, and Christy would soon be a teenager as well.

"Yeah, I had to buy Connor a whole new wardrobe for school this year; he'd outgrown everything. I hope I don't have to do that too many more times," Kathy stated.

Kathy and Trish had joined in on the dinner preparations as the women visited together. Tantalizing smells wafted from the kitchen, and the men occasionally risked getting their hands slapped to come in search of something to nibble on.

"They're getting vicious out there!" Don teased as he emerged from the kitchen with a pickle in each hand. "I just about got stabbed with a pickle fork by your wife," he motioned toward Cory.

"Next time I won't miss," Trish called from the kitchen, causing the men in the living room to laugh.

"Sounds like a challenge!" David yelled back jokingly.

About quarter after one, David was called and put to work slicing the turkey in the overcrowded room. With everyone's help, the feast was finally on the table and the gang was seated. David asked his father-in-law to ask the blessing, and Mike made sure to remember his daughter and family so far away in Africa. Thankfully DJ was doing much better and was able to celebrate Christmas with his parents and a couple other missionary families on the compound.

Everyone lingered over their meal. By the time they were done, most decided that they were too full for dessert and that it should be saved until later. This brought a groan from Connor, who always seemed to have room for more food, but he was appeased with a few Christmas cookies from one of the many platters lining the crowded counters.

When the food was put away and the dishes done, the families gathered once again in the living room to open presents. All the cousins and siblings had drawn names months ago to see who they would each buy a present for, and these gifts were distributed and opened first. Then Joyce and Mike passed out a present to each of their children, in-laws, and grandchildren. Everyone graciously thanked one another for their gifts. When the exchange was finished, the ladies went to dish up and serve dessert.

"Oh, I'm still so full," Cory commented, rubbing his stomach when his wife handed him a plate of apple pie and ice cream. "But I'll suffer," he added quickly and grabbed the plate before his wife could pass it to the next person.

"What a martyr," Trish commented dryly as she returned to the kitchen.

After dessert the kids headed off in different directions to play with their toys, while the adults congregated around the kitchen table to play games. Throughout the afternoon, the kids made frequent appearances in the kitchen, however, to sneak more goodies from the abundance to be found.

"It's good that your kids have some time to play with other kids," Don commented at one point as they were dealing the next hand. "I know some homeschoolers in our area who are too isolated, and they don't know how to interact with the other kids in the youth group very well. They're kind of strange and don't fit in."

Cassy looked at her brother in surprise. "Maybe they spend more time with their family than their peers, but that doesn't make them weird," she stammered.

"No, but I don't think they get out much, and they don't seem to have many friends. They need more time with their peers; it's not good for them," Don clarified. "Their parents are overprotective, I think. Connor says they really stand out in the youth group."

"Sometimes it wouldn't hurt for parents to protect their children a bit more, and for their kids to have a little less influence from their peers," David cut in calmly, sensing his wife's agitation. "It could keep a few more teens out of trouble."

"Yeah, maybe, but they go way overboard," Don insisted.

The cards were dealt and David reached under the table to grasp his wife's hand in reassurance and the matter was dropped. It was only a few comments, but Cassy could still feel the sting of them later that night as she got ready for bed. She was probably over-reacting, and maybe Don wasn't inferring anything about their kids in particular, but it sure felt that way, and Cassy was frustrated.

"I don't know why Don had to say that," Cassy said to David when they were alone in their room. "I know that as a public school teacher he doesn't agree with homeschooling, but I wish he would try to understand it!"

"Don't take it so personal, I don't think he was trying to hurt you, Cassy; he's just concerned. You have to realize that a few months ago we didn't understand it either."

"I know," she admitted reluctantly. "It's just that I've come to see how backwards our society is in placing the importance of peers and the youth culture way over family. I've seen how some of the other teens in our homeschool group interact with their parents, and it's a great thing. I want that kind of a relationship with my kids, but you sure don't see it very often in our society."

"Why would you?" David responded simply. "Kids spend most of their week with their friends in school, in after school sports and activities or just hanging out. Even in church they are in their separate classes and youth group. Most wouldn't be caught dead sitting in the pew with their parents on a Sunday morning instead of with their friends. It's hard for them to have a lot of time left to develop much of a relationship with their parents and siblings at home, and it's labeled as a generation gap and considered normal. I don't think there is anything normal in God's view about having teens so dependent on their peers that they look to them for direction in everything from what clothes to wear and what music to listen to, to the attitudes they develop and the activities they choose to be involved in. Our society has disjointed our families to the degree that they no longer know how to interact or communicate with each other and they no longer feel the need or desire to fix it. They think it's normal, and to them a family that is cohesive and not peer dependent, is weird or isolated."

"So how do you say that to Don without stepping on his toes?"

"Sometimes you can't," David stated simply. "And if people don't want to hear it, maybe you just have to show them and hope that they'll see it for themselves. Unfortunately, by then their kids may be grown and they won't have a chance to build that relationship while their kids are young."

"Teresa Henderson said that she spent a week at a music camp with Jamie where the kids and parents all stayed in big dorm rooms. She said she realized just how much her daughter didn't fit in when she listened for a whole week to the talk, moral values, and attitudes towards parents expressed by the other kids, and saw the behavior and dress of the other teen girls. She said she was never so glad that her daughter didn't fit in with her peers! It's not that she couldn't talk to them, it's just that she felt no pressure to fit in with their culture and was okay with being different and standing up for what she believed. She said that Jamie visited just as comfortably with the other parents as with the other students, but she did stand out, and Teresa was glad."

"I would be more concerned with parents who did want their kids to fit in to the youth culture of today, especially among non-Christian peers," David agreed. "I wouldn't want my kids battling that for so many hours a day. No matter how good they are, some of it is bound to rub off."

"It's all starting to make so much more sense to me and it suddenly seems so obvious, that I think everyone else should see it too." Cassy climbed into bed beside her husband. "It's weird. I guess God has been changing my perspective, and I've hardly noticed it was happening." She turned over and snuggled against her husband as he enfolded her into his arms.

"God has us on a journey; let's just see where He takes us," David whispered against her hair.

Cassy nodded as she gave a tired yawn.

18

Queen Esther Comes to Visit

Over the holidays the Knights spent some time with David's family as well, but as New Year's celebrations faded away, Cassy once again got out the schoolbooks. It had been good to have a break, though the holidays had been busy in a different way. However, it was time to get back into the routine of school. Swim lessons would be starting soon and would run for eight weeks on Tuesday afternoons, so Cassy had decided to bump her Tuesday afternoon schedule to Friday, now that Reader's Theater was finished.

With all the Christmas preparations and baking, Cassy felt she had let some of the kids' work slide a little and she was struggling with guilt. She felt the need to catch up so that no one could call into question the quality of education she was providing her children. They had all enjoyed the time baking and decorating Christmas cookies, which other years Cassy had tried to accomplish while the kids were in school. However, at times it was still difficult for the new homeschool mom not to hold herself up against the public school schedule, let alone the fear that if someone else knew she'd had her children baking cookies while most kids were in school, they would consider her lax.

That first week back to "school," Cassy was reading her kids the story of Esther. When she was done, she decided to get them to re-enact the story. She gave them a bit of time to organize and plan while she went to the kitchen to go through the mail and balance the checkbook. When the kids were ready, they called their mother into the living room.

Finding a seat in her favorite chair, Cassy got settled and each child introduced their respective characters. Anika stepped forward wearing a paper crown and a blanket, which was tied around her neck and hung down in a long train.

"I'm the king," she announced, "but I can't say his name."

"I'm Esther," Kimberleigh curtsied as she stepped forward, and then returned to her spot in the line.

"I'm Haman and also the king's guard," Jeremy bowed.

"And I'm Mordecai," Nicole added.

Anika took her place on a kitchen chair set in the middle of the room, and Jeremy came to stand before her. "Find me a new queen!" she commanded her brother.

Jeremy bowed. "Yes, Your Highness," and he walked to the corner, where Nicole and Kimberleigh waited. Kimberleigh had a winter scarf wrapped around her head and face. "Let me see," Jeremy pulled the scarf from his sister's face. "I guess you're pretty...sort of."

Kimberleigh slapped her brother's arm. "You're supposed to say I'm beautiful!"

"Whatever," Jeremy mumbled under his breath. "Come with me." Cassy smothered a chuckle as Jeremy grabbed his sister by the arm and started to drag her away.

"No! Not my Esther!" Nicole moaned.

"Don't take me away!" Kimberleigh reached toward her cousin, Mordecai, as Jeremy pulled her further. "Oh how dreadful, what will become of me? A poor innocent girl, ripped from my home by an evil guard..."

Jeremy glared at his sister. "She didn't say that!"

"She might have," Kimberleigh insisted, and Cassy shook with silent laughter.

Jeremy stopped in front of Anika, who was still seated on her throne.

"You wi'w be my new queen," Anika announced, as she stood on her chair to place a paper crown on Kimberleigh's head.

With that Jeremy waltzed over to where Mordecai stood and commanded haughtily, "I am the great Haman; bow down before me."

Standing her ground Nicole declared, "I will bow only to my God."

"You wicked Jew, I'll get you for this!" Jeremy stormed back to the king. "King, there is an evil group of people in your kingdom who don't listen to you. Can I kill them?"

"Ki'wing is bad!" Anika shook her head.

Jeremy nudged his little sister. "You're supposed to say yes!" he whispered.

"Okay, yes, but it's sti'w bad," she insisted.

Kimberleigh had taken a seat to the side of the room and Nicole went to stand before her. "Esther, the wicked man, Haman, hates me, and now he's going to kill all the Jews—you have to do something!"

"But if I go before the king, he may kill me." Kimberleigh raised the back of her hand to her brow in despair.

"You will die anyway," Nicole told her matter-of-factly. "You're a Jew. God may have brought you here for such a time as this!"

"Okay, I'll see what I can do." Kimberleigh let out a heavy sigh. "Get all the people to fast and pray for me so I won't suffer the king's wrath and die," she pleaded. Hurrying to Anika's throne in the middle of the living room, she whispered to her little sister and motioned her to the couch.

Anika lay down on the couch and started tossing and turning. "I can't sweep. Servant, come read to me," she called out.

Nicole marched over to the couch with a thick red dictionary and flipped it open. Clearing her throat loudly, she began. "O King, the wonderful Mordecai once saved your life from an evil plot."

Anika stared questioningly at her oldest sister and Nicole whispered her next line. "How was he rewarded?" she repeated.

"He hasn't been, O King," Nicole answered.

"Bring...what's his name?" Anika shielded her mouth with her hands and looked again to her sister.

"Haman," Nicole whispered back.

"Oh yeah, bring Haman to me," she commanded. Nicole left and Jeremy marched over to the couch, where his little sister was now sitting. "What wou'd you do to reward someone?" Anika asked him.

Jeremy turned and gave a haughty smile to his audience of one. Looking back to his sister he declared in a loud voice, "I would dress him in fine clothes and lead him through the streets and make everyone bow down to him."

"Go and do that for Nicole!" Anika stomped her foot and stretched out her arm to point at her brother.

"It's for Mordecai, not Nicole," Jeremy corrected.

Anika gave her brother an impatient look. "Nicole is Mordecai!" she informed him.

With a huff, Jeremy stomped over to Nicole and led her around the living room by the arm, telling the would-be bystanders to bow down to Mordecai. Finally, they concluded with Esther going with apprehension before the king to request his presence, along with Haman's, at her banquet. Anika held out a silver baton to her sister and accepted. When Jeremy and Anika came before Kimberleigh for the banquet scene, Kimberleigh threw herself down before Anika.

"Please, oh King, don't let me and all my people be killed!" she wailed.

"Who wou'd do that?" Anika demanded.

Kimberleigh leaned back on her knees to glare and point at Jeremy. "This evil man, Haman," she spat.

Jeremy gasped and covered his mouth with his hand.

"Ki'w him!" Anika proclaimed.

"How come you don't say killing is bad when it's my turn?" Jeremy asked his sister, and at her giggle, he turned and slunk from the room.

The kids all lined up in front of their mother and bowed. They were rewarded by her laughter and enthusiastic applause.

"Well done!" she commended. "You make an awesome king." Cassy patted Anika on the back as she jumped into her mother's lap with a grin.

"That was fun," the little girl admitted.

"I should have videotaped it for Daddy to see."

"Can we do it again for him when he gets home?" Anika begged.

"If you want to."

So that evening the performance was repeated once again for their greatly amused father. Cassy could tell that he was enjoying getting to share bits and pieces of his family's adventures when he could. She knew he was glad that his children were enjoying their studies of different Bible stories and ancient civilizations.

⌘ ⌘ ⌘

The weeks seemed to fly by, filled with stories about the rebuilding of Jerusalem as well as Alexander the Great and the mighty empire of Ancient Greece. There were occasional outings with the other families and afternoons working in their science binders, learning amazing things about God's creation. Some weeks Cassy struggled with interruptions to their routine and the discouragement of not accomplishing all she had intended, but for the most part, she was enjoying her new lifestyle and was learning alongside her children.

Often she just needed a word of encouragement from her husband or another homeschool mom to help her adjust her expectations and focus on the task God had called David and herself to accomplish. Most important was God's command to train their children in obedience and in godly character, as well as to give them a solid foundation to stand on in their walk with the Lord. Second to that came the academics. Slowly Cassy was noticing the subtle changes occurring in the dynamics of her family, and she liked what she saw.

Looking at the calendar, Cassy could hardly believe that February was almost over. David's birthday was on Saturday; he would be thirty-five. Cassy had invited David's family over for supper Saturday evening, but she hadn't had time to get his presents yet. She was longing for a shopping day with Sarah. Though she saw Anthony and Sarah regularly at church and for the occasional get together on weekends, she missed the impromptu shopping sprees she'd had with her sister-in-law. Cassy felt too conspicuous taking her school-aged children around the mall during school hours and imagined that everyone who saw them might report her for truancy. Besides, she felt guilty if she "skipped school" to go shopping, so she usually tried to fit in any errands, or even grocery shopping, after normal school hours. However, this often meant her trips were rushed in order to get back in time for supper, so most trips into the city were delegated to Saturday.

Cassy decided she would check with Lauren to see if the kids could stay with her on Wednesday so that she could spend a leisurely day shopping for David's birthday. Lauren was quick to agree, and in no time Cassy had Sarah on the phone to ask if she would like to join her. Sarah was more than glad to go, and she decided to find a babysitter as well so that they could enjoy a quiet day together.

"David's been talking about getting a laser level, and I thought I might look for one for his birthday. Do you know much about them?" Cassy asked Wednesday morning when she picked up her sister-in-law.

"Not really, but it sounds simple enough. How many different kinds of laser levels could there be?"

"Well, I hate shopping for tools because I don't know what David's looking for. Maybe we can look for the level first and get it out of the way; then we can shop for the fun stuff."

Fifteen minutes later, the women were meandering down the aisles of a building supply store looking for something that said "laser level" on the package. To her consternation, Cassy discovered a whole row of odd shaped contraptions alongside the traditional levels, all claiming to be some sort of laser leveling device.

"Great! Now what?" Cassy moaned as she picked up a bright orange, hand-held device and studied it. "This one says it's a laser level and AC/stud finder. Bonus!"

Sarah laughed. "My motto is to go for the most expensive one—it should be able to do the most things, and if it's wrong, at least he'll be impressed that you picked out such a good tool!"

"Oh sure, that one is almost a thousand bucks!" She pointed to one claiming to be an "automatic self-leveling pendulum rotary laser." "I'm going to ask someone for help," Cassy decided after she'd spent half an hour reading packages. "I don't have a clue what any of these do." She went to the end of the aisle and managed to flag down an employee.

"Can you tell me what the difference is between all these types of laser levels? I'm looking for a birthday gift for my husband who works in construction, and I'm not sure which one would be the best."

The middle-aged man gave a knowing smirk and proceeded to explain how the different models on the shelf worked. "Some of these are what's called self-leveling laser levels. They take the guesswork out of making sure your instrument is level by using gravity and projecting a beam through a prism which hangs down like a pendulum. If you are using an optical vial or are leveling your laser manually, and you are out by just a fraction when you set your scope at the beginning, that error is magnified the further your beam is projected. This self-leveling laser works both horizontally and vertically simultaneously and comes with a remote," the man helpfully pointed out.

"Then you have rotary lasers which spin in a 360° circle so that the diode looks like it is projecting a solid line instead of a single point. If your husband is using it inside, you will probably want to get some laser goggles to help him see the line, and a laser detector if he is using it outside. You just set the detector to the frequency of the laser, and the faster the laser rotates, the further away the detector can pick up the beam. Most rotary levels have different speeds so you can adjust it to suit your distance, or you can slow it down if you are not using a detector to allow your eyes to actually see the line better. Some have multiple beams, or what's called a split beam, using a half-silvered mirror to split the beam and shoot a point straight up to use as a plumb line."

By now Cassy's eyes had glazed over, but she tried to at least look like she knew what the man was talking about. She could hear Sarah snicker quietly behind her and she brought her elbow back slightly to give her a nudge. The clerk didn't seem to notice and kept right on talking.

"Cross line lasers project perpendicular beams for aligning vertical and horizontal corners. They're great for hanging cabinets and for finishing work. This one has a magnetically dampened compensator in it to self-level the laser more quickly."

"Oh, that's nice," Cassy commented politely before throwing a dumbfounded look over her shoulder at Sarah, causing her sister-in-law to snicker again.

"Some laser levels have an automatic shut-off or a flashing alarm to let you know if it goes out of level, and they all list their degree of accuracy and range on the box. The accessories are over here." He pointed to the shelf behind him. "If you have any more questions, just let me know."

Cassy graciously thanked the man for his help, and when he had gone, she turned back to Sarah. "Did you get all that?" she asked hopefully.

"You mean all that magnetically dampened whatever, and pendulum stuff? Not a chance! I didn't know levels could be so complicated or that they come with accessories," she exclaimed.

"I should have asked Anthony about it before I came," Cassy moaned.

"You want me to call him on his cell phone?"

Cassy nodded gratefully, and after talking with her brother-in-law for several minutes, she made a decision and headed for the checkout.

"Men never know what we go through trying to buy them tools," Cassy declared once they were in the van. "I don't think they ever have to buy us anything that is so complicated."

Sarah laughed in agreement. The rest of the day the ladies meandered around the mall shopping together, and Cassy picked out a few shirts for David's birthday as well. They enjoyed a nice lunch and the chance to sit and visit awhile without interruption. As a whole, the day was a welcome break, and when Cassy dropped Sarah off later that afternoon, she felt refreshed.

⌘ ⌘ ⌘

On Saturday Cassy spent the day preparing for company, and she was looking forward to the evening. She'd made a big pan of lasagna, David's favorite, and everything was ready by the time their guests started to arrive. It was an enjoyable supper together. After the table was cleared, Cassy served black forest cake and ice cream for dessert, and everyone retired to the living room. When it came time to open presents, Cassy waited anxiously as David opened the laser level she'd purchased. Ripping the paper from the box, David's eyebrows shot up in pleasant surprise.

"Perfect! That's just the kind I wanted." He looked at his wife appreciatively.

"Good." Cassy breathed a sigh of relief. "Just don't ask me to explain how it works." She threw Anthony a big smile.

David thanked everyone for their presents, and soon the kids dispersed to go play. The adults visited together, and at a lull in the

164

conversation, Laura turned to Cassy, who was sitting near her.

"So, how's the homeschooling? Are you getting tired and ready to send them back to school yet?"

"No, I enjoy having them at home," Cassy responded without hesitation. "I feel it's been great for our family, and I'm glad I can be teaching them biblical values."

"Yeah," Laura admitted, "our school does some of that too. Not using the Bible of course, but they have all these units on teaching values and ethics. I think it's so good they have seen the importance of kids learning good morals and have added it to the curriculum."

Remembering the book Lauren had lent her, Cassy hesitated before answering—unsure of whether to say anything. "I used to think so too, but I've come to realize that we need to be careful what kinds of values the schools are teaching and what perspective the teachers are coming from."

"Oh, I know, but they just teach core values that everyone can accept, like honesty, self-esteem, respect and tolerance. Things like that."

"Yeah, but whose standard are they using?" Cassy challenged gently.

"What do you mean?"

"I mean, if they aren't basing it on the Bible, whose standard are they using? How do you teach ethics apart from the Bible? So often what the schools are teaching is situational ethics and that morals are relative. Their perspective of certain values might not be at all in line with Scripture, like if they're using respect and tolerance as a means to teach that you have to accept all beliefs and ideas as equally right or as a framework to push the homosexual agenda," Cassy explained.

"I think for the most part, they're just teaching basic concepts. The schools want to teach against things like racism and bullying and to help kids develop a good self-esteem, and there's nothing wrong with that. They may teach the acceptability of homosexuality in sex education classes, but my kids know that it's wrong. You can't take an example of what one teacher may have taught and lump all the teachers together in the same boat," Laura said a bit defensively.

"I just mean that the curriculum itself comes from a nonbiblical perspective and you have to be careful. You said there's nothing wrong with teaching self-esteem, but does the Bible teach that we are to think highly of ourselves, or is that man's idea? Are the schools teaching our children that they are all good people and should feel great about themselves apart from God, even though they are living in sin?"

Laura stared at her sister-in-law skeptically. "They're just teaching the kids a little self-confidence," she responded with a tinge of annoyance. "We have some really good teachers, and I'm sure Mandy and Mark would tell us if they were teaching all that stuff."

"It's just something to be aware of, because I believe the Bible teaches that our confidence and sense of worth should be found in Christ, not ourselves. It's all so subtle, but it undermines our need for a Savior and could encourage kids to believe in themselves rather than God. I never thought about it too much when our kids were in the system either, but I read a book recently that really challenged me in this area. It stressed the importance of making sure your kids are learning their values from a biblical perspective and not from non-Christian teachers and friends. It just made sense," Cassy said quietly, then dropped the subject. She noticed Sarah shaking her head thoughtfully from across the room.

It was hard for Cassy to know just how much to press the subject, but she hoped that Laura would at least consider it. She felt it was important. One thing Cassy did notice was that she was feeling more confident in defending their decision to homeschool, but she still fretted over what their families thought and whether her stance would alienate them. Cassy cared about her nieces and nephews and just wanted to know they were being taught the truth, but she knew if she wasn't careful she might offend her family, and she didn't want to do that. All she could do was pray for wisdom.

19

Homeschool Conference

The big, provincially sponsored homeschool conference was fast approaching, and Cassy could hardly wait. She and David had discussed the prospect of homeschooling next year, and both agreed that it was something they wanted to continue. Cassy had heard so much about the conference from Lauren and some of the other moms, and it sounded exciting. A month ago she had made arrangements for the kids to stay with Sarah and Anthony for the two days, and her sister-in-law had kindly offered to have them spend the night. Thankfully Cassy accepted, as it would be late Friday night by the time she and David got home, and the conference would start early again on Saturday. The flyer she had received gave a short biography of the various speakers and a description of the many workshops. Cassy sat up late one evening reviewing the list once again in an effort to decide which workshops she was most interested in. They all sounded great.

Finally the day arrived, and Cassy made sure that the kids' bags were ready to go before the family sat down to enjoy breakfast together. She was glad that David had taken the day off to join her. She had noticed that some of the workshops were geared especially for the fathers, so she had assured him he would not be the only dad there. David hadn't needed any convincing. He seemed anxious to hear some of the speakers as well and to get a bigger picture of the homeschooling movement they had so recently become a part of.

"Finish your breakfast; we've got to get going," Cassy urged Anika. The little girl was excited about getting to spend a night at her cousins' and had hardly touched her toast.

"Okay, Mommy." Anika paused in her nonstop chatter long

enough to take a bite.

"Are you going to buy us a bunch of new books?" Kimberleigh took advantage of her sister's momentary silence to inquire.

"Well, I don't know what all we'll get, but I'm sure we'll find a few things," Cassy reasoned.

"I wish I could come and help pick them out," Nicole said wistfully.

"You're not old enough to come," Cassy reminded her daughter. "Besides, it will be long days and we'll be listening to a lot of speakers. I'm sure you'll have lots of fun with your cousins."

Nicole nodded in agreement. "I know. I love helping with Samantha, and she's so funny now that she's learning how to walk. I just wish I could do both." She drained the last of her milk and rose to put her dishes in the dishwasher.

"Do you think they would sell microscopes there?" Jeremy's tone was hopeful.

"I don't know; what would you use a microscope for?" Cassy wasn't sure she wanted to know.

"To study bugs 'n' things," Jeremy mumbled under his breath before stuffing the last of his toast into his mouth. At his mother's grimace, the boy looked pleadingly toward his father.

David just laughed. "We'll have to see about that one."

Within half an hour the Knights had dropped off their kids and were on their way to the nearby convention center. The building was already thronging with eager homeschoolers when David and Cassy entered and joined the line to pick up nametags and their packet of material. Lauren had told her that it was a large convention, but the new homeschool mom was still amazed at the number of parents and teens in the crowded hall. Once they had received their conference packet, the couple made their way to the main auditorium for the opening session. Scanning the room, Cassy was pleased to see the huge percentage of dads in attendance.

"We should find a seat." David clutched his wife's elbow and steered her toward some empty chairs.

Cassy glanced at her watch as she sat down. The first session would be starting momentarily, and she flipped through the conference guide she'd received while she waited. It contained lengthier descriptions of each of the sessions scheduled throughout the day, and Cassy skimmed them.

"This looks like a good one." She pointed to a workshop aimed at encouraging new homeschoolers.

"They all look good," admitted David who had been reading over her shoulder.

A few moments later, when a leader from the provincial association stood to introduce the main speaker, Cassy flipped her program shut.

For the next forty-five minutes, the Knights listened attentively as Jeff Sanders shared the importance of instilling in our children the courage and conviction to stand up in a society which runs so counter to Christ's teachings. Cassy found him to be dynamic and inspiring and was sorry when he wrapped up his talk and sat down. His wife, Anne, would be sharing in one of the later talks, and Cassy wanted to be sure to hear her. Together the Sanders had been homeschooling their seven children for sixteen years. Once again Cassy opened her schedule to check the time of Anne's workshop—it was the one she'd seen for new homeschoolers, and it wasn't until after lunch. Suddenly Cassy became aware of the mass exodus taking place around her, and she looked up in surprise.

"Where is everyone going in such a hurry?" She turned to her husband beside her.

"They just announced that the exhibit hall is open. I suppose people are anxious to get shopping," he guessed.

Looking back at the schedule, Cassy saw that there was an hour break before the next session. "There aren't any workshops right now, so let's go check it out."

All the couple had to do was follow the crowd, and soon they were entering a massive hall filled with booths. Cassy stopped and stared, dumbstruck at the sheer volume of resources surrounding her. More experienced homeschoolers brushed past her with lists in hand, clearly on a mission to find what they'd come after. Just then the overwhelmed first-timer felt a tug on her arm and turned to see Lauren's friendly smile. She sighed with relief.

"Where do I begin? I never knew there were so many books and things to choose from!"

"Come, I'll take you to one of my favorite stores. We can start there," Lauren offered kindly.

"Everyone looks like they're in a race," Cassy observed as she took her husband's arm and followed her friend.

"Some people are." Lauren laughed. "They know exactly what they want and that supply is limited, so they want to make sure they get it while the getting is good. Many families do the bulk of their shopping for the next year while they're here because they live a fair distance from a homeschool curriculum store. It saves on postage costs and allows them to look the books over first instead of buying from a catalogue."

"I guess I never thought about the scarcity of homeschool stores before. I'll appreciate the fact that we have one reasonably close, though it doesn't compare to all this!" Cassy waved her hand to indicate the variety of retailers represented in the room.

"Some are specialty stores that carry just one line of curriculum, and some are booths set up by colleges or other organizations. It's not quite as overwhelming as it looks, but you'll find lots of things here that they don't carry at the store I took you to," Lauren explained.

By now they had reached one of the largest booths in the room and Cassy was amazed at the expanse of shelving, books, and educational supplies carted in by the retailer for the conference. She noticed that a short line was already forming before the tables set in front where three computer stations were arranged to handle the business.

"I can't imagine hauling all this stuff here and setting it up for two days!" Cassy exclaimed.

"By the stacks of books people haul out of here every year, I'm sure it's worth it," Lauren reasoned.

"I'm going to go take a look at the science equipment over there while you two shop," David informed his wife before making his way to the far corner of the booth.

"He's going to buy a microscope, I know it," Cassy hissed when her husband was out of earshot.

"What's so bad about a microscope?"

"It's not the microscope. It's the fact that Jeremy wants one so he can study bugs with it!" Cassy's face wrinkled in disgust.

Lauren laughed. "You're going to have to give in if he likes them so much."

"Jeremy is enthralled with them, but they totally gross me out. I don't think I could stand helping him with it."

"That can be David's job," Lauren consoled.

Trying her best to forget about the idea of studying bugs, Cassy set about looking down the long rows of historical novels and classical literature. There were so many and it wasn't long before she was juggling an armful of books. Each one she picked up sounded so good that Cassy had a hard time choosing. Lauren recommended a few book series and authors that her family especially enjoyed, and the two women compared their selections as each of their piles grew. Most of Cassy's choices were from the time period following the early church and leading up to the Crusades, but a few just sounded like interesting character-building stories she thought the kids would enjoy.

Cassy also managed to collect some math books for each of the kids, but she was surprised how quickly the hour had gone. Noticing the lineup at the front tables, she hurriedly went in search of her husband while Lauren headed to get in line. David had discovered a science kit with an assortment of neat experiments on light, energy, and matter, which he thought Jeremy especially would like.

"No explosive stuff, or things that will destroy my kitchen, I hope!" Cassy eyed the box suspiciously.

"No, it's pretty harmless, I think."

"That's what I thought about Diet Coke and Mentos," Cassy mumbled. She quickly showed her husband the books she'd picked out as they made their way to the end of the line. At least David didn't have a microscope—yet!

As soon as the couple had paid for their purchases, they collected their bags and hurried from the room. David was headed to the workshop for dads, so at the top of the stairs leading to the conference rooms the husband and wife parted company. Lauren had promised to save Cassy a seat in the history workshop. She rushed down the hall looking for the appropriate room. It was by now a few minutes past eleven, and Cassy hoped she hadn't missed too much.

Quietly slipping into the open door, she located her friend. Taking a seat beside Lauren, Cassy deposited her bags in front of her chair and caught her breath. The speaker had already started her talk on how to teach history using what she called "living books," and Cassy soon found herself absorbed in the topic. It sounded like the same idea that Lauren had shared with her at the beginning of the year, but now Cassy could understand it a little better after having experienced it for herself.

Andrea explained that a "living book" is a book that brings history to life through true-to-life stories, or one that provides in-depth information about a topic, place, event, or time period. In contrast, a textbook breaks information down into small, isolated bits consisting of dates and facts, without delving into the depth of character, lifestyle, and circumstances surrounding the person or event. Textbooks are usually a compilation of many authors, instead of the specialized work of a single author.

Throughout her talk, Andrea gave many examples of how to discuss the issues, moral decisions, beliefs, and consequences contained within the books you read with your family, to use that opportunity to teach your children right from wrong. She provided a handout with a whole list of "living books" she recommended, and Cassy tucked the list into her purse so that she wouldn't lose it. The workshop reinforced and developed more fully the concepts Cassy was trying to use in her own teaching, and she was glad she had come.

Following the workshop, the two women met David by the top of the stairs to discuss lunch options. When they discovered the long lineup at the concession downstairs, they decided to head out to a drive-through at one of the fast-food restaurants down the road. That way they could also leave their purchases in their vehicles instead of carrying them around all day.

"You sure you don't mind if I tag along?" Lauren asked her friends as they headed for the door.

"Don't be ridiculous!" Cassy said. "Besides, you don't want to wait in that lineup. I sure don't know how I'm going to get time to look at all the stuff in that exhibit hall and get in on the workshops. There's just too much to take it all in!"

"I know. The first year is always overwhelming, but you get used to the different distributors and who carries the curriculum you like best, so it gets easier. They do record all the sessions as well, so if you need more time to shop you can skip a couple of sessions and order the CDs to listen to later. I often do that so I don't feel too rushed looking over curriculum."

"That sounds like a great idea!" Cassy agreed as they reached the parking lot.

"Where's your car?" David asked. "You can go stick your bags in your vehicle and then we'll pick you up there with the van."

Lauren pointed out the row she was parked in and then hurried away.

It didn't take long before they succeeded in getting some lunch, and the threesome ate their burgers as they drove back to the convention center. Cassy was glad to see that they'd have half an hour left to browse in the exhibit hall before the afternoon sessions started up. She still wanted to hear Anne's talk for new homeschoolers, but she thought she might skip one of the later workshops and order the CD as Lauren had suggested.

By the end of the next session, Cassy had pages of notes full of ideas and suggestions for next year. Anne's session was very practical and full of insight. Cassy and David were enthusiastic as they exited the room and headed back downstairs. Together they meandered through the hall for the rest of the afternoon, stopping to look at whatever caught their attention.

"It's so amazing the amount of resources available to homeschoolers, I can't get over it!" David told his wife, as he scanned the shelves crammed with books, science kits, games and videos in one booth.

"I know." Cassy nodded. "There's so much to choose from." She handed the bag she was carrying to David and stooped to look through some books on a lower shelf.

They had just come from the Creation Science booth where they had picked up a number of books and DVDs for the family. Now Cassy was focused on looking through language arts curriculum, so David made his way around the stuffed bookshelves, glancing at the titles as he walked. Spotting a table in the corner with a few microscopes, he headed over to take a look. Carefully studying the specs for the different models, David compared prices and selected a middle-of-the-line microscope that would have plenty of magnification for what Jeremy wanted. Nearby was a shelf with study guides for all kinds of plants and animals, so David scanned through them until he located a book on insects. It was loaded with colorful pictures and an abundance of facts. Carrying his selections back to the area where his wife was still looking through workbooks, he stopped beside her.

"What do you think of these?" David held up his find, a huge smile on his face.

Glancing up, Cassy saw the microscope and shook her head. "I knew it!" She stood up to check it out. Spotting the book on insects, she wrinkled her nose. "Not exactly my favorite topic of science," was all she said.

"I know. I thought it would give me the opportunity to do something with Jeremy, and I know he'd love it."

"That would be great. As long as I don't have to look at them, it's fine with me," Cassy relented. "It's bad enough looking at bugs life-size without blowing them up even bigger!"

David just laughed. When Cassy had made her selections, they headed to the checkout table to pay for them. David made another trip to the van to lighten his load before coming back to find his wife. The couple fully enjoyed the rest of their day and the evening session with Jeff Sanders entitled, "Keeping the Vision."

It was late by the time they headed home, but they were excited about what they'd heard and were feeling pleased with all their purchases.

By the end of the second day, Cassy and David both felt like their heads were spinning from overload, but they were greatly encouraged. Richard had been able to join Lauren for Saturday, so the couples stopped at a nice restaurant for supper before heading home. It felt good just to sit down and visit together, but they didn't tarry too long after the meal. It had been a wonderful weekend, and they were anxious to get back to the kids and show them all they had found.

⌘ ⌘ ⌘

"Did you get a microscope?" Jeremy asked the moment he was in the van.

"Yep!" David acknowledged.

"Really? Aw, cool!" their son whooped, clearly surprised at his good fortune. "Where is it?"

"At home already," David informed him. "We bought it yesterday." He turned to his wife with a smile.

That night the girls eagerly hovered over all of their new books, taking turns looking through them. Anika was excited to see the nice picture books that were part of her program for learning to read. They were full of all kinds of short stories, including Bible stories.

Jeremy hadn't gotten much further than the microscope and his book on insects. He could hardly contain himself as he carefully inspected how to adjust and focus the lenses. When the children were finally settled down enough to head to bed, Jeremy said good night and headed off, his new book tucked under his arm. David followed his children down the hall to pray with each one before tucking them in.

"Dear Jesus, thank You for my microscope, and thank You for the fun time we had at our cousins. Help us to have a good sleep. And Lord, thanks for convincing Mom and Dad to homeschool us—in Your Name, Amen," Jeremy prayed before giving his father a hug good night.

Later, when Cassy headed to bed herself, she noticed a dim light filtering out from under her son's door. She slowly opened the door to check on him and found his bedside lamp on. Her son had fallen asleep, and in his hands he still held his precious book. As much as she hated insects, she was glad her husband had gotten it for him. Gently Cassy lifted the book from his lax grip and set it on the stand beside his bed. Flipping off the lamp, she quietly exited the room and closed the door behind her.

20

Anika's Surprise

Spring had come early this year, and the leaves were already budding out on most of the trees. The kids were all taking advantage of the milder weather to get outside as much as possible. One bright morning, Cassy decided to pack a picnic lunch, take her science teacher guide, and head out into the woods behind their house to collect specimens. They had been studying plants, and this seemed like the perfect opportunity to take their studies outside. Of course the kids were thrilled with the idea and all chipped in to pack sandwiches, apples, cookies, and bottles of water for their excursion.

Although their property only consisted of a few acres, it backed onto a coulee with a small creek running through and a stand of trees they had dubbed "the woods." Cassy carried the sack lunch while the kids bounded ahead and down the gentle slope toward the trees. It was so good to see the fresh green grass and the first few wildflowers starting to appear. Upon reaching the creek, the excited children located a fairly level spot to spread the blanket Jeremy had slung over his arm, and they settled themselves for the spontaneously planned picnic.

"Ooh, look at that bird." Nicole pointed to a Bohemian Waxwing that hopped along the ground, inspecting the picnickers from a safe distance. "Can I give him a piece of bread?" she asked tentatively.

Cassy scanned the sky for any sign of seagulls before giving assent. Nicole plucked a crust of bread from her sandwich and flung it in the bird's direction, causing it to flutter away. It wasn't long, however, before the Waxwing was back and cautiously making its way toward the offered morsel.

Jeremy plucked up a caterpillar crawling along the edge of their blanket and placed it on his leg while he ate. Cassy cringed but held her tongue. As they finished their lunch, the family was rewarded with a close-up view of a bluebird when it landed briefly on the ground to clutch a piece of dry grass in its beak, before taking flight once again in route to the new nest it was building. It was so peaceful out here by the creek. Cassy had rarely come to the coulee. She was enjoying the little haven and listening to the water gurgle nearby.

"What are we supposed to collect?" Kimberleigh wanted to know.

"I want you to see how many different kinds of leaves and flowers you can find, and then bring them back to the blanket so that we can try to identify them using my book." Cassy motioned toward the teacher's manual beside her.

"Can we bring bugs too?" Jeremy asked hopefully.

"Not this time. I don't have your insect book with me."

"We could bring them home."

"We don't have anything to carry them in," Cassy reasoned.

"I could put them in this bag," Jeremy held up the empty plastic bag from his sandwich.

"Let's get the leaves first, and then I'll see," Cassy finally relented. "But if you bring back any bugs, they'll have to stay outside until your father gets home!" she was quick to clarify.

"All right!"

"You're disgusting!" Kimberleigh flung at her brother.

One by one the kids left the blanket in search of leaves. Anika was still munching on a cookie as she tagged along and plucked small new leaves from a sapling and ran them back to her mother. There wasn't a huge variety of trees in the area, but with the added specimens of bushy plants and a small assortment of early wildflowers, the pile was growing.

"I have that one already," Nicole informed Anika as she plucked several leaves from one plant.

"So, they're pretty," the little girl declared and went on to the next bush.

When they were finally done, the kids huddled on the blanket and started sorting their specimens, grouping duplicates together as much as possible. Then they spent the next hour flipping through the colored charts in their mother's nature manual, identifying as many as possible with Cassy's help. Among the specimens identified was the soft furry branch from a Staghorn Sumac tree, the tip of a branch from a Balsam Fir, and leaves from a Laurel Willow, Poplar, and Saskatoon. Jeremy got excited when he correctly identified the broad, circular leaf of a Wild Ginger plant.

"I think this one is a Birch," Kimberleigh declared, holding up a teardrop shaped leaf with a pointed tip to compare with the chart.

"No it's not; look at the smooth sides. A Birch is more jagged," Nicole corrected. "This leaf is rounder and looks like an Aspen." They studied it together and finally agreed.

"Wook at this weaf. It's my favorite!" Anika held up the variegated fernlike foliage of a Jacob's Ladder plant.

Next came the identification of the small sampling of wildflowers they had discovered, and the girls marveled over the delicate petals and intricate design of the tiny blossoms. As they studied the flowers, a Boreal Chickadee settled on a low branch nearby and entertained them with its happy song.

"Can I go find some bugs now?" Jeremy wanted to know when he had gotten tired of the flowers.

"You collect a few while we pack up, but keep them away from me," Cassy warned.

Finally everything was gathered together and the family headed back in the direction of the house. Anika still carried a small cluster of Prairie Crocus and Blue Violets in her clenched fist, while Jeremy gloated over his cache of ants, worms, and beetles. Cassy tried not to look at the squirming insects her son held and made sure they were stashed in a safe place far from the back door until David came home to help him with the microscope.

The little nature adventure was a huge hit and was repeated several times that spring.

⌘ ⌘ ⌘

Later that week, Cassy grabbed a blanket and ushered her children out to the backyard to sprawl in the warm sunshine to read. She was glad the neighbors were too far away to see them sitting outside during school hours. Cassy had been reading about the life of Christ and His commissioning of the disciples from the book of Matthew.

"All authority in heaven and on earth has been given to me. Therefore go and make disciples of all nations, baptizing them in the name of the Father and of the Son and of the Holy Spirit, and teaching them to obey everything I have commanded you. And surely I am with you always, to the very end of the age." Cassy finished reading at the end of chapter twenty-eight.

Anika tugged on her mother's sleeve. "Mommy, I want to do that."

"You want to do what, sweetheart?" Cassy looked into her bright, blue eyes, unsure what her five-year-old daughter was referring to.

"I want to fo'wow Jesus and have Him with me a'ways."

At her daughter's unexpected reply, Cassy felt tears rush to her eyes. "Do you understand what it means to follow Jesus?" she carefully questioned, knowing that Anika had heard the Gospel message many times before but wanting to make sure she understood it.

"Uh-huh. Jesus died for me too, right? I need to believe in Him and ask Jesus to forgive me for the naughty things I've done," she stated simply.

"That's right. Jesus died for you and He loves you very much." Cassy pulled her precious daughter onto her lap.

"Then you can be God's child just like us!" Kimberleigh motioned to her other siblings on the blanket with a huge smile.

"And if you believe in Jesus, that means He'll forgive your sins so that you can go to Heaven someday with Him." Nicole scooted closer to her little sister.

Cassy closed her Bible and, right there in the backyard, she took her daughter's hands, and together they listened while Anika prayed a simple but heartfelt prayer that soared straight to the heart of God. When David came home later that evening, a jubilant Anika met him at the door.

"Guess what I did today, Daddy?" Anika danced excitedly in front of him, while Cassy stood in the doorway of the kitchen watching.

"You went to the moon," David teased his youngest.

"Nope," Anika said with a giggle. "I decided to fo'wow Jesus just wike His disciples—onwy I'm sma'wer!"

David squatted down and scooped his little girl up into his arms and hugged her tight. "That's way better than going to the moon," he declared, his voice thick with emotion. "That's the best surprise you ever gave me!"

"God wuvs me just wike you do, Daddy," Anika whispered into her father's ear, and his tears spilled over.

"Even more, sweetie. He loves you even more!"

21

The Zoo

B y mid-May, Cassy was feeling tired, but she was pleased with how their year had gone. It was a Thursday afternoon, and she sat in the now familiar spot on the couch reading once again. This time it was a novel set in the time of Nero and the persecution of the early church. The kids had grown unusually still while she read.

"Did Nero really kill people just because they believed in God?" The idea was new to Jeremy, and he looked shocked.

"Many of them," Cassy admitted sadly. "He would have been ruling when the Apostle Paul was killed, but there were many more Christians who were put to death in horrible ways at that time."

"I'm glad that doesn't happen anymore," Nicole said with relief.

Cassy looked down at her young family and sighed. "Unfortunately, in many parts of our world it still does happen," she stated gently, momentarily closing the book in her lap.

"What!" Kimberleigh cried. "Why don't people stop it?"

"It's not quite as easy as that, because in some countries their leaders follow different gods and hate Christians."

"Why?" Kimberleigh asked.

"Well…" Cassy paused to collect her thoughts. "For one thing, because Christians believe that Jesus is the only way to have a relationship with God and go to Heaven, and that the Bible is God's Word. That means all other beliefs are wrong, which makes people mad. You have to remember that Satan is behind this too, and Satan hates God more than anyone. He wants to stop the Christians from believing in Jesus."

"And does he?" Jeremy wanted to know.

"No!" Cassy emphasized. "In fact, most times, when Christians have been persecuted, it has made Christianity spread. You see, Christians know Jesus is worth dying for and that they will go to be with Him in Heaven. Persecution can make a Christian's faith stronger, which is hard for people around them to understand. It can sometimes bring others to a faith in Jesus too because they see that the Christian is willing to die for what they believe."

"I'm glad bad people don't want to ki'w us." Anika snuggled closer to her mother.

"Me too, sweetie, but we still have to learn how to stand up for our faith here in Canada. Sometimes we forget to do that." Cassy rubbed her daughter's back gently.

"So what countries are killing Christians now?" Nicole asked.

"Well, I'm not really sure. We could look on the internet if you want to know," Cassy suggested.

"Yeah," the kids shouted in unison.

With that they were soon crowded around the computer, watching while Cassy did a search for the Voice of the Martyrs website. They read through news clips and articles on the persecuted church around the world, and even Cassy was surprised at the extent of what was happening that she had been oblivious to. They decided to get their globe and stick pins in the countries where Christians were being persecuted so that they could remember some of them when they said their prayers. Silently Cassy wondered how the average Christian in Canada would fare if they were suddenly subjected to prison, torture, or death because of their faith. Her heart went out to the families they had read about whose husbands and fathers had been beaten and put in prison, or for those who'd had family members killed. How naive and complacent she suddenly felt. The children were subdued as they finished their lesson.

On Friday Cassy got the kids to help pack a picnic lunch as they hurried to get ready in the morning. They were meeting some of the other families at the zoo for the day, and she didn't want to be late. Everyone was to meet at the gates at ten o'clock so they could enter together under a group rate. Recently Cassy and her children had been studying the classifications of animals and their habitats, and in the kids' science binders they had some charts to be filled out at the zoo—identifying animals by class, filling in the type of habitat they were from and what they ate. This fieldtrip came in perfect timing, and Cassy made sure that each child had their binder before heading out the door.

The morning was overcast, but as she pulled out on the highway, Cassy was hoping it would clear as the day progressed. Arriving at the zoo entrance about fifteen minutes early, they didn't have long to wait before the group could all go in. Already most of the families who had signed up were accounted for.

Once inside, different families paired off and headed in all directions. The Knights opted to stick together with the Andrews, and Lauren's children helped read signs and gather the appropriate information for Nicole, Jeremy, and Kimberleigh.

"Let's do the giraffes," Kimberleigh decided when they came to the giraffe pen. "I like them!"

Nicole was the first to identify Africa as the continent of residence for the graceful, long-necked creatures, and they each proceeded to write *Giraffe* on the top of the next chart and then color in Africa on the small world map.

"They're a mammal," Jeremy yelled out next. "That one's easy."

"Giraffes eat leaves," Kimberleigh added, "but I don't think they live in a forest."

"No, they live in grasslands," Nicole said.

"They have wong, bwack tongues," Anika commented as she watched one giraffe snatch leaves from a tree just outside its pen.

Nicole included the observation in her space for listing distinctive characteristics.

No one spent too long watching the lions and tigers. Though they were beautiful, majestic creatures, there was not much to hold the kids' interest as the large cats all lounged lazily in the grass, barely moving except for an occasional flick of a tail. At some of the cages, however, the kids lingered as they watched the different antics of the animals inside. They especially enjoyed the playfulness of the monkeys and chimps. One black chimpanzee sat on a narrow ledge right against the glass, and Anika situated herself in front of it and waved.

"Wook, he waved back," she said in astonishment.

Soon all the boys were crowded in front of the chimp, jumping up and down and making faces. Whenever the animal would mimic one of their actions, they would all howl with laughter.

"Watch this," Christian called out. He curled both arms under and scratched his sides, making monkey noises. The chimpanzee just curled back its lips and screeched at the boys, making them laugh all the more.

"I like the baby chimps," Brianne declared. "Look at that tiny one cuddled by its mother."

"Aw," Nicole cooed softly.

None of the kids were anxious to leave the primate house, but eventually they moved on. In the reptile house, the girls stayed only long enough to complete their five pages on reptiles and then rushed through the rest.

"They're disgusting!" Nicole avoided looking in the cages as she walked past them.

"They're cool!" Jeremy countered.

"Yeah, I like them," James agreed, but the girls were unconvinced.

"I'm ready for lunch," Kimberleigh moaned.

At the mention of food, the boys suddenly lost interest in the snakes and they all headed outside to find a picnic table. Some sat at the table, while the remainder lounged on the grass to enjoy their bag lunches. It was still cloudy, but at least it wasn't raining. The kids all debated about which animals were the best and why, and though they had several favorites, they all agreed on the chimpanzees as the most fun. When they'd finished lunch, they packed up their garbage to deposit in a nearby trash can and continued on their tour.

Finally at three o'clock, the gang decided they'd had enough and it was time to go. Cassy decided to pick up some pizza and a video on the way home for a family movie night. There was a new movie out that had received good reviews from a couple of Christian organizations, and Cassy thought it sounded like one their family would enjoy. She was tired after walking around the park all day, and it would be nice to curl up on the couch and relax for the evening.

By seven o'clock that night, the kids were all in their pajamas and sprawled on pillows on the floor for the event. A couple bowls of popcorn were stationed within reach, and Cassy curled up against her husband to watch the show. Anika soon grabbed her pillow and joined her parents on the couch, settling herself in the cozy spot behind her mother's legs.

"No Shasta!" Jeremy scolded as the dog eyed the large bowl of popcorn sitting on the floor.

With a whine Shasta lay down beside her playmate and looked imploringly up at him with her big brown eyes. She was rewarded with an occasional kernel of popcorn tossed in her direction throughout the movie.

When the show was over, David carefully slid from beside his wife and came around to scoop up Anika, who had fallen asleep somewhere near the middle of the film. Gently he carried his daughter off to bed.

"Time for bed for the rest of you too," Cassy directed those on the floor when her husband had disappeared down the hall.

"That was a good story." Nicole stretched sleepily and rose to leave. "Good night, Mom." She crossed the room to give her mother a hug and kiss. "Thanks for the nice day."

"You're welcome, Nicole." Cassy hugged her daughter back.

"Yeah, thanks, Mom," Kimberleigh echoed as she said good night.

"Can I get one of those iguanas like at the zoo?" Jeremy asked after giving his mother a kiss.

"Nice try Mr.!" Cassy swatted his behind.

"Just checking." The boy grinned and headed for his room.

22

The Accident

One morning, as Cassy was just getting the kids' books off the shelf, the telephone rang. Setting the books on the table, Cassy sighed and contemplated ignoring the call so she wouldn't be delayed in getting started with schooling, but at the persistent ring she reluctantly crossed the kitchen to answer it. She was surprised to hear Anthony's voice on the other end.

"Oh good, you're home." There was obvious relief in his voice.

Cassy gripped the receiver tightly in apprehension. "What's wrong?" she asked hesitantly. She could hear Anthony take a deep breath before continuing.

"I don't want to frighten you, but there's been an accident at the job site, and David took a fall." Cassy let out a frantic gasp and Anthony hurried to reassure her. "I think he's all right. He was knocked unconscious at first, so I was afraid to move him on my own, and I called an ambulance, just as a precaution."

Anthony paused, and Cassy was sure there was something more he wasn't telling her. "How bad is it?"

"I'm not sure, Cassy, but David was regaining consciousness as he was being loaded into the ambulance, and I'm just following them to the hospital right now. Are you going to be okay to drive, or do you want me to call Sarah to come get you?"

"No, I'm on my way," Cassy declared frantically as she hung up the phone and yelled for the kids to come. She was shaking and tried to calm herself as her children came scurrying into the kitchen at her urgent call.

"What's the matter, Mommy?" questioned Nicole, who seemed to detect the panic in her mother's face and the tears threatening to spill over. She hurried to her mother's side.

"Hurry out to the van, and I'll tell you on the way," was all Cassy could say as she gave her daughter a quick hug and ran to grab her purse and keys. Thankfully, she could hear Nicole ushering her siblings out the door, and in a moment Cassy joined them. Her legs were trembling so bad Cassy felt like she would collapse, and it was a relief to take her seat behind the wheel. She wasn't sure what lay in store for her at the hospital and hardly knew how to pray, but her mind cried out silently to God as she turned the keys in the ignition and swung the van out onto the road.

"What's wrong?" Anika whimpered, and Cassy noticed her children's muffled sobs from the backseat for the first time.

"I'm sorry I scared you." Cassy tried to calm herself for her children's sake as she sought for the right words to say. Taking a deep breath, she continued. "Daddy's had a bit of an accident, and he's at the hospital. He's going to be all right, but we're going to go see him and cheer him up," Cassy tried to mask the fear in her voice and prayed with every fiber of her being that she was telling the truth.

The drive into Red Deer seemed to take forever, but finally she pulled into the crowded hospital parking lot. Cassy snatched the first spot she came to and her door was open before her keys were even out of the ignition. Quickly she ushered her children into the hospital and toward the Emergency Room. Anthony met Cassy at the door and gently took her arm to lead her to a seat in the busy waiting room.

"I haven't heard anything yet, and I couldn't get a hold of Sarah," he whispered in Cassy's ear as he sat her down in a chair in the far corner of the room. There were only four vacant seats together, so Nicole and Kimberleigh scrunched together on the chair to one side of their mother and Jeremy quietly took the seat beside them.

"How's my big girl?" Anthony lifted Anika up and settled her on his knee as he took the last seat on Cassy's left.

"Is my daddy awright?" Anika ignored his question as she stared up at her uncle with sad, blue eyes.

Cassy could see that Anthony was fighting for control, and he looked away for a moment before answering. The gesture frightened her.

"I think he's going to be just fine. The doctor is looking after him right now, and the nurse will let us know as soon as we can go see him," he finally answered.

"Can we pray for him?" Nicole asked quietly as she nudged her mother. Cassy's heart melted as she turned and saw the silent tear slip from her daughter's eye and follow the wet trail down her cheek.

"Sure we can," Cassy reached to draw her children close as they huddled together and each said a quiet prayer for their father. When they were done, Cassy eyed her brother-in-law beside her.

"Can I talk to you?" she mouthed silently. She had to know what had happened, but she didn't want to talk in front of the children. They were scared enough.

Anthony nodded. "I'm going to take your mother to see if we can find out how your daddy's doing. Is that okay?" he asked the kids. At their nods, the two rose. Anthony settled Anika on his chair and turned to Jeremy. "Look after your sisters," he said, giving the young boy a nod.

Jeremy solemnly nodded back.

Anthony escorted Cassy over toward the receptionist's counter, and when she questioned him about the accident, he briefly explained what had happened. "We were placing a gable, and David was standing on a partition wall waiting to anchor it. The gable broke loose, and he fell."

"No, Anthony, I want to know the details. That's my husband in there, and I need to know what I'm facing." Cassy's voice was shaking, and she could tell that Anthony was holding back. He glanced over her shoulder toward the kids and shook his head. Cassy glanced back to make sure her children were okay and then looked Anthony straight in the eye, trying to read his thoughts. "Please Anthony, you were there. I need to be prepared for the worst possible scenario."

Anthony brushed his hand over his face as though trying to wipe away the raw emotion he was so desperately fighting to hold back. "Yes, I was there, and you don't know how helpless I felt when I saw what was happening and couldn't do a thing to stop it," he said huskily. I was on a ladder against the side wall waiting to position the corner of the gable, and it swung out of my range when it fell. Even if I could have reached it, I couldn't have stopped a four-hundred-pound gable from…from…" Anthony stopped and looked at Cassy. She could see he didn't want to continue.

"It's not your fault, Anthony. Just tell me why it fell and what happened to David." Cassy was shaking visibly, but she was managing to hold her tears in check.

Anthony put out a hand to steady her. "You don't have to hear this."

"Yes, I do," she answered with steely resolve.

Anthony sighed. "The gable was being lowered by a crane, and a gust of wind caught it. Tom tried to steady it with the guide rope below, but the crane cable worked loose and released the gable before it had been lowered into position. There was nothing we could do to keep it from falling and hitting David. It caught him on the side of the head and knocked him off the wall." At Cassy's faltering intake of breath he paused once again, his face full of regret. "He was starting to regain consciousness, Cassy, and once the paramedics got the bleeding under control, it didn't look so bad." At her lack of response Anthony gripped her arm. "You gonna be all right?" he asked with concern.

"Yes." Cassy's head was swimming and she couldn't think. "Can we just ask the receptionist if she can find out anything for us? I can't stand this waiting."

Anthony questioned the woman at the desk, and she promised to try and get some information as soon as possible. For now it was all they could do, and the two returned to their seats. The kids were upset, and Cassy was kept busy trying to comfort them, though it felt like her whole insides were being twisted into knots. Silently her heart was crying out to God. It seemed like an eternity before the receptionist motioned Cassy back over to the counter, but in actuality it had been less than an hour.

"Mrs. Knight," the woman informed her when Cassy appeared at her desk, "your husband is with the doctor right now, but it looks like he's going to be okay." A wave of relief flooded over her, as the words of the receptionist sunk in. "He suffered a couple of broken ribs, some nasty lacerations on his head which are being stitched up, and he has a concussion. He should be out soon, and you can see him. The doctor said that the X-rays and CAT scan showed no signs of internal bleeding, and his ribs were a clean break so they didn't puncture his lungs, which is good." The receptionist smiled at Cassy's words of gratitude. "He was very lucky from the sounds of the report," she added.

"Luck has nothing to do with it!" Cassy assured the woman, who just nodded. She hurried back to where Anthony was waiting with her children.

"We should be able to see Daddy soon," she consoled them as she explained what the receptionist had told her. Together they breathed a prayer of thanksgiving.

Within twenty minutes, David's parents came striding into the waiting room to give Cassy a hug and to wait with the anxious family. Anthony had called them when he had first gotten to the hospital, and they were relieved to hear the good report. Finally a nurse came and called for Cassy. With a smile she offered to take Cassy to see her husband, and soon she and the children were ushered into a small curtained room down the hall. They were rewarded by a tremulous smile from David.

"You scared the life out of me," Cassy whispered as she neared the bed, the tears finally falling unchecked at the sight of her husband's smile. David reached his arm out to encircle his wife and winced in pain at the movement.

"I'm okay," he assured her, "don't worry. I'm a bit stiff is all."

Cassy could see by his tightly wrapped chest and the thick, sterile bandages across the side of his head, which were already revealing dark bruising around the edges, that he was more than stiff, but she was so thankful he would be all right.

"Daddy, I can't see!" Anika complained from the side of his bed, and David carefully cocked his head to view his children while Cassy bent to lift their youngest daughter.

"It's good to see you guys." David's smile wavered as he fought for control. "I'm going to have to hire some nurses to wait on me for a few weeks until I can get back to work. Know anyone looking for a job?" he questioned and was rewarded with a chorus of answers to the affirmative.

190

"I'w do it, Daddy," Anika pleaded. "They have to do schoo'!"

At this David chuckled and was immediately sorry as pain shot through his side.

"We can all take turns," Nicole insisted, and Cassy agreed.

After giving the family a few moments alone, David's parents and Anthony asked for directions and made their way down the hall to see for themselves that David was all right.

"Boy, you'll go to any extreme to get out of work," Anthony teased as he made his way to the crowded bedside.

David gave his brother a lopsided grin. "I could think of better ways to spend a holiday," he countered ruefully. "The doctor says no heavy lifting for a few weeks, though, and we've got a lot of jobs lined up right now," David's brow was creased with concern.

"We've got a full crew going; we'll be okay," Anthony placed his hand gently on his brother's shoulder. "Just don't go trying this stunt again, you hear me!" Anthony's voice wavered slightly as he looked intently into David's eyes.

"I'm not planning on it," David assured as he blinked back a tear that threatened to escape.

Cassy had not missed the penetrating expression in her husband's eyes as he met his brother's gaze, a look acknowledging the magnitude of what could have happened, mixed with a deep gratitude. But Cassy already knew she had much to thank God for.

"We're sure glad to see you're all right!" Jean said from her spot at the foot of the bed, and Paul reached over to lightly grasp his son's arm.

"Thanks for coming, Mom and Dad." David nodded toward his parents. Stiffly he lifted one hand to his bandaged head and closed his eyes a moment, his brows furrowed.

Cassy guessed that his anesthetic was wearing off, and she gently squeezed his other hand.

"We shouldn't all be in here right now, but we had to at least peek and see how you were doing." David's mother turned toward her husband. "We should go and wait for Cassy in the waiting room," she whispered.

"Take it easy," Anthony said before following his parents out.

"Thanks," David called after them.

Cassy and the children stayed as long as possible before a nurse came in to shoo them out. She informed them that they would be moving David to a room and keeping him for observation overnight, but Cassy could see him in his room later. If everything went okay, he would be able to go home in the morning. With reluctance Cassy motioned for her kids to leave.

When they returned to the waiting room, Paul and Jean offered to take the children home and stay with them until Cassy was ready to come, and Cassy gratefully accepted. Anthony departed soon after to head back to work, and Cassy remained at the hospital until visiting hours were over that evening. David was sleeping restlessly when she left, but the nurses assured her they would be checking on him at regular intervals throughout the night to monitor his concussion. Cassy was tired as she headed home to relieve her in-laws so they could go home.

⌘ ⌘ ⌘

The following morning Cassy brought David home just before lunch. The kids scrambled around him as she helped her husband walk stiffly to the couch where he could lie down. Nicole positioned a couple of pillows behind his head and Kimberleigh brought him a blanket. When he was settled, Cassy went to the kitchen to fix something to eat.

Not much schoolwork got done that week, but Cassy didn't care. She was busy just looking after her husband, who was very sore and was finding it hard to sleep. Her mind couldn't focus much on workbooks at the moment, and the kids didn't seem to mind the extra break.

By the following week, however, David's pain was easing a bit and Cassy decided to start up her routine once again. She helped her husband get settled in the recliner, which he found to be the most comfortable on his sore ribs, and brought him a book to read before calling the kids to the table. David was situated where he could still see into the kitchen and hear what was going on, or get Cassy's attention if he needed something.

"I'm not sure how to do this problem," Kimberleigh said, looking up from her math book.

"Wet me see." Anika scooted sideways on her chair to peer over her sister's arm.

"You can't do it," Kimberleigh told her.

"Maybe I cou'd. I know what four pwus four is and I'm pretty smart!"

Cassy heard David chuckle from the living room, but it was cut off abruptly by his sharp intake of breath. How long would it be before her husband could laugh without his ribs hurting? she wondered. Cassy glanced up to make sure he was all right before answering her daughter. "Just a minute, Kimberleigh. I can help you when I'm done helping Jeremy."

"I can help her," Nicole offered instead, and she got up to check out her sister's math book.

Kimberleigh pointed to a line of squares on her page, each one divided into nine blocks—three across and three down. Some of the blocks contained a number and some were empty, in which Kimberleigh was to fill in the missing addition facts.

"I know, I've done some like this only with multiplication in my book," Nicole informed her. "You just have to start with a row that has two numbers in it and fill in the number that is missing. Each row should add up to equal the number at the end of the row, so what number would you have to add to six to equal eight?"

"Two," Anika shouted out before Kimberleigh responded.

"Right, good job," Nicole congratulated her little sister.

"See, towd you I was smart!" Anika beamed at Kimberleigh.

"Okay, you help me," Kimberleigh encouraged, and together the three girls filled in the rows of addition puzzles. The older girls gave Anika a shot at each row before Kimberleigh wrote in the answer, and though Anika sometimes had to count it out on her fingers, she got most of them right.

When they were done, Anika ran out to where her father was sitting. "Daddy, I was doing Kimmy's math!" she boasted.

"I heard you." David smiled. "You were doing really well!"

Anika beamed and climbed up on the arm of the recliner. Gently patting her father's shoulder she asked, "Can I get you anything, Daddy?"

"No, I'm fine." David smiled at his daughter, but at her look of disappointment he changed his mind. "Well, actually, I could use a drink of water."

"Okay." Anika slid from his chair and ran to the kitchen.

Later, when the kids had finished their language arts pages, Cassy selected a Bible verse and the kids all sat copying it in their best penmanship. Anika went around the table and had each sibling read the verse aloud to her. It was found in John 10:11, and when they were finished writing, Cassy went on to explain the context of the passage.

"Who is the Good Shepherd?" she questioned.

"Jesus," Jeremy was first to answer.

"And who are His sheep?"

"We are," piped up Nicole. "And Jesus laid down his life for us because He loves us and wants us to belong to Him."

"That's right, and this passage talks about the fact that if we belong to Him, we will recognize Jesus' voice and will want to follow what He says is right. Sometimes it can be confusing because the world will try to tell us all kinds of things that don't agree with God's Word, but we need to learn to tell the difference and know what the Bible says so that we can follow Jesus' voice," Cassy finished off. "Now, whose turn is it to hang their verse on the bulletin board?"

"Mine." Jeremy grabbed his paper and went to tack it up.

"Okay, pick up your books and put them away while I get lunch," Cassy directed, and everyone started to collect their things.

Again Anika bounded out to where her father sat. "I can remember our verse a'w by mysewf! Wanna hear it?"

"Sure." David closed his book and eyed his daughter expectantly.

"I am the good shepherd." Anika paused and thought for a moment. "The good shepherd ways down his wife for the sheep," she finished excitedly.

David smiled. "Well, now that's an interesting rendition of the verse. I never heard of a shepherd laying down his wife for the sheep before," he teased.

"Not his wife, Daddy." Anika glared sternly at her father. "You know what I mean!"

David held the pillow in his lap against his ribcage and tried not to laugh. Anika stayed to chat with her father and was soon joined by her siblings. When Cassy called that lunch was ready, they hurried out to the kitchen. It had become the habit over the last week to eat in the living room so that David could stay where he was most comfortable. Nicole carried her father's plate out to the TV tray beside his chair, while Kimberleigh brought him a glass of juice. Soon they were all settled and waiting for their father to say the blessing.

Later that afternoon, David leaned back in his chair and listened in as Cassy read to the children. She was reading *Freckles*, by Gene Stratton-Porter. Cassy had picked it up at the homeschool conference on recommendation by Lauren, and the kids were enthralled with the story of the crippled young man who was working in the Limberlost Forest to protect the trees for a lumber company. The noble character of the youth and his love of nature made for a heart-warming tale.

"Daddy's sweeping," Anika whispered when she looked up and saw him sitting with his eyes closed.

David's eyes flew open. "Am not! I heard every word," he defended himself.

Cassy smiled and continued reading. She finished the chapter she was on before dismissing the kids to go play. When they had disappeared outside, Cassy turned to her husband across from her.

"How are you feeling?" she inquired.

"Restless and like I need to get up and do something," he responded grimly. "The pain isn't quite so bad now, but I can still hardly lift my left arm. If I'm careful not to lift my shoulder, I'm okay."

"Well, the doctor said it would take awhile and that you shouldn't be doing much. Between the broken ribs and concussion, it's been good for you to just rest." Cassy got up to inspect the cuts on her husband's head. They were healing nicely. "Just try to be patient a little longer," she advised.

⌘ ⌘ ⌘

By midweek David was getting around a bit more, though he was still very sore and careful of his movements. He'd been back to see the doctor to get his stitches out, and the doctor was pleased with how the gashes on the side of his head had healed. The bruising and swelling had gone down, and even if there would be some scarring from the lacerations, most of it would be covered by hair. David was now off the heavy painkillers and anti-inflammatory medication and could get by with nonprescription pain medication. The doctor warned him not to do too heavy of work for a couple of weeks yet and let him know that it would be a month or more before the broken ribs would be fully healed.

David hated being idle and insisted on doing what he could around the house. When Cassy thought he was overdoing it, she would encourage him to take a break and send him back to his chair in the living room. This didn't usually last long, however, before David was up again and puttering in the garage, or doing some light yardwork. Often he would collect a few specimens to bring in for Jeremy to study under his microscope, and the two would spend an hour together taking turns looking through the lens at the minute details of different bugs.

Now that David was getting around more, Cassy knew he was feeling antsy to get back to work. Not that he hadn't enjoyed his weeks at home with the family, but Cassy knew it bothered her husband to be sitting at home when Anthony had his hands so full right now. Every evening David called his brother to see how work was going, so it didn't surprise her when he was back on the job less than three weeks after his accident, doing what he could to oversee construction and help out.

23

Year End

By the first weekend in June Cassy was feeling ready for a change in routine from schoolwork. She longed to get outside and get the yard and flowerbeds in shape. Usually she was much further along by now, but she just didn't seem to find the time. Between all of their nature walks and David's accident, the kids hadn't quite finished off their workbooks, but Cassy was ready to be done. Looking back over the year, she felt they had accomplished a lot, and she couldn't believe the growth in her kids. Jeremy's attitude toward his studies was the most dramatic of the changes, but she could notice subtle changes in all of their attitudes and in how well they got along. More importantly, Cassy felt closer to her children than ever before, and she could see how they had all grown spiritually. After talking to David, they agreed to call an official end to their school year. Though the schools would not be out for three weeks yet, the Knights felt comfortable being done early.

Cassy spent the next few afternoons weeding the flower gardens and planting bedding plants while the kids played outside, and often one or more of them would offer to come and work alongside of her. Cassy smiled when she heard Kimberleigh softly singing one of her favorite songs while she worked. It wasn't long before the flowers were all in, and Cassy rose from her cramped position and pulled off her garden gloves. After watering all the new plants, she walked over to check the vegetable garden, which the kids had helped her get in a couple of weeks ago. Anthony had offered to come till up the ground for her the Saturday following David's accident so that she could get her garden planted on time. Walking along the edge of the rich, dark earth, Cassy noticed the first sprouts poking up through the soil. She loved this time of year!

It rained fairly steady for the next several days, and Cassy was glad she'd gotten the flowers in when she did. On these long, wet afternoons, Cassy would often discover the kids sprawled on couches and chairs all over the living room quietly reading. She was shocked the first time she found her son voluntarily curled up on the couch along with his sisters, book in hand. Not wanting to be excluded, Anika would bring out some of her favorite books to look at, or she'd convince one of her siblings to read to her. One afternoon Cassy noticed Nicole trying to help her little sister sound out the words for herself, and she smiled quietly as she watched from the doorway.

The girls had also discovered the intrigue of using Jeremy's microscope, and one evening they bombarded their father with leaves, flower petals, twigs and an assortment of tiny articles that they wanted to observe under the lens. Taking turns they picked different items to view and waited for David to bring them into focus.

"Neat, look at all the tiny veins in this leaf!" Kimberleigh exclaimed.

"Wet me see!" Anika nudged her sister's elbow. When Kimberleigh stepped back from the table, Anika climbed onto the chair and squinted into the eyepiece. "Neat!" she echoed.

"Now you guys need to try looking at an ant, it's really cool," Jeremy insisted.

"No way!" Nicole cried.

"Aw come on, I looked at all your stuff."

"Yeah, but our stuff isn't disgusting," Kimberleigh informed him.

"Just one peek, please." Their brother wasn't about to give up.

Finally the girls agreed, and Jeremy instantly ran outside to find a likely specimen. Within minutes he was back, holding a dead ant in the palm of his hand. Depositing it on a glass slide, he looked into the eyepiece and worked to get it into focus. He adjusted the position of the slide under the lens several times before he was finally satisfied and stepped back.

"Did you get it focused?" David asked his son.

"Yep!"

Kimberleigh was the first to take a tentative peek at the insect. "It's sort of cool," she conceded when she saw all the detail on the ant's head, "but I don't like him staring at me!" Kimberleigh stepped back to give Nicole a look.

When they'd all had a turn, Jeremy called to his mother, who was just finishing up the supper dishes, "Hey Mom, wanna come see this ant? The girls all looked, and they didn't think it was so bad."

Cassy surprised her son when she grudgingly agreed. She knew her phobia of bugs and snakes was unreasonable, but she couldn't seem to get over it. Slowly Cassy dried her hands and crossed to the kitchen table. Jeremy stared up at his mother in expectation, while the girls just looked at one another in unbelief. Hesitantly Cassy stood in front of the microscope, trying to psych herself up to look through the lens. Finally she bent down and squinted through the eyepiece.

"Oh, yuck!" She jumped back almost immediately after peering into the ant's large eyes. "I don't think that will help me like them any better," she declared as she shuddered and moved away from the table.

Jeremy let out a laugh and David held a finger to his lips to shush his son, but Cassy noticed the smile behind her husband's finger. The kids looked at several more specimens before putting the microscope away.

Cassy had found her favorite chair in the living room to curl up with her book, and she glanced up when her husband entered. She could tell that his ribs were still bothering him by the way he walked, though he rarely said anything about it. It was good to see him getting around so well, but she hoped he wasn't overdoing it at work.

⌘ ⌘ ⌘

That Sunday after church the Knights headed to Trish and Cory's for dinner. It was Cory's birthday, and Kathy and Don were coming down as well. Cassy was looking forward to the afternoon visit. They had a nice meal together, and after cake and ice cream the kids headed downstairs to the family room.

Sixteen-year-old Connor immediately plopped on the couch and switched on the TV, while Kiera went to get some cards to play a game. Anika didn't know how to play, so Nicole offered to let her little sister sit on her lap and help. Soon the kids were comparing notes about what they were doing in school, and when Jeremy announced that they were done for the year, Christy looked at him skeptically. She was in the midst of studying for final exams.

"How can you be done?" she quizzed her cousin.

"Because Mom and Dad said we are," Jeremy stated.

"That's because they don't do real school," Connor said, turning away from the TV screen long enough to look at his cousins.

"We do too!" Kimberleigh declared in an injured tone. "My mom teaches us at home, and it's way more fun than school!"

"You just sit at home all day. I bet you don't even have any friends," Connor answered.

"We have lots of friends," Nicole defended quietly.

"Real ones?"

"No, we make them up," Jeremy shot back. "Of course we have real friends."

"Whatever." Connor shrugged and turned back to the show he was watching.

"Don't mind him." Christy motioned to her brother. "So what's it like having your mom teach you at home?"

It was the first that any of their cousins had asked them about homeschooling all year, and the Knight children enthusiastically shared with them what they'd been doing. Daniel and Justin were impressed that Jeremy had a real microscope, and Jeremy promised to show it to them the next time they came over. Christy asked lots of questions, but she seemed surprised when her cousins said they didn't have regular tests.

"How does your mom know what grades to give you?" she wanted to know.

"Oh, we don't get report cards anymore," Nicole said. "Mom can tell whether we understand what we are doing and she says that's all that's important."

"That doesn't make sense." Christy, who was in seventh grade, shook her head. "How can you have school without grades and report cards?”

“How does your mom know how to teach you everything when she’s not a real teacher?” Kiera inquired.

“My mom is rea’wy smart!” Anika replied seriously, making her siblings smile.

“If she doesn’t know something, she just looks it up,” Nicole added simply. “Teachers don’t know everything either, and sometimes they can be wrong.”

Her cousins just stared at her doubtfully.

Later on the way home, the kids shared bits of the conversation with their parents. Cassy was annoyed when she heard the comments Connor had made, but she was glad her children didn’t seem too upset about it. It sounded like they had been able to share a bit about homeschooling with their cousins, and she hoped that her nieces and nephews understood it a little better. At the same time, Cassy had come to realize that it’s very hard to understand what homeschooling really involves unless you’ve tried it. Throughout the year she’d seen all different approaches to homeschooling and knew that for each family it looked a little different, but that was okay too. Cassy was just so thankful they had discovered what worked well for them.

⌘ ⌘ ⌘

The following Saturday was the final family get together for their homeschool group for the year. The picnic was being held at the Hendersons’, and everyone was to bring salads and dessert to go along with the hamburgers supplied by the association. The Hendersons had a large acreage with lots of room for group relays and for the kids to run around. Cassy was glad that, after another week of rain, the forecast for Saturday called for warm temperatures and sunshine. For once the forecast was right, and Saturday afternoon proved to be beautiful.

When the Knights arrived, there were already a number of families milling around the yard or visiting at the tables which had been set up beside the house. Cassy crossed the yard to deposit her plate of cookies on the crowded table of desserts, while David followed with the small cooler containing her salad. Before long a rowdy game of soccer, featuring the kids versus their dads, was started at the far end of the yard. As David turned to go join in the game, Cassy gave her husband a look of warning.

"You shouldn't be playing," she cautioned.

"It'll be all right; I'll take it easy," and with a grin he was off.

Cassy found a chair among a group of women who were visiting and watching from a safe distance. There were way more players on the field than the rules allowed, and the teams were uneven in both size and number, but no one seemed to care. Cassy shook her head ruefully as her husband raced around the field. He wasn't going full speed, but she still worried that his ribs were not completely healed yet.

A few of the kids had brought their baseball mitts and were playing catch, while others formed a circle to toss a Frisbee. Some of the smaller children simply chased one another around playing tag. There was plenty to choose from, and Cassy's children were soon spread around the yard.

When the hamburgers were ready, one of the dads gave a loud whistle. By then the kids were starving and came running. Mr. Henderson asked the blessing, followed by a bustle of activity as everyone found a place in line. Cassy enjoyed the conversation around their table as they ate. It was good to have these times when the dads could be a part of the activities and the group could interact as a whole.

Later that evening the gathering had grown smaller, and the families who remained crowded around a glowing bonfire. The temperature had dropped somewhat and the fire brought welcome warmth.

"So, how was your first year homeschooling?" Teresa leaned toward Cassy, who was situated beside her.

"Oh, where do I begin?" Cassy laughed. "I've learned so much through the year and it has been such a neat experience. It's not really at all what I'd first expected."

"What do you feel you've learned most?"

"Well," Cassy thought for a moment, "for one thing I learned to be flexible. It's not really about keeping pace with the school system and following their structure."

Teresa smiled and nodded. "Good, what else?"

"The greatest part of it all is the growth I've seen in our family as a whole; it's been great! God kept His promise," she added thoughtfully.

"What do you mean?"

"Before we started, I was worried about giving up so much of my time, and I felt God tell me that if I gave of myself for His glory, that He would go with me. And He has!"

"So are you going to do it again next year?"

"You bet!" Cassy responded confidently. "I wouldn't miss this for the world!"

Author's Note

Although this story is not specifically about our family, it is a reflection of our journey. After two years of battling God's call to homeschool, we finally pulled our daughters out of the Christian school and brought them home. Our oldest, Jessica, had just completed second grade, and Jylisa had just completed kindergarten. (Justina and Tamara have never attended formal school.) Now, after fourteen years of schooling at home, I can honestly say that we have never regretted that decision and have no desire to turn back.

At this time Tamara is in grade ten, Justina in grade twelve, Jylisa graduated two years ago, and Jessica graduated four years ago. Though Jessica and Jylisa both took part in a homeschool graduation ceremony with their friends, neither received a government diploma, because we had chosen not to align ourselves with the government curriculum. Instead, we have chosen a wide variety of Christian-based resources and have grounded our daughters in their faith through teaching a Christian worldview, the providence of God throughout history (from the Bible right through to the current events unfolding before us), and by using science curriculum that honors God. We have also instilled in them a heart for missions and reaching out to their community with the Gospel message, and have concentrated on developing godly character and the life skills they will need as wives and mothers someday. Since graduating, Jessica and Jylisa have continued to study and work from home and minister alongside of family.

My husband and I have allowed our children to follow key areas of interest and to build on their strengths. Actual grade levels mean little to us, as we are not necessarily following what is prescribed by the government for each age. Three years ago our twelve-year-old was studying a very heavy course in advanced biology and human anatomy alongside her older sister. Not that we were naive enough to believe that she would fully understand everything in the text, but because we allow our children to pursue topics of interest even if they're difficult and don't fit the government guidelines.

This has been a long journey for us. We are not perfect, and we have made many mistakes along the way. However, I believe God has richly blessed our family for stepping out in this act of faith. And like in my story of the Knight family, early in our homeschool journey we discovered an organization that has helped guide our family down the path of truth. Through many resources from Answers in Genesis, now Creation Ministries International in Canada, we have been able to teach our girls to defend the authority of Scripture. Starting in Genesis, with its foundation for the doctrines of sin, death, redemption, marriage, and man's relationship with God, we have learned that if we cannot trust Scripture as written when it comes to the beginning and the age of the earth, etc., we might as well throw it out. It has given us a much sharper pair of glasses for viewing the rest of Scripture and to stand strong when we see it being twisted in other areas to suit the current trends in our culture.

It is impossible to condense and try to fit our experience gained over fourteen years of homeschooling into one year in the life of the Knight family. I have attempted to bring some of that journey into the story through the experiences and advice of Cassy's homeschool friends, which is a very real part of the homeschooling community. And though we as homeschool families all approach our schooling a little differently, because our families and goals vary, we can learn from one another. This story is just the beginning. The sequel, which is in process, will follow the Knights through the teen years and courtship. For now I hope you have enjoyed this peek through the window of our journey, and that it will encourage you, wherever you are, to take more time to instill God's truth into your family. God Bless!

—*Elizabeth Wiens*

The Fallacy of a
Neutral Public School System

By Elizabeth Wiens

One doesn't have to search far in order to discover some very distressing statistics in regards to the spiritual condition of our Christian teens today. According to one study conducted in 2006 by The Barna Group, 61% of young adults in their 20s who attended church as teens, no longer actively attend church, read their Bibles, or pray. Unfortunately, most continue this pattern into later adulthood. So why are teens walking away from the faith when they leave home?[1]

In a separate study, The Barna Group asked teens what factor would most influence them in making a moral or ethical decision. Surprisingly, the answers given by "born again" teens closely mirrored the answers of the general teen population. Only 12% claimed that the Bible would be their biggest influence while 10% followed the values taught by their parents. On the other hand, 34% said they would make a moral decision based on whatever feels right or comfortable in that situation and 13% based on whatever would produce the most positive outcome for them personally. (The remaining percentages dealt with other people's expectations, thoughts and actions.) When asked whether they believe there are moral truths which are absolute and unchanging, 76% believed that moral truth depends on the situation, and 15% said that they didn't know. Only 9% agreed that moral truth is absolute and unchanging![2]

What do these stats tell us about the next generation if they are a true reflection of where our "Christian" teens are at? What influences are drawing them to reach these conclusions? One major influence in our children's lives is school, where our children spend a huge portion of their day. In this article, I will not be focusing on the pull of the largely non-Christian peer groups our children are immersed in at school, which we are all aware of. Instead, I want to comment on the trends within our school systems themselves and what is being taught in many classrooms.

There is a huge push in our nations' schools to conform to a global curriculum being promoted worldwide through a division of the U.N. called UNESCO (U.N. Educational, Social and Scientific Organization). The purpose of this global curriculum is to draw our children more and more in line with the movement towards a global community and a one-world government.

> In order to achieve their new planetary civilization, globalists understood early on that they would have to influence the world's educational systems. Only by reeducating our youth to embrace a new set of cosmic values—referred to by Gorbachev, Muller, and other New Agers as the "Global Ethic"—could their political efforts succeed.
>
> Understanding the important role of schools in the development of children, the U.N. embarked on a vigorous campaign to replace traditional Western curricula, which had promoted a strong sense of national identity and a Christian ethic. They proposed a new international curriculum promoting the concepts of world government and pantheistic religion. This new curriculum, it was hoped, would turn children into "global citizens" who would not only embrace the new order but would actively work to help bring it about.[3]

This new approach to education clearly involves undermining children's biblical worldview and values, which are unacceptable in the new world mindset. The author of this new global curriculum was Robert Muller, a long-time member and highly influential man in the U.N. In 1989 Robert Muller won the UNESCO Peace Education Prize for developing his World Core Curriculum. In his book, *New Genesis: Shaping a Global Spirituality*, Muller claims, "Yes, global education must transcend material, scientific and intellectual achievements and reach deliberately into the moral and spiritual spheres."[4]

Robert Muller is a blatant promoter of the New Age Movement, and many of his philosophies for education are based on Alice Bailey's writings. Bailey was a prolific writer of the 20th century, who wrote her books using occultic transchanneling under the direction of her demonic spirit guide, Djwal Khul. Her work, as well as the World Core Curriculum and much of the U.N.'s material, was published through a company she founded called Lucifer Publishing Company. The name was later disguised by changing it to Lucis Trust. (Check out www.lucistrust.org if you want to see what occult beliefs and spiritual values this company is promoting in our schools!)

If you think Muller's curriculum is harmless, consider what he said while speaking to school children at a Global Citizenship 2000 Conference in Vancouver, British Columbia, in the spring of 1997. Muller was introduced as a "planet elder," and he went on to encourage the children with much hype and environmental propaganda, to remember that they were global citizens and sons and daughters of the sun and "Mother Earth." He told the students that they must:

> consider the Earth as being number one, your Mother…behave correctly towards the Earth….You are not children of Canada, you are really living units of the cosmos because the Earth is a cosmic phenomena…we are all cosmic units. This is why religions tell you, you are divine. We are divine energy…it is in your hands whether evolution on this planet continues or not.[5]

UNESCO has also developed the International Baccalaureate Program, which integrates earth-centered religious philosophies of the U.N.'s Earth Charter throughout the curriculum. The Earth Charter is an internationally accepted document spearheaded by a very powerful Canadian, Maurice Strong, and widely promoted by Gorbachev and Al Gore under the umbrella of the U.N. It originates from the philosophies of Gaia, or earth worship, and it lays the groundwork for a one-world government based on communist ideology and New Age beliefs, as well as world population control through abortion. This document is housed in the "Ark of Hope"—a replica of the Ark of the Covenant, painted on all sides with cultic images. The Ark of Hope is also home to thousands of pictures and "Earth prayers" contributed by artists and school students worldwide in affirmation of the Earth and its "ten commandments."

The International Baccalaureate Program is being used in over 650 schools across the States and Canada, and the philosophies of UNESCO and the Earth Charter are being taught worldwide. Professor Philip Vander Velde, who teaches "Foundations of Education" at Western Washington University wrote:

> ...unless a new faith...overcomes the old ideologies and creates planetary synthesis, world government is doomed...Nation-States have outlived their usefulness, and a new world order is necessary if we are to live in harmony with each other...The task of reordering our traditional values and institutions should be one of the major educational objectives of our schools.[6]

Canada and the U.S. are big players in UNESCO. You don't have to look very hard to find UNESCO's educational philosophies immersed in the curriculum guidelines across both Canada and the U.S. Words like: *multiculturalism, globalism, pluralism, values clarification, Outcome-Based Education, tolerance, lifelong learning, metacognition, creative or critical thinking* and *consensus building* pop up throughout every grade level and almost every course.[7] Though at first glance some of these words may appear innocent enough, we need to realize that they mask underlying concepts.

To understand the effect of what is happening, parents need to be aware of what the concepts behind these words mean. For instance, some parents may think that it is great that their school is teaching values, but what kind of values are they teaching if they are not using the Bible as the basis? I have read extensively on the changing philosophies within public education, and the underlying purpose in the "values clarification" curriculum is to undermine traditional parental values and to bring student's values in line with new universal values, or anti-biblical values. This means biblical morals and the word *sin* is out, biblical faith is labeled as *hateful*, and belief in absolute truth is considered *intolerant*. The new standard is situational ethics and acceptance of all value systems, except biblical Christianity.

One can understand that Christian parents may not be fully aware of the subversive attacks their children face in school concerning their biblical values. But many Christian parents willingly relinquish their responsibility to teach God's standards concerning sexual behavior in favor of public school sex education courses, where it is well known that the school system blatantly defies Scripture in what it teaches. These classes not only promote the acceptance of fornication, homosexuality, and abortion, but they do so with explicit and graphic material and props that break down natural inhibitions and encourage experimentation. It is hard to understand why any Christian would knowingly allow their children to be indoctrinated with such unbiblical moral values and not see the harm in this. Is it any wonder that the sexual and moral behavior of our Christian teens is what it is today?

Consider also one high-profile concept taught in today's schools that is often overlooked by Christians—the emphasis on self-esteem. This concept comes from secular psychology, not the Bible, though "Christian psychology" has falsely bought into the idea. Man's elevation of self, and the belief that we are great in and of ourselves cannot be supported by Scripture. Search the Bible for yourself and see if you can find the concept that God wants us to have pride in or exalt ourselves. It is only in our weakness, when we humble ourselves before Him, that God can use us. Though we have been created in God's image and are objects of His love, we are still sinful creatures in desperate need of a Savior! We are lost without Christ and have replaced the sense of humble awe we should hold for God, with an unhealthy self-absorption and self-love. Children are being taught to think too highly of themselves and to believe in the power and goodness of self apart from God. This teaching totally ignores the concepts of sin, guilt and judgment, or that we are to find our worth and strength in God alone. Second Timothy 3:1-2 states, "But mark this: There will be terrible times in the last days. People will be lovers of themselves..." this is not a good thing! It is time for all parents, if they have not already done so, to take a closer look at what values are being taught in the public school system with great determination and consistency.

Ultimately, UNESCO's goal is to "promote the growth of a common outlook,"[8] and to accomplish this, they must "reconcile opposing philosophies" and "uncrystalize our dogmas."[9] One popular method being used to achieve this and other ideas within the classroom is the huge movement toward what is called *consensus building*. Rather than being able to take a stand on individual values and convictions, students are encouraged to work together in discussing problems and moral dilemmas presented in class, and to compromise and come to a consensus that is acceptable to the group. This is also called *collaborative decision making*. In other words, let's make up our own standards of right and wrong. What kind of pressure are these activities putting on our Christian children to conform?

Another movement within our schools is to move more and more away from teaching history and the lessons learned from history, to teaching multiculturalism. The focus is on the world as a global community, not independent nations, and teaching a wide variety of world cultures and belief systems to promote pluralism and a blending of cultures. All practices and belief systems within a culture are presented as equally true and acceptable, regardless of what the Bible declares as absolute truth, or what the Bible proclaims to be sin. The objective is a pluralistic society and the material presented is very biased to bring children in line with the desired worldview. Is that our objective as Christian parents? We are to love people from all cultures, while at the same time discerning truth from Satan's lie and declaring sin to be sin. If children no longer see these belief systems as wrong, there is no longer a need to direct a lost world to the Truth. Are we aware of what our children are facing and being indoctrinated with? Our school systems are not what they were a generation ago. They were always humanistic, but the attack on our children's faith and values is much more intrusive today.

What about Outcome-Based Education (OBE)? It sounds noble for a school to set a goal of outcomes to be reached before graduation, but what are those outcomes? Unfortunately, in the global curriculum the desired outcomes are more concerned with attitudes, behaviors, and beliefs than with academic knowledge. And if those outcomes are not reached, then the push is to send the non-conforming child to remediation. If you don't think the school teaches attitudes and beliefs, just look into your government curriculum guidelines and see how many times those two words are mentioned.

According to Professor Benjamin Bloom, the Father of OBE, the new "purpose of education and schools is to change the thoughts, feelings and actions of students."[10]

Now, using OBE, the focus is on teaching students *what* to think, more than on teaching them a thorough understanding of the facts. Bloom realized that "Students armed with facts and strong convictions resist manipulation."[11] The curriculum is therefore made up of carefully chosen bits of information and teachers are trained to facilitate discussion and challenge fixed beliefs in order to achieve the end result desired.

> Well aware that knowledge is the foundation of all true thinking, Dr. Bloom had discovered a process that could control the *outcome* or end product of thinking, which was often an opinion or value judgment. By censoring a student's knowledge base, the teacher could direct the student's thinking. Bloom's process works. Through biased information, carefully designed hypothetical stories, and pointed Socratic questioning, students are persuaded that their home-taught beliefs and values are incompatible with the needs for the next century.[12]

This new approach can be clearly seen in our government curriculum guides. Under outcomes for social studies on the education.gov.ab website, it states that:

> The goal of social studies is to foster the development of values and attitudes that enable students to participate actively and responsibly as citizens in a changing and pluralistic society. Attitudes are an expression of values and beliefs about an issue or topic.[13]

So much for the goal of teaching the facts of history, let alone teaching God's providence in history! The goal is now a global mindset, with attitudes and beliefs consistent with a pluralistic society. Researcher Berit Kjos claims:

> ...today's change agents don't seem to listen. They have changed the rules and revised our history. Good and evil have been turned upside down— and our children are learning to love the latter.[14]

I cannot go into the details and many unbelievable examples of

213

how this is being accomplished in North American schools and around the world, but you as parents need to be aware of what is happening in our schools if you don't want your children to become one of those statistics mentioned at the beginning of this article. Is it surprising when our children spend so many hours a day under the influence of secular school systems, to discover that so many of them do not hold a truly biblical worldview?

A key approach to accomplishing this change in values is by developing what is termed "critical thinking" skills in our children. This may sound good, but it has nothing to do with reasonable thought grounded in facts. So, what is the educational system's new definition for critical thinking? In 1987 Raymond English, Vice President of the Ethics and Public Policy Center, told the National Advisory Council on Educational Research and Improvement that:

> [C]ritical thinking means not only learning how to think for oneself, but it also means learning how to subvert the traditional values in your society. You're not thinking "critically" if you're accepting the values that mommy and daddy taught you. That's not "critical."[15]

When this style of critical thinking is combined with a curriculum which revises history and distorts the truth through textbooks which present limited facts from the desired perspective, then asks leading questions and expects students to come to a consensus, one can see how effective it might be. Students are encouraged to make decisions and solve problems without having all the information. They need the truth and they need the freedom to stand on their convictions. As parents we need to look beneath the surface and study the content and techniques our schools are using to realize that things are not as they seem. Don't be deceived.

Most parents and teachers still believe that critical thinking refers to *factual, logical thinking.* But they have been misled. It actually means the opposite. School fliers explain that this term means teaching students "to think for themselves." Instead, this psychological strategy *limits* factual knowledge and independent reasoning. It encourages myths, imagination, and group synthesis—the tools for manipulating a child's values system.[16]

Teaching students to "think for themselves" means that our children are being taught to question the values they may have been taught at home and to create their own values based on the politically correct, "universal values" being presented. There is no sense of absolute truth—truth is decided by majority vote or through compromise. In this system God's Word not only has no authority, but it is completely ignored or outlawed. Berit Kjos claims in her book, *Brave New Schools,* that:

> To mold world-class students, social engineers are testing the latest techniques in behavior modification on our children...children must either reject their *old* home-taught faith or stretch it far beyond biblical boundaries to include the world's pantheistic, polytheistic belief systems.[17]

Following is a quote from Dale Wallace, a Calgary schoolteacher, taken from a letter he sent to the *Calgary Herald.*

> In education, forces outside the child—such as parents—would gladly influence the child and mould them. They want them to attain certain standards and uphold certain beliefs. True education must unshackle itself from the manacles of parental influence.... A child's mind must be stroked and allowed to expand and not struck down and made into a print of a previous mind.[18]

Are all teachers like that? Thankfully no, but the system itself encourages this mentality and, unfortunately, many teachers are simply teaching the curriculum and philosophy they have been taught to use without realizing what is behind it.

Similarly, the education system's definition of metacognition includes: "Critical self-awareness," "conscious reflection" and the process where, "students become *knowledge creators* and contribute to a shared understanding of the world we live in—a key feature of democratic life and *commitment to pluralism*"[19] (emphasis mine). The New Age belief is that we are all part of one cosmic force, and by meditating or channeling, we can join consciousness with one another and become a part of this cosmic deity. Many of these New Age occult practices and philosophies are creeping into our schools through the introduction of yoga, meditation, visualization, and cooperative consciousness exercises.

The idea behind lifelong learning, contrary to the inferred meaning of developing a lifelong *love* of learning, involves instead a desire to instill in our children a permanent humanistic value system and multicultural viewpoint that will go with them for a lifetime. In promoting Muller's new World Core Curriculum, Gloria Crook states,

> ...A School can begin with any age-group of children; however it is hoped that *children will be taught the Curriculum from birth and throughout life*; the interdependence of all existence will be foundational to their thinking for a lifetime....Ideally, the school *will begin at birth, with the parents having used the Balanced Beginnings Program prenatally*; and will continue through the secondary level. In this structure, the student will move directly into college with no break in the continuity of presented perspective.
>
> By that time, there will *be an understanding which overrides all false concepts* which are still held among much of the general populace of the world—concepts which have bred separative and prejudiced behavior for most of human history.[20]

These educators know that, if they have our children long enough and the teaching is consistent, they will be successful in indoctrinating them for a lifetime! What "false concepts" and "prejudiced behavior" do you think they are trying to eradicate? As stated by Alice Bailey when describing this new form of education she was working toward, "It will be apparent to you, therefore, that the whole goal of the future and of the present effort is to bring humanity to the point where it—occultly speaking—enters into light."[21]

Parents, these educators are trying to extinguish the only true Light—that is, Christ! They want to replace that Light with Satan's deceptive lies. Alice Bailey's goal was to rewrite the textbooks and establish a system that would usher the next generation into the cosmic consciousness of the New Age movement. Remember, her work was the foundation upon which Robert Muller built his World Core Curriculum our schools are following.

In our Post-Christian society, which mocks biblical values and where truth is relative, we need to be more aware than ever of what our children are up against. It is not enough that they come from Christian homes and go to church on Sunday. We need to be alert and actively engaged in the battle for their souls on a daily basis! As parents we have the God-given responsibility to bring our children up in the nurture and admonition of the Lord and to be sure that they have a solid foundation to stand on by the time they leave our homes. So what influences might your children be facing that could undermine their faith? Are your children being asked to "trade truth, facts, and logical thinking for myths, U.N. values, and the consensus process?"[22] The push to get all teachers in line with this new curriculum is real. Catherine Barrett, former president of the National Education Association, years ago foretold the changes coming.

> Dramatic changes in the way we will raise our children in the year 2000 are indicated, particularly in terms of schooling.... We will need to recognize that the so-called "basic skills," which currently represent nearly the total effort in elementary schools, will be taught in one-quarter of the present school-day...when this happens...and it's near...the teacher can rise to his true calling. More than a dispenser of information, the teacher will be a conveyor of values, a philosopher....We will be agents of change.[23]

If you find these ideas hard to believe, you should read more about the people behind the movement, and books like *Brave New Schools* by Berit Kjos or *The New World Religion* by Gary H. Kah. These concepts are just the tip of the iceberg. It is impossible in this short space to present and expound upon the host of unbiblical philosophies penetrating our schools, but I hope that this gives you the desire to pursue the issue further if your children are in the system.

> "See to it that no one takes you captive
> through hollow and deceptive philosophy,
> which depends on human tradition and
> the basic principles of this world rather than on Christ."
> —COLOSSIANS 2:8

Notes

[1]The Barna Update: *Most Twentysomethings Put Christianity On The Shelf Following Spiritually Active Years.* September 11, 2006. The Barna Group of Ventura, CA. www.barna.org

[2]The Barna Update: *Americans Most Likely To Base Their Truth On Feelings.* February 12, 2002. The Barna Group of Ventura, CA. www.barna.org

[3]Gary H. Kah, *The New World Religion* (Noblesville, IN: Hope International Publishing, Inc., 1999), p. 171.

[4]Robert Muller, *New Genesis: Shaping a Global Spirituality* (Anacortes, Wash.: World Happiness and Cooperation, 1982), p. 8. Taken from an article by Carl Teichrib, "Social Engineering for Global Change," www.forcingchange.org

[5]Gary H. Kah, *The New World Religion*, p. 187. Taken from a speech addressed to the Global Citizenship 2000 Youth Congress, Vancouver, BC, April 5, 1997. (Transcribed from an audio tape recorded by Carl Teichrib.)

[6]Berit Kjos, *Brave New Schools*, (Eugene, Oreg.: Harvest House Publishers, 1995) p. 34. Taken from Philip Vander Velde and Hyung-Chan Kim. Eds., *Global Mandate: Pedagogy For Peace* (Bellingham, WA: Bellwether Press, 1985), p. 76.

[7]www.education.gov.ab.ca/k_12/curriculum/bySubject/elem2005.pdf

[8]Julian Huxley, *UNESCO Its Purpose and Its Philosophy* (Washington DC: Public Affairs Press, 1947), p. 60. Taken online at www.crossroads.to/quotes/globalism/julian-husley.htm

[9]Ibid., p. 61.

[10]Berit Kjos, *Brave New Schools*, p. 13. Taken from Benjamin Bloom, *All Our Children Learning* (New York: McGraw-Hill, 1981), p. 180.

[11]Berit Kjos, *Brave New Schools*, p. 61.

[12]Ibid., p. 67.

[13]www.education.gov.ab.ca/k_12/curriculum/bySubject/elem2005.pdf.

[14]Berit Kjos, *Brave New Schools*, p. 24.

[15]Ibid., p. 21.

[16]Ibid., p. 111.

[17]Ibid., p. 34.

[18]Dale Wallace, *Calgary Herald*, "Letters to the Editor," April 16, 2005.

[19]www.education.gov.ab.ca/k_12/curriculum/bySubject/elem2005.pdf.

[20]Gary H. Kah, *The New World Religion*, p. 181.

[21]Ibid., p.184.

[22]Berit Kjos, "The UN Plan for Your Mental Health," 1999. Article taken from www.crossroad.to/text/articles/MentalHealth2-99.html.

[23]Gary H. Kah, *The New World Religion*, p. 191.

About the Author

ELIZABETH WIENS and her husband, Gary, have four daughters and live in Alberta, Canada. Their family has enjoyed working together in children's ministry for almost sixteen years while serving full-time with Child Evangelism Fellowship. They are now ministering with GoodSeed Canada.

Elizabeth feels passionate about God's call for parents to purposefully mentor their children for Him. She and Gary have been homeschooling their family for fourteen years, and Elizabeth is involved in homeschool leadership in her community. In her spare time, she enjoys writing and doing research—seeking biblical answers to life's issues. She has previously published a novel entitled *Destined For Eternity*, which she coauthored with her twin sister. Currently Elizabeth is working on a sequel to *Bringing Them Home*, following the Knight family through the teen years and courtship.

You may reach Elizabeth via email at: **gbwiens@shaw.ca**

For more info:
http://elizabethwiens.com
www.oaktara.com

LaVergne, TN USA
17 March 2010
176209LV00001B/11/P